THE SHOWMAN'S GHOST

CANDACE ADAMS

Copyright © 2021 by Candace Adams

All rights reserved.

No part of this book may be reproduced in any form or by any electronic or mechanical means, including information storage and retrieval systems, without written permission from the author, except for the use of brief quotations in a book review.

CHAPTER ONE

June 8th, 1918

No joy in the world compared to that of a child's when the circus was in town. *Entrance of the Gladiators* titillating sound playing on the calliope mounted on a carved, painted wagon with big wheels pulled by horses could send a young heart racing with delight. The mouthwatering smell of peanuts, popcorn, and hot funnel cakes permeated the air. The clowns cartwheeled and flipped, pulling flowers from their caps with happy, smiling faces, reminding each grown up what it was like to be a child, the woes of life left behind.

Trumpeting elephants walked in line, their trainers' watchful eyes never faltering. Tigers paced in gilded cages, horses with colorful feathers in their manes pranced at the head of the parade. There were strongmen, lifting more than any ordinary man could ever hope to heft, making little boys vow to grow strong themselves. Acrobats tumbled down the streets with their limbs seemingly made of rubber, their faces glowing with shimmering makeup, the envy of every young girl watching.

Roustabouts traveling with the troupe erected the big top. The dominating canvas structure was large enough to house a three-ring act, animal menagerie, and seating for all. The tent painted in the traditional red and white stripes, holding secrets within that must be seen to be believed. The clowns paraded outside, ushering in the crowd.

There was nothing quite like the circus.

On this day, the circus troupe was in Chicago. In a week, they'd move on.

"Put your backs into it, men! Get those poles up!" A shirtless man with a dark tan encouraged the others while pulling hard on a rope attached to the center support. The heavy material of the tent fixed to the top of the pole. It took ten men and two elephants with lines attached to halters to get it off the ground.

"Henry! Get those beasts moving!" The man called out to the elephant trainer, directing the animals what to do. "We need this set up before the rain comes down."

Ominous clouds began rolling in shortly before the train stopped. The occasional thunderclap drowned out the voices of the workers struggling to have everything ready before the downpour.

"They're doing the best they can, Gregory." Henry patted the larger of the two females on her leg and whispered encouragement into her big ear. She raised her trunk and gave a rumble, acknowledging her trainer. The elephants only responded to Henry. "They're still groggy from the train ride."

The elephant's grey hide was wrinkled and thick, their feet wide and heavy. Both beasts possessed soft brown eyes and fixed them on the man giving them delicate touches and gentle commands, eager to please him. Henry smiled at them each time they obeyed.

The main mast went up without a hitch. The smaller poles made up the outside ring of the structure, and the red and white striped canvas was stretched taut across them. At each side, massive flaps were pulled back with rope, granting access to the tent's inside, where other workers assembled the three rings for performances.

"Get the trapeze up, men! The Wards need somewhere to fly. The kiddies will be expecting them!" Gregory projected his voice from across the space.

"Yes, sir!" A chorus of gruff male voices erupted, expertly executing their orders.

They completed the last of the work as the first droplets began to fall.

Henry stood at the front of the tent by himself with his arms crossed over his broad chest. The animals were fed and watered and left to rest. Raindrops hit the ground hard enough to bounce back and soak the hem of his trousers from where he stood just inside. He didn't mind the water and wind. There were plenty of clean clothes in his trunk. It was the smell of the fresh summer storm, wet flower petals, the sound of the leaves swaying in the trees fighting to stay attached. Those were the moments that calmed his soul.

"What are you doing out here all by yourself, Henry?"

The young man was startled, jumping a little at the voice that surprised him. The ringmaster, Charlie, was a cat-like man who exuded grace in every step he took. Henry often thought his boss should wear a bell around his throat to announce his presence. He tended to pop up where there'd been no sign of him before. The ringmaster was a lanky kind of man who was always finely dressed in an array of bright colors. He wore his face painted the traditional way of a clown during shows, even though he wasn't one himself, and garbed his body in the long red waistcoat with golden threads and buttons with a top hat pulled low over one eyebrow.

"I'm just listening to the storm, sir." A bolt of lightning shot across the sky. The fingers illuminated the treetops of the dark landscape beyond the clearing they'd settled in for a moment before thunder disrupted the gentle pattering sound of the droplets. "I find thunderstorms very relaxing."

Charlie nodded, fixing his gaze on a mud puddle forming outside the opening of the tent. "The clowns aren't going to like all this mud. They won't be able to do their usual tricks and flips."

"They'll just have to take it inside then."

Charlie grunted in response, mimicking Henry's stature, crossing his arms before him. "I hope the new acts can get it together. We have a reputation to protect. Baldy's worried."

"About what?" Henry dropped his arms to his sides and turned to the man.

"The two new clowns who joined at the last stop." The ringmaster continued to stare at the mud, his brow furrowed. "He said he smelled liquor on their breath. I confronted them, but they both assured me they weren't drinking. That's the last thing we need. The public already has a set opinion about carnie folks, and it's not a very high one."

Henry nodded. "You want me to keep an eye out?"

"If you don't mind. The more eyes on them, the better." Charlie gave up on staring at the puddle. "If they step out of line here, I'll send them on their way before we head to Hammond. Clowns are a dime a dozen. I'd rather not have the headache and be short-staffed for a while."

"That's understandable."

A bald man with a great round stomach sauntered his way between the two men. Both Henry and Charlie scooted to either side, allowing him space. Most people thought the extra inches around the middle of the man was part of the clown costume he wore. An inflated inner tube perhaps, but it was just Baldy. Fate granted him a body as round as it was tall, and he didn't fight it. Kids loved poking his belly with their tiny fingers and listening to the chuckles he produced at each stop. The clown was the one everyone went to with their problems, and he always conveyed great words of wisdom for anyone who cared to listen.

"Good evening, Baldy." Charlie gave the man a warm smile. "Are the clowns set up for the first show of the evening?"

"We are, and we're ripping to go." Baldy placed his hands on his stomach; they didn't quite meet in the middle. "I sent Smiley to set up the ticket booth. Everyone else is getting into costumes and makeup. The Wards are on the wires practicing. It's going to be a great show, sir."

"Very good." Charlie grinned, turning his attention to the sky above. "So glad I can rely on all of you to do your jobs. How's your wife and boy doing with the circus train life, Baldy? Are they ready to go back to Wisconsin yet?"

"Just fantastic, sir." Baldy's eyes lit up whenever someone mentioned his family. The clown was elated to have them both with him on tour. Before Charlie took over, it was forbidden to bring loved ones on the train. The old ringmaster was of the mindset that distractions would ruin the show. It didn't stop the man from drinking himself into an early grave, though. The new ringmaster was second in command for years and was happy to fill the other man's shoes when he passed. Charlie believed people would do a better job if they weren't worried about what was going on at home. The clown was the first performer to invite his family aboard, and so far, it had gone off without a hitch. Not many who traveled with the troupe had families. Long distance relationships tended to not work out. But Baldy was a testament to perseverance and the power of true love.

Henry was the second to bring his family onboard. No one talked about his wife, Diane, though. She'd stayed with the train for three weeks before packing her bags and going home to her mother. According to her, she got motion sickness from the train. Henry seemed to believe her, but no one else did. She left behind the couple's six-year-old boy, Allen. The child was quiet and kept to himself most days. The other performers all thought Henry and Diane would split up, but they kept writing letters to each other, pretending everything was fine.

The rain was beginning to taper off. The time between lightning and thunder went from being almost instantaneous to half a minute in-between, signaling the storm moved further away. The sky brightened where the dark clouds were receding. Charlie looked at his pocket watch, snapped the face closed, and dropped the thing back inside his pocket from whence it came.

"Right on time."

The doors slid open on the train cars sitting behind the big top. Many clowns, all in various forms of dress and makeup, sprung forth like a colorful volcano. Max Neitzborn, the strongman with his handlebar mustache and bald head, leaped out behind them in his one-piece leotard. The rest of the troupe, some three-hundred men and women consisting of performers, trainers, and other workers, stumbled out at their leisure.

"Ringmaster Charlie?" Gregory approached the men from the side. He was no longer shirtless, adorned in a costume like the ringmaster's but with less flair. No one out staged Charlie. "You should get ready, sir. A crowd is beginning to gather. Rusty is starting up the calliope, and the food tent is churning out the treats. The souvenirs are all in place for the kiddies as well. They'll move them inside if the rain returns."

Henry watched the man and wondered if he'd ever cracked a smile in his life.

"Thank you, Gregory." Charlie dismissed his second in command and turned to Baldy and Henry. "I guess our moment of peace has expired, boys. The show must go on."

Charlie turned on his heel and headed towards his private tent to prepare himself for the opening of the show. The ringmaster's job was to welcome the crowd and introduce the acts. It was up to him to get everyone excited while keeping his crew in line. He executed his position effortlessly, and everyone respected him immensely. His second, Gregory, couldn't be any more different from him. While the performers adored him, he was a very no-nonsense man. He led the men with military efficiency. Nothing much was known about his past, but many speculated he'd been a deserter. The way the man stood and walked, the timber of his voice, and the way he flinched each time a soldier in uniform attended a show, spoke volumes. The Great War was just winding down, and the circus was as far as a man could get from the gunfire and death of the battlefield.

Baldy turned to Henry, pulling on his bright red suspenders and rocking back and forth on his heels. "It's so nice having Martha and my boy here. Putting on my makeup doesn't take half the time that it used to. Plus, she can see behind my ears."

Henry glanced at the man and saw both his ears wiggle back and forth.

"How the heck do you do that?" The elephant trainer burst into long peals of laughter. "I don't think that's natural, Baldy. You should see a doctor before those things fall right off your head."

Baldy slapped his thigh and laughed. "Son, I've been doing the clown act for twenty years. If they haven't fallen off by now, they won't. Besides, I'd just have Martha sew them back on for me. She's a force to be reckoned with when it comes to needlework."

Henry looked at the man thoughtfully. "I have a few uniforms that need darning. You think she would help me out?"

Baldy nodded his head enthusiastically. "My Martha is a peach, a real peach, Henry. I'm sure she would take care of that for you. Say, I've meant to ask you, my boy just turned eleven last week, and I think it's high time he got a job. What do you think about him helping you clean up after the animals?"

"Can he shovel shit?" Henry smirked. "Elephants make a lot of shit."

Baldy pulled on his suspenders again. "Seems like a task he couldn't possibly mess up. I'll send him over to your train car after the show."

"What's your boy's name?"

"Reginald." The clown looked mighty proud. "Named for his grandfather on his mother's side. It's a good strong name. He'll be ringmaster someday, mark my words."

"Every good ringmaster should learn the proper way to shovel his fair share of shit."

Both men laughed.

CHAPTER TWO

May 5th, 2018

The smell of burning coffee brought Kristina flying out of bed and into the kitchen in a panic. The electric machine sitting on her granite countertop was programmed to start brewing at six, and her alarm should've gone off shortly after, at six-thirty. But it hadn't. Instead, a nostril burning stench replaced the fragrant aroma of Columbian coffee beans. The clock on the microwave showed nearly an hour passed since the time she should've been getting ready for work.

Chucking the sludge out of the carafe into the garbage can, Kristina set the glass container gingerly in the sink. She filled it with dish soap and hot water from the tap to clean the burned mess. It did nothing for the smell.

Creepy circus music nearly made her jump out of her skin. The ringtone her colleague set on her phone days before caught her off guard. She thought she'd changed that already. Placing her hand over her heart to slow her speeding pulse, Kristina groaned when she took the phone off the counter and saw the name on the screen. She begrudgingly accepted the call.

"Yes, Jason?"

"Kristina? Are you okay? I just saw this maniac dressed like a clown running out of your apartment complex! He didn't attack you with balloon animals, did he?" Jason snorted at his joke.

"That's so not funny. You know I hate clowns." Switching the phone to her other ear, Kristina shut off the water and leaned her butt against the sink. "This whole thing's dumb. I shouldn't have taken this job."

"I think hate isn't the right word. When the boss showed us the slideshow of the train wreck, you looked like you were going to pass out." Jason reminded her. "How can anyone be afraid of clowns? They're so cheery."

Kristina rolled her eyes. "Listen. They might wear a happy face, but they're creepy. Ever since I was a kid, they've unnerved me. It probably didn't help that my brother hid under the bed dressed as a clown when I was a kid and grabbed my ankle as I climbed into bed."

Jason gasped. "Seriously? That's amazing!"

"Yeah, you would say that." Kristina sulked. "You weren't the one curled up in the fetal position in the corner peeing on yourself. That was the most terrifying moment of my life, and I never lived it down."

"Wow, Kris. I didn't take you for such a fraidy cat."

Kristina pressed her lips together in a frown. "You act like you aren't afraid of anything."

Jason chuckled. "That's because I'm not. I'm a bonafide badass."

"Yeah, okay. Tell that to the spider who was hanging out in your desk drawer that you made me kill for you." Kristina recalled the shrill cry her friend made when he discovered the creature. She wanted to tease him more for it now, but the upcoming event was still heavy on her mind.

Jason hit his horn, and a slew of obscenities followed the intrusion of noise. Kristina could imagine the determined set of Jason's jaw as he navigated around the slower vehicles in his path. He'd never been one to obey a speed limit, and it'd gotten worse since he'd bought the bright yellow Mustang convertible a month ago. He'd told her about a turbo something or other and insisted the only way to drive the car was fast. "I swear no one has anywhere to be today. You'd think it's a Sunday. Anyways, not to change the subject from eight-legged freaks, but I'm going to be at your place in about ten minutes as long as this slow ass truck gets out of my way."

Kristina rushed back to the bedroom with the phone pressed to her ear. There wouldn't be any time for a shower or getting her makeup perfect. The stylish black dress she'd laid out the night before hung on the back of her closet door on a velvet hanger meant to keep it in place. Stripping out of her pajamas, she carefully balanced the phone between her ear and shoulder while dressing.

"You're early!" Kristina exclaimed, wiggling into the tight-fitting sheath, smoothing it down over her flared hips and adjusting her breasts in the built-in cups. "I'm not even dressed yet."

"That's hot." Jason cursed again, and his blinker began to click in the background. "I'm pulling up in front of your place. Ready or not, here I come." Jason had been on a mission to see her naked since he'd started work with the newspaper six months ago. Kristina wasn't sure if he was just flirtatious or if he had a real interest in her. With all the heat laced comments he made towards her; he'd never asked her out. She was beginning to think it was just his personality to talk that way.

"You wait outside, Jason. Don't you dare come in here before I'm ready! The door is locked!" The line went dead in her hand, following his deep laughter.

Once clothed, Kristina pulled her dark-brown hair into a messy bun and secured it with pins. She then rushed into the bathroom to apply her makeup frantically. Under her eyes, heavy bags stood out in stark contrast to her otherwise smooth complexion from lack of good sleep. Dabbing on concealer with a sponge, she appraised herself. "Not fantastic, but not half bad either."

Back in the bedroom, the boots she'd chosen to go with the dress lay beside the bed. She took them in her hand and carried the pair into the living room just as Jason began pounding on the door. "Baldy the Clown here! Come out, come out, little girl!" A deep chuckle emanated from his throat, growing into sick, cacophonous laughter. He slammed his fists against the door, rattling the slab beneath. *Bang! Bang! Bang!*

Kristina jumped, her breath catching in her throat. Even though it was apparent it was him outside the door, the raspy voice Jason used made her nerve endings come alive. He wasn't aware of the nightmares about the painted-up horrors she'd been having since being selected to cover the one-hundred-year memorial service, and she wouldn't tell him either. That would only increase the amount of shit he would dish out.

Her boss chose her for this damn job because she had a stellar reputation for getting the best photos. Jason got the job to learn from her. The few menial shoots he'd done to date by himself were only mediocre at best, and everyone hoped he'd glean a thing or two from her. Kristina wasn't concerned. The two clicked immediately upon him accepting employment, and they'd been thick as thieves ever since.

Rolling her eyes, she abandoned the boots in front of the couch and stomped towards the lunatic making a nuisance of himself. Kristina put on a show, not wanting him to know how much he'd frightened her.

"Oh, I'm so scared. Whatever will I do with a big scary clown at my door?" He laughed in the hallway on the other side of her apartment door.

Steeling herself for whatever prank he was about to pull, Kristina counted to three. She jerked the door open and was sprayed in the face by water originating from a plastic daisy attached to his shirt pocket. Jason erupted into laughter, smacking his thigh heartily.

"Seriously, Jason! I just did my makeup." She wiped the trail of liquid rolling down her cheek. "We're running late as it is."

"I'm sorry," he said. "I had to do it. You should've seen your face."

He made more snickers at her expense. Sometimes Jason could be a real asshole.

"I'm so glad I'm a source of amusement for you." Kristina sulked into the kitchen and tore a paper towel from the roll, gingerly patting her cheek. Jason followed, leaning on the center island, watching her clean up his mess.

"Oh, come on, Kristina!" Jason shot her one of his prize-winning smiles and pushed off the counter. "It was just a joke. Don't take it so seriously. You look beautiful. Besides, this is a sad event. If you look like you've been crying, you'll fit right in." Jason wrinkled his nose and searched for the source of the foul smell that just hit him.

Kristina knew what he smelled. "I didn't wake up on time. I burned the coffee."

"Dreaming about the circus?" he asked. "I could put on a clown suit for you if it would make you feel better. You know what they say about a guy with big shoes." Jason wiggled his eyebrows in her direction.

"I hate you so much right now." Kristina tossed the paper towel into the trash and glared at her friend. Before long, a grin broke the corners of her mouth, and she turned her face to keep him from seeing.

"I see that little smile!" Jason maneuvered himself around her and looked into her eyes. "You can't hide it from me. It was the thought of me in clown shoes that did it, wasn't it?"

Kristina pushed his chest with her fist. "Leave me alone. You're a bully."

"Come on. We're gonna be late if you don't stop messing around." Jason casually strolled around the island towards the door. "We don't have time for your silly games today, Kristina. Pull yourself together."

Bursting into laughter, Kristina went to grab her boots and slid them onto her feet, zipping them on the inner side. "My silly games. That's rich, Jason. You're not wearing that stupid flower to the event, are you?"

He shrugged. "Why not? Boss man Sullivan said there are going to be clowns and stuff there. Might as well blend in with the crowd, right?"

Kristina's heart skipped a beat. A wave of fear washed over her body, leaving a thin layer of perspiration on her forehead. She swirled her tongue around the inside of her mouth, wetting the suddenly dry space. "This is going to be awful."

She'd known people would be attending in costume, but she'd put it out of her mind, focusing instead on the job itself. Everything about those painted up jesters jarred her senses. Maybe it was because she didn't have any idea what was really under the smiling faces. John Wayne Gacy played a clown, after all, and he wasn't funny. No one could know what a clown's real intentions were, what they plotted under all that makeup, what nefarious plans they were concocting. Even the clothing they wore was suspect, with big baggy pants hiding God knows what.

"I think it's going to be a blast. I never saw the circus as a kid." Jason pulled the door open and waited for her to join him. "I've only ever seen it on TV."

"Lucky."

Jason raised an eyebrow. "You're really sour about this."

"Let's just get it over with, please." Kristina stooped to grab the black bag containing her Nikon camera and an assortment of lenses before passing through the open door. "I'm going to need a strong drink after this is over."

Jason closed the door and turned the handle making sure it locked behind him. "I'm sorry about the flower. I knew you had a thing about clowns, but I didn't know it was that bad. That was insensitive of me. Forgive me?" Jogging ahead, he turned and walked backward in front of her so he could bat his eyes and implore for forgiveness.

Kristina had never seen a man with irises the color of his. They were blue but looked lavender under bright lights and rimmed with a thick, dark circle around the edges. Jason attracted attention everywhere he went. Today, he wore a pair of khaki dress slacks with shiny leather shoes, one large buckle over the top of each. His shirt was a light purple that played with the strange color of his eyes. The stupid, water-spouting daisy must have had a tube going down the inside of his shirt with a bulb full of liquid he could squeeze at an unsuspecting victim. Kristina hoped he'd emptied it when he aimed it at her.

"If I make it through this thing, you can make it up to me by buying the first round of drinks."

Jason grinned. Little lines around his eyes deepened with the expression, giving away the big secret that he'd left his twenties behind the previous February. Kristina wasn't far off from that milestone herself.

"Deal. But if yours tastes funny, I swear I didn't do it." Putting his hands up in mock innocence, Jason turned and faced forward.

Three more steps and he would've taken the stairs backward. He'd been to Kristina's place enough times to know the length of the hallway without looking. One flight of stairs later, and the foyer door opened to a beautiful, sunny day. The early morning dew still coated the stationary cars parked on the street. The birds chirped, announcing the return of blue skies as the night faded into memory.

Kristina covered her brow with her hand, shielding her eyes from the intrusive rays of the sun.

"I'm parked over there." Jason gestured to the left where the Mustang sat behind a small beat-up Ford Focus. Crossing the short distance, he opened the door and bowed. "Your chariot, m'lady."

Rolling her eyes, Kristina handed the bag off to Jason and slid into the passenger seat, feeling the buttery leather beneath her thighs. The car still smelled brand new with a hint of the leather protectant he slathered onto the dashboard. While the outside was bumblebee yellow, the inside was all black. It had a touchscreen mounted between the air vents beside the steering wheel. She wouldn't have chosen it for herself, but she appreciated the luxury.

Her vehicle bit the dust a few weeks prior. The thing went in for routine maintenance, and she'd never brought it home again. When the dealership called, she expected them to say the car was ready to be picked up from getting the oil changed. She hadn't expected when the clerk explained it needed four new tires, a fuel pump, and brake pads. It was already fifteen years old, and she couldn't justify spending that much money on a car that was past its expiration date. When they'd offered her five-hundred dollars to take it off her hands, she'd agreed. The only problem now was finding the time to purchase a new one. In the meantime, Jason valiantly offered to be her chauffer and it was working out perfectly, at least until he showed up with water-spouting daisies.

At least she'd been able to scope out Showmen's Rest Cemetery before it crapped out on her. She wanted to get a feel for where she'd be taking photos for her next job, even though the place scared the hell out of her. She'd hated it and wasn't in any hurry to go back today. Ever since she crossed the threshold between the two elephant statues, she'd felt uneasy like something watched her from the shadows. The feeling persisted after she'd gotten home and the days after.

The creepy feeling wasn't all she got from that place. When she'd reach the center, surrounded by the stones of the unknown dead, Kristina had the distinct impression of someone embracing her. While it felt warm and caring, it only further terrified her, and that was the tipping point for her to leave. She hadn't been back since.

Jason dropped the bag into the trunk before opening his door and taking the driver's seat. He turned the key in the ignition, and the powerful engine roared to life. He stepped on the gas pedal a few times, smirking at her with his bottom lip between his teeth, listening to the revving noise. *Men and their toys.*

Kristina turned away from him and glanced out the window. Her apartment was on the second floor— the first set of windows on the building's right side. She already imagined how good it would feel to take off her dress clothes and slip into a bubble bath, far away from the circus performers she'd be mingling with for the day. As her mind drifted, she caught a flash of movement in the living room window. Jason backed up to make space to pull out of the parking spot. The curtain moved again.

"Wait!"

Jason hit the brakes causing Kristina's head to bounce forward. She brushed the hair out of her face and squinted at the windows above. Someone moved around in her place, first one window, then the next. It was in her bedroom now, an unmistakable silhouette of a person walking.

"What's wrong? Did you forget something?" Jason asked, concerned.

"Someone's in my apartment!" Kristina rolled the window down to get a better look, worried the black tint was somehow causing her to hallucinate. "Look! There he is again!"

A person strolled through the living room, his body swaying from side to side in a strange lumbering gait. Jason leaned over her trying to ascertain what she saw.

"I don't see anything, Kristina." He unclipped his seatbelt to lean over further. "You sure you saw something?"

The curtains parted. A white face stared out with a terrifying grin. The lines in the face paint done sharply with harsh edges instead of a gaily flowing hand. Kristina screamed, pushing herself out of her seat and into Jason's lap on the driver's side. Time froze as her eyes focused on the creature leering at her from above. Her skin broke out in a thin film of sweat, her limbs pulsing with the need to run. It looked at her, staring into her eyes. He waved one white gloved hand from the window, wagging his fingers.

"Do you see that? Do you see him? There's a fucking clown in my living room, Jason!"

Jason looked perplexed. He wrapped his arms around his friend, continuing to look past her to the rooms above. "Kristina, I don't know what you're seeing, but there's nothing there."

Looking into his face as he spoke, Kristina felt baffled by his dismissive words. Her whole body quaked, teeth chattering. She looked back at her window. Nothing was there. The curtains were still. No face looked back at her. She squinted, looking for the person she knew was there moments before. The bedroom window was just as empty as the living room, as if she'd imagined it all.

"Do you need me to go check it out? I have a baseball bat in the back. I'll knock the asshole out for going into your place and scaring you. You call the cops, and I'll go look." Jason started to open his door, reaching behind the seat for his weapon.

"No, it's fine." Kristina slid back over the center console into her seat. Her voice still held a tremor, but she felt bad for scaring him. It must have been a trick of the light, or her mind playing games with her. She hadn't realized she was that stressed out over this. "There's nothing there— guess I'm just jumpy. Don't worry about it."

"You sure? I really don't mind going up there." Jason looked concerned.

Kristina shook her head. "It's okay, I promise. I'm sorry for being a pain."

"This job's getting to you, huh?" He pulled the shifter into drive and lurched forward. "You should've said no to the job if it was going to bother you this much."

Kristina sighed. She looked out the window again and caught her reflection in the side mirror. Her skin looked pasty white from terror. She took a deep breath, counted to three, and released it. He was probably right. How the hell was she going to do her job if it had her afraid of her own shadow? One last glance at the window showed everything was well. Then she noticed the figure behind her in the mirror.

Standing in the middle of the street waving the grotesque white hand was the clown she'd seen in her apartment. The air rushed out of Kristina's lungs in a whoosh. She turned in her seat and looked out the rear window and saw nothing. Facing forward again, she squeezed her eyes shut until she saw starbursts behind her lids. *There's nothing there. There's no clown. Everything's okay.*

CHAPTER THREE

June 8th, 1918

"Come one! Come all!" Ringmaster Charlie's voice boomed over the throng of onlookers lined up to enter the big tent. The flaps were pulled open to the side with a thick rope and tied off on stakes hammered into the soft wet ground. Melodic calliope music wafted across the field, mesmerizing the crowd. "Get your tickets ready folks, and Baldy here will be happy to stamp each one!"

Baldy giggled and wiggled his ears, taking the first girl's ticket in his gloved hand.

"Gee, mister, is that your belly under there?" A little boy poked Baldy's pudge before turning crimson and ducking his face into his mother's skirt.

"Woo-wee!" Baldy loudly exclaimed, hopping up and down from each elongated foot. "That tickles! Do it again!" Leaning down with a grin, Baldy encouraged the child to poke him once more.

The mother pushed her son forward with a gentle hand, keeping her palm on his shoulder to bolster his bravery. With a determined expression and his tongue pressed securely between his lips, the child made a fist and extended his pointer finger. He gasped in shock when the clown threw himself backwards in a peal of laughter, kicking his feet in the air above him.

"That's a pretty funny clown, isn't he, Daniel?" The mother guided the boy through the opening of the tent while the boy smiled from ear to ear.

Baldy composed himself and took the next ticket. No one else poked him, but plenty of children gazed at the man in awe. Offering a plethora of strange faces and ear wiggles, the clown did all he could to make sure he made a lasting impression on each person he met.

Everyone crowded inside the big top; the band fired up, and the entrance music was in full swing. Baldy took one flap while Gregory took the second, closing the tent for the show to begin.

"How can you handle all that touching?" Gregory took his post in front of the door to make sure stragglers didn't try to sneak in without a ticket while Baldy deposited the handful he'd taken into a large wooden box seated on the ground beside the canvas. "Children are so dirty. They all pick their noses, and who knows what else."

Baldy slapped his thigh. "And that right there's why you never married, Gregory. What woman would want to saddle up with a man who doesn't like kids?"

"I didn't say I don't like them," Gregory said indignantly. "Besides, I have plenty to offer a woman that doesn't involve knocking them up."

"Oh yeah? Like what, pray tell?" Baldy hefted the box from the ground and tucked it under one arm. It was scarcely noticeable under his girth and the frothy, puffy clothing of his costume.

Gregory shrugged. "I can take care of them in the sack. I just make sure to pull out before I sire any little monsters of my own."

"Monsters!" Baldy's great stomach bounced under his laugh. "They're hardly monsters if they're reared correctly, my friend. Look at my Reginald."

"What about him? He's still a child."

Baldy wasn't smiling anymore, but his painted-on grin gave the illusion that he was. "Reginald's wise beyond his years. He's a good boy. And I don't think I've ever seen him eat a single booger. Some of the roustabouts, on the other hand, I think they might still eat them."

Gregory scoffed. "Well, you ain't kidding there."

"I better get inside." Baldy tipped his head with the tiny hat attached at the top to the second in command and gave his ears a wiggle. Gregory was the only person among them who didn't get a kick out of that trick, but the clown never tired of trying to make him smile. "Those other clowns get lazy if I don't keep a close watch on them."

Taking the wooden box from the clown, Gregory nodded. "I know the feeling. I feel like nothing gets done around here if I'm not breathing down the men's necks. Have a good show, Baldy."

The rain had stopped completely, and the earth quickly sucked down the water pooled on the surface. In its place, thick mud with footprints from many sets of shoes remained. The clown's own soles were caked with mud. Taking them off carefully by the door to the tent, he slapped them together, getting the big pieces off before sliding them back on over his bright red stockings. His fingers grazed the large patch on the knee of his trousers fixed by Martha the night before. Baldy couldn't help thinking of her beautiful face in the light of the lantern as she pushed the needle through, again and again, humming a sweet song to Reggie, who slept at her feet.

He'd really gotten lucky with that woman. She would be in the crowd tonight with their son as she always was. She was his biggest fan.

Baldy snuck through the flap of the tent and made his way to the front of the crowd. His men, the clowns, cartwheeled across the ring. Smiley held one of the new guys, who juggled brightly colored balls, on his shoulders. Laughter rang out from every corner from excited onlookers.

Ringmaster Charlie was on his podium, whip in one hand, overseeing the tomfoolery. Lights trained on the tumbling forms; drums pounded at the right moment to add suspense to each fall. Baldy grabbed a bucket of water and showed it to another clown with a grin. When the other investigated the depths, Baldy poured it over his head and did a victory dance to the surprise of gleeful faces.

A tiger roared from beyond. That was the clowns' cue to vacate the spotlight. Baldy whistled, and the group took a bow, exiting to the right and left, each doing their own dance with a different goofy expression.

Fireballs erupted from the front of the stage in an organized line meant to distract and amaze. The drums played at a fierce pace getting louder and louder until they stopped altogether. The ringmaster, with his face painted white and a big red, exaggerated mouth, walked onto the stage. His steps were slow, his stride long, with his hands clasped behind his back. When he reached the center, he turned and faced the crowd, looking toward the ceiling. The room went silent, waiting for him to speak. One could almost hear the flurry of beating hearts, the excitement for what was to come. Charlie brought his face down. He glanced from left to right, greeting each person on a personal level.

"Ladies and gentlemen," he started. "Boys and girls." Charlie grinned and looked down at the younger members of the audience. "There's only one place in the world where you can see a great Siberian cat. A cat so fantastic with bright orange and black stripes. Many of you would call this cat a tiger, but he's so much more." Charlie swept his hand before him, spreading the feeling of magic to everyone watching him.

Baldy stood at the right of the stage, just out of sight. The large cage holding the tiger was on wheels, and he and three other clowns were poised to push the pen in on Charlie's signal. "Get ready boys, it's almost time." The men grunted in response and placed their hands in the proper spots.

Charlie drew out the pause to make sure everyone paid attention. "You see, this particular tiger's the only one in existence who knows how to jump through a ring of fire without burning its fur." Mouths dropped open; the crowd whispered amongst themselves. "It's true! I swear to all of you!"

Baldy raised one gloved hand into the air. "Brutus, push out the ring!"

The clown of the shortest stature carried the large ring out onto the stage and fitted the pole it attached to into a large red box that held it upright. Pulling a match from his large red pants, he struck the thing against the sole of his shoe and held it to the ring that had been lying in kerosene backstage. Flames shot out, wrapping around the circle entirely. Gasps of shock and wonder went through the people watching. Another set of clowns leaped from the other side of the stage carrying twin platforms. One was set on either side of the burning ring.

Charlie turned back to the crowd, satisfied he had everyone's attention. He drew back the whip in his hand and cracked it into the air. "Bring out Khan, the Burning Tiger!" The whip cracked three times in rapid succession, and he turned to the right of the stage where the cage with the pacing animal stood. The tiger's trainer pulled himself on top of Khan's enclosure as the clowns began to push.

When they came into view of the audience, Khan's handler stood to his full height with his arms extended over his head, and his feet spread wide apart to keep his balance. Charlie tossed him the whip as he made his exit.

A woman screamed when the front of the cage fell open, and the animal stepped out, his large paws stretching on the stage. He yawned, showing the rows of sharp teeth inside his mouth. The whip cracked in his direction.

"Khan! Come!" The tiger roared and swiped at the whip, claws coming within an inch of the man's hand.

Baldy knew it was part of the act, but the audience didn't He was sure he saw a woman faint clean away against her husband's shoulder. Khan knew to swipe when given the command, *come.*

The whip cracked again. "Advance!"

The tiger leaped onto the first platform, his tail twisting below him. The trainer pretended to explain to the beast what he must do. Children in the crowd laughed when the great animal turned his huge face away from the man as if he wasn't interested in complying. Another trick, a well-placed command to make the beast look away.

Baldy surveyed the crowd from where he stood. Everyone sat on the edge of their seats. Charlie sauntered over beside him and removed his top hat. "You think that old cat will give him any trouble tonight?"

Baldy shook his head, not looking away from the tiger. "Doesn't seem like it. I told Frank to stop keeping bits of steak in his pocket during shows. That works just fine during training, but the tiger needs to focus on performing and not eating during shows. Seems to be working out fine tonight."

Charlie chuckled. "So that's why Khan kept biting at Frank's pocket during the last show."

"Yeah, he wanted the meat."

Charlie leaned in close to Baldy. "Why aren't you my second in command? You know more about this show and all the acts than even I. No one here could keep things running better than you if something were to happen to me."

"That's a mighty fine compliment, sir, but being a ringmaster isn't for me. I just want to make kids happy." Baldy motioned to his men to get ready to remove the cage. The tiger executed his leap perfectly onto the platform on the other side and waved his paw in the air to the crowd on Frank's cue. "Knowing how to do something and wanting to do it are two different things. I'm happy with the life I have."

The men rolled out the large cage with Frank feeding Khan meat through the bars. "You did a good job tonight, you pretty kitty you."

Baldy slapped the man on the back. "I see I was right about not keeping the meat in your pocket."

"Aye. Didn't have an issue this evening thanks to your intuition." Frank shook the clown's hand before following the cage outside to take care of his tiger.

"I better get out there. Looks like Jenny and her brother are up on the wires waiting for their introduction."

Charlie rushed out before eliciting a response from the clown.

The rest of the show went perfectly, leaving all in attendance elated at what they'd seen.

A HANDFUL OF THE PERFORMERS CELEBRATED ANOTHER WELL-DONE SHOW. Charlie looked down on alcohol consumption after losing the previous ringmaster to the bottle, but he never stopped the crew from enjoying a drink or two after a show. Drinking before a performance was prohibited and grounds for expulsion from the troupe, though.

Huddled around a large table in a local tavern, the group who assembled tried to keep to themselves. Dressed in ordinary clothes, all the day's makeup washed away; the men tried to blend in the best they could.

"You know that asshole Charlie accused me of drinking before a show." No one was sure of the man's name who spoke. He'd joined the circus at the last stop with a buddy, and the two hadn't been overly friendly with anyone unless they wore a skirt. "What business is it of his if I have a swig off the flask to calm my nerves? Last time I checked; this was a goddamn circus. No one expects us to be a damned proper lot. It's not like Queen Victoria would be in attendance. We ain't gonna have to bow or any of that shit. We're clowns. If I'm drunk, it would make my performance all the better." The man laughed and clinked his mug against that of his friends.

"Aye, he asked me if I'd been partaking too." The friend took a drink and slammed the mug down on the table. "I need this job, so I assured him I'd never do a thing like that when I'd been told not to. But you bet your ass as soon as that freak turned his back, I pulled out my flask and took a drink. And then I held it up in a toast to the ringmaster and had another, all right behind him. He's too stupid to know I did it."

Gregory sat at a table behind the men. With a cigarette hanging off his lip and his hat pulled down low over his eyes, he listened to the conversation without interjecting himself. He'd wait until the men stepped outside—no sense bringing attention to any of them in there. The circus troupe needed to be mindful of how they presented themselves in public. They carried a reputation of being lowlifes, of thieving and raping and moving on before the law could catch up with them. If Gregory approached them inside, they could all be arrested, and Charlie needed him.

The rest of the performers seated with the two newcomers looked uneasy. Excusing themselves one by one, soon all that was left was the two troublemakers.

"I have to take a piss," the first man said.

"Don't you be going back to Miss Adelaide's tent!" His friend yelled after him. "I already had to apologize to her once for your bad manners."

Getting up from the table and turning his empty mug upside down, the man stumbled towards the door. Gregory quickly stood and followed. Outside, while the man unzipped his fly to urinate against the side of the building, Gregory grabbed him from behind, lacing his arm around the man's throat.

"Drinking before shows with a complete lack of regard for the wishes of the boss, huh?"

The man's stream shot off wide in an arc. "What business is it of yours?"

Gregory ripped his hat from his head with his free arm and tilted the man's face toward him. "I'm sure you were introduced to me on your tour. I'm second in command, and I'm telling you your time with the troupe is over. This will be your one and only show with us. You and your friend in there can find your own way home."

The man they'd left behind in the tavern fell out the door and landed on his face beside them. "What are you guys doing? Why are you behind him like that?" he asked Gregory. "Are you guys making some kind of exchange?"

Gregory rolled his eyes in disgust. The man accused them of scandalous sexual activity—right outside a public place, nonetheless. Placing his palm on the back of the first man's head, Gregory slammed his face into the side of the tavern and let his body sink to the ground to rest in his own piss.

"What did you go and do that for?" The second man was on his feet and advancing.

Gregory turned and faced him, stepping into the light from the door as he did so.

"Mr. Gregory, sir, I'm sorry I didn't recognize you." The drunk man suddenly sobered up, realizing his employment was about to come to a crashing halt. "We were just joshing in there, sir. We didn't do any of those things we were saying. We were just trying to sound tough. You know how men are when they're drinking."

Gregory stepped towards the man.

Laughing nervously, the second man put his hands up and scooted sideways, out of reach. "I swear to you, it won't happen again. We just wanted to fit in, that's all."

"Go back to the train and pack your bags—both of you. I want you gone before the train leaves this evening. If I ever see either of you again, I'll make you wish your mother had never spread her sorry legs to make you."

"Yes, sir." The man shivered, staring at Gregory in terror. The first man was coming to with mud and piss covering his face and clothes. "You're going to pay for this!" he squealed. "We'll leave your puny little circus but mark my words. There won't be another show."

"You keep your threats to yourself. I don't give a damn what you have to say on the matter." Gregory stomped away from the two men to inform Charlie what had occurred and to make sure everyone knew those men were no longer welcome after they'd collected their belongings.

"He thinks he's so big and bad." The man with mud covering his body spat on the ground. "I'll show him. He's not as tough as he thinks he is." Attempting to wipe his mouth on the sleeve of his shirt, the man became even more irritated when he only managed to smear more filth across his lips.

His friend giggled, watching him get angrier. "He is big and bad. He put you right down on the ground with no trouble."

The dirty man's face turned crimson where his flesh was still visible. "You're just going to let him treat us like that?"

The other man shrugged. "I got a bad back. I can't fight him."

"Bullshit. You're just scared." Dirty man squared off against his friend. The other man flinched. "I got something special for him. I have something that's going to really ruin his night."

The circus train lay just ahead. Most of the troupe was already settled into the cooler tents they'd erected earlier in the day, and the men didn't see anyone else hovering around. Not even Gregory.

"What are you going to do?" The second man pulled the door of the sleeping car where their meager possessions were stowed open and hopped inside. "You gonna let their tiger out? Now that would be a sight to be seen."

"Even better. I'm going to make sure their train doesn't go anywhere."

The other man's head tilted to the side. "How are you going to manage that?"

Jumping into the car and opening the little trunk he'd pushed under a cot, the dirty man pulled out a glass bottle with a clear fluid inside. "This stuff does more than help you wipe that paint off your face. This shit's magical. Mix it with a little saltwater and you really have something special."

"You're going to make sure the train doesn't move with vinegar?" The other man looked at his dirty friend, perplexed until he erupted into laughter. "What are you going to do? Pickle their wheels?"

Rolling his eyes and sneering, the dirty man jumped down, careful not to drop the bottle. "Don't you know what vinegar and saltwater does to iron, you idiot?"

The other man shook his head back and forth.

"It rusts it. Almost instantly. Get me that bag of salt out of your bag you put on everything and some water from the barrel outside."

Rushing to obey, the other man brought back everything the first had requested.

"I'm gonna crawl under the train and pour this all over their brakes. If the brakes are stuck, the train doesn't go anywhere. If the train doesn't go anywhere, they miss shows. If they miss shows, I'll have my revenge for how that fool just treated us. Now you keep a look out and make sure no one sees me." The dirty man ducked under the train car, and his friend took his post next to the door, scanning the darkness for any movement.

CHAPTER FOUR

May 5th, 2018

Kristina didn't allow herself to look in the mirror again during the drive. The thought of seeing that painted face looking back at her, the bright red mouth, the pointed teeth made it hard to take a breath. The paralyzing fear enveloping her refused to wane, even as the apartment complex fell out of sight. Not since her brother's cruel joke had she felt anything as debilitating as the fear she'd felt today. Everything about the clown felt so real, right down to the frilled collar around his neck. There was no way her brain could've made something up with that much detail.

Jason drove like a bat out of hell, as per the usual, all the way to the Illinois border. He kept his hard rock music to a dull thud in the speakers, the bass vibrating the door even though Kristina couldn't make out the song. He looked at her every so often, making sure she was okay, but he didn't bring up what happened when they left the apartment building. Kristina thought he must think she was insane. But, true to his best friend status, he didn't prod her about it. He knew her well enough to know she would bring it up if she wanted to talk.

The cemetery was in Forest Park, Illinois. On a good day, the drive should've taken forty-five minutes from where they were in Hammond, Indiana. Thanks to Jason's lead foot, they made it there in thirty. The parking area was full of all manner of vehicles. Some of them were whimsical, painted in bright colors denoting the owner's circus ties. An old firetruck made to look like a cage on large wheels with a tiger pacing inside took up the rear of the lot. The mural was expertly done, right down to the snarl on the big cat's face. Kristina could imagine the roar emanating from the beast's throat and a flick of the long orange tail behind him.

Jason held the door open for her to step out of the low sitting car.

"How do you manage not to get pulled over driving like that?" She smoothed the hair away from her face, adjusting a few pins that shifted during the ride. He slammed the door shut once she was clear of it.

Kristina was a minimalist girl. Naturally pretty, she never applied more than a little concealer, liner, and a hint of shadow to her eyelids. She thought she looked silly with lipstick on, and her long auburn hair was straight as could be. Her dress attire for work tended to be on the conservative side and almost always in dark hues. When she was on a job, she preferred to blend into the background rather than garner any attention. She was there to take pictures, not be in them.

Jason, on the other hand, preened whenever anyone gave him a second glance. He enjoyed being the star of the show. Going out of his way to speak to everyone, he rarely left an event without a number or two in his pocket from the women who found him attractive. To Kristina's knowledge, he never called any of the women he flirted with.

Struggling with the camera bag, Jason took his place at her side as they walked through the cemetery's iron gates. "I'm just a lucky person, doll."

"Your luck's going to run out someday, and you're going to be in a world of hurt." Kristina smiled at a man standing inside the gate with a clipboard in his old, wrinkled hands.

"You must be the photographer, Miss Kristina Perdue. How are you today?" The old man took her hand in his with a warm greeting. "I bet we'll get a front-page story for the anniversary with you taking the pictures. I've seen your work. You're very talented." The man's eyes glittered with appreciation as he released her fingers and gripped onto his list anew.

"That's very kind of you to say. I want to do right by all of you with these pictures. This was a horrible tragedy, and the victims deserve no less than the best." Kristina smiled warmly, banishing the remnants of the ghostly clown's memory to the deepest recesses of her mind. "This is my colleague, Jason Asher. He's going to be helping me out today."

Jason took the man's hand when offered and thanked him.

"No need to thank me, young man. The people who died in that crash deserve to be known. With your help, they will be. Thank you for your diligence in this matter."

"We're just doing our jobs, sir. I'm glad you think so highly of us." Kristina crossed her arms at the wrists across her lower belly demurely. More people waited to enter behind them. Giving the man one last nod, they stepped out of the way so the others could pass. The old gentleman shook each person's hand, greeting them by name.

"This place is great," Jason whispered against Kristina's ear. This was his first visit and he was like a kid in a candy shop.

Somehow, the four large stone elephants at each corner of the burial site looked more foreboding and ominous to her than they had the first time she'd visited. From what she'd read, their trunks were down in mourning for those lost during the wreck. Showmen's Rest was ironically purchased only a few months before the accident by the Showmen's League of America, the group paying for their services today. Fifty-three of the performers killed that night were buried here in a mass grave below their feet.

Kristina fought with herself not to look down. The last thing she wanted to see were the stones for those people. Labeled "Unknown Man or Woman," each with a different number, it was unnerving to think of all the families who lost a loved one and never knew what became of them. Only a few of the stones bore names, and none held the person's real identity. Instead, they said Baldy or Four Horse Driver. These were the only names the survivors knew them by. It was unfortunate.

Jason touched Kristina's elbow. She jumped and pulled her arm away quickly.

"Geez, sorry." Jason took a step away with his hands up. "I didn't mean to scare you, Kris, but that man over there's waving us over."

Kristina wiped the sweat off her brow and took a deep breath. *You need to stop. There isn't any reason to be reacting the way you are. Nothing bad's happening to you. People are going to think you're insane.* "Where?" she asked.

"Over there." Jason raised his hand and pointed to the far right of the podium set up for the speeches that would be made later in the day. The man sat with a pleasant looking woman beside him. Both wore a cheery grin and wore clothing from the time period of the accident. The man was in overalls, baggy pants, black boots, and a rail worker's cap, the woman in a long dress with a feather in her hair, which was piled loosely on top of her head. The couple was well-aged —at least in their early sixties.

"That's Norman Caster and his wife, Beatrice. He's the president of the Showmen's League." Kristina waved back politely and started towards them. "They're the ones who requested me personally, so be on your best behavior."

"When am I not?" Jason chuckled.

Kristina made her way across the expanse with Jason in tow, careful not to step on the stones. She was never a superstitious person, but there seemed to be something sacred about the markers, and she didn't want to accrue any bad karma for walking on them. The heels of her boots sank into the soft turf, and she was mindful of balancing her weight on her toes to keep from getting them dirty or breaking her neck. She thought of her feet sinking into the ground where the dead performers' ghosts waited to pull her under. She could see their twisted, burned hands grabbing her ankles and yanking her down with them where she would be trapped forever.

That's enough of that! Kristina scolded herself silently as she took a deep breath and began to walk faster.

Norman rose from his seat, leaning heavily on a cane, as they drew near. Holding his hand out to Kristina first, he grasped her hand in a feeble grip that shook slightly. "I'm so happy you both could come and honor our lost brothers and sisters with us today. It's hard to believe it's been a hundred years since they were taken from us." Norman then shook Jason's hand and settled himself back down at his wife's side.

"It's a pleasure to have you both here," Beatrice said from beside him. When she nodded, the plume bobbed on her head, brushing across her forehead. She scratched the spot it'd touched absently as if it'd left a tickle there.

"The pleasure is ours." Kristina smiled at the couple, turning on her professional voice. *No clowns here. I'm perfectly safe.*

Jason watched her as she spoke, waiting for the cue to add anything in. She didn't leave much for him to say.

"It was great fun preparing for this memorial," Jason started. "I generally don't care for doing sad events. It doesn't suit my style, but you're all such an exciting group of people. It was a blast researching the circus and learning about the history connected to it. I even changed Kristina's ring tone to circus music, and she's terrified of clowns."

Norman laughed a great belly laugh, holding his sides. Beatrice smirked with a dainty hand over her mouth.

Kristina gave Jason a look to warn him he'd said too much and wondered how she would compensate for his lack of professionalism. She felt her face grow hot, and she clenched her fists at her sides to calm herself. They'd have to have a long talk about what's acceptable to say in front of clients and what's not. Fortunately, the couple didn't seem to be offended by what he'd said.

"Young lady, don't look so embarrassed. The circus isn't for everyone, but everyone is for the circus. Give it time. We'll grow on you." Norman fought off his giggles to speak. "You'll be an honorary clown by the end of the day."

Kristina's breath caught when he mentioned clowns. Remembering the one she'd seen in her apartment earlier that day, she felt a wave of cold as it enveloped her body. "Thank you, sir. I look forward to meeting everyone and hearing the speech you've prepared. I'm sure it's going to be riveting."

Norman chuckled again. "I'm not sure about riveting. I'll settle for decent. I'm not as young as I once was, Miss Perdue. My brain doesn't work quite as well as it used to. Getting my thoughts out on paper is becoming harder and harder the older I get. I'm glad I was around to see the one-hundredth anniversary, but I fear this might be the last one I attend. It may be time to pass down the gavel. My grandfather died in the crash, but my father survived. I don't know if you knew that or not."

"I wasn't aware, Mr. Caster." Kristina tore her mind from the clowns who could be waiting beneath her feet to focus on his words more closely.

"Were you on the train?" Jason asked.

"I wasn't even born yet when it happened. I'm old but not that old!"

Beatrice laughed out loud this time. "Honey, you don't look a day over thirty."

"Thank you, my love." Norman turned back to Kristina and Jason. "My dad, Allen, was a porter on the train. My grandfather, Henry, was an animal trainer. He worked with the tigers and elephants. Fortunately for our family, my grandfather's body was thrown away from the crash on impact. His neck broke, and he died instantly, but he wasn't burned. They were able to recover him, and his remains were given back to my grandmother for burial. She laid him to rest in the family plot, but when I became the president of the Showmen's League, I had his casket exhumed and relocated here. I think he'd be more at peace to be with his crew. He lived with them nine months out of the year for thirty years, ever since he was a young boy. Then he died with them. It's only fitting that he rests with them as well. His gravesite is right here beside us." Norman pointed down to the ground beside his chair. A flat stone was pressed into the ground in the same style as all the rest.

Henry Caster, born June 8th, 1868, died June 18th, 1918.

Beatrice crossed herself and mumbled a prayer beneath her breath. The feather in her hair bounced back and forth each time she dipped her head. Kristina found herself watching the thing, transfixed by the hot pink color.

"What about your father?" Jason asked. "Is he buried here as well?"

Kristina shot him another look.

"My father was never the same after the accident. Or so I've been told at least." Norman took his wife's hand when she offered it to him. "He took to drinking. It was heavy alcoholism by the time I came into the world. He worked with the circus on and off during my childhood. He got into lots of trouble and tended to beat my mother when he was home. He finally left for a tour to California with the troupe, and when they returned, he wasn't with them."

"I'm sorry to hear that." Kristina furrowed her eyebrows wishing Jason hadn't brought up the negative memory for the man.

"No need to be sorry," Norman said. "I was only five when he disappeared for good. It didn't dissuade my decision to join the troupe when I was old enough." The old man grinned.

"Norman here was the best elephant trainer to ever work for the Hagenbeck-Wallace circus," Beatrice proclaimed proudly.

"Shhh, woman," Norman chided. "Don't you say that in front of my grandpappy." He grinned at her lovingly.

On the other side of the podium, the band finished setting up, and a melodious circus tune began to play. Norman's face softened to a whimsical grin. He tilted his head back and closed his eyes, listening to the song drifting across the cemetery.

"Oh, boy, hearing that," the old man didn't open his eyes. "It brings back so many memories. Good and bad. Like the smell of all the carnival food when the boys would start cooking at the beginning of the day, the sound of roustabouts directing their crew what to do when the big top went up. The way the canvas tents looked when they came off the train folded into impossibly small squares before being opened." Norman wrinkled his nose. "It also reminds me of what it was like to get pooped on by an elephant and smelling like dung for a week no matter how many showers I got. You remember that, Bea?" He turned to his wife, who fanned her face with a gloved hand.

"I sure do. You tried to climb into my bunk smelling like that."

Norman turned back to Kristina and Jason. "Bea was an acrobat. You ever seen a woman who can fold herself into a pretzel? My Bea could." Norman wiggled his eyebrows and grinned. Beatrice slapped his shoulder.

"Don't you go telling them stuff like that. It was a very long time ago. I'm lucky I can buckle my own shoe these days." Beatrice held one dainty foot out before her, showing a short-heeled slipper with a small buckle on the side. "Sometimes I have to have my husband do it for me. I just can't get down that low anymore."

"It's been an honor to grow old with you, Bea. I'll buckle your shoe anytime you need me to." Norman took the hand she'd tapped his shoulder with and pressed it to his lips. Bea giggled and pulled away. "We've been married for forty years. Hers are still the only shoes I'd buckle."

The couple did a great job of chasing away Kristina's trepidation, but they couldn't hang out with them all day. She needed to get the camera ready and start snapping photos. She also needed to be sure she explained every step to Jason so he could file the knowledge away for a time when he would be on his own.

"Mr. and Mrs. Caster, it's been such a pleasure chatting with you both. Thank you for choosing us to capture every moment for you. We'll check in with you later in the evening to get your feedback and to give you the information to access the online photo album that'll be uploaded after the event." Kristina smiled at the couple, reciting the words she knew by heart that she said to every client.

Norman laughed. "Don't go all professional on us now, Miss Perdue. We're a goofy, fun-loving bunch. You'll do much better with the attendees to remember they respond better to those who are real with them. If you try to sound too smart, they won't be bothered with you." Beatrice slapped his shoulder again.

"I'll remember that, sir." Kristina knew the man wasn't saying it to her because he felt displeased but because he wanted her to lighten up and have a good time while she was there. Having a good time wasn't in her job description, though.

Tugging on Jason's arm as the couple went back to a conversation amongst themselves, Kristina decided to get a few pictures of the band before they got too far into their set. The music they played sounded well-rehearsed. The players were all veterans of the circus scene and even boasted a portable calliope on a cart of sorts that could be taken anywhere. As far as Kristina was able to research, that was almost unheard of since circus's stopped doing parades. Everything was transported on big trucks now instead of the slower, more cumbersome trains, and everything went up in the dead of night.

Other things changed too. Circuses were no longer permitted to use animals in their shows. The animal rights groups finally got their way, stating it was cruel to make the creatures perform because it wasn't in their nature to do so. Every circus with animals had to give them up to sanctuaries to live the rest of their lives in enclosures mimicking what it was like in the wild. Kristina agreed with them. She wished someone would do away with the clowns as well, no special enclosures, though. A simple eradication would suffice.

"Where are we headed next?" Jason asked.

"I need to get a few good pictures of the band," I told him. "They're an important piece to the ceremony. The newspaper wants a full-size photo featured with their calliope."

"Oh, okay. They only play circus music, right?"

"As far as I'm aware." Once again, Kristina walked on her toes, crossing the field above a mass grave. Her gut rolled, picturing the skeletons beneath her feet.

"What happens if they run out of circus music and start playing Van Halen? You think they could do some Van Halen on that thing?" He pointed to the mobile calliope.

"That would be very inappropriate." Kristina rolled her eyes. She loved her friend, but sometimes she was concerned about his level of professionalism.

Pausing for a moment as Jason bantered on about classic rock and how it was appropriate everywhere, Kristina was alarmed to feel the same warmth she'd felt on her first visit rush over her like a warm blanket. She couldn't put her finger on it, but it reminded her of chocolate chip cookies, and bedtime hugs from someone who loved her very much. It was so different from the paralyzing fear she'd felt everywhere else that she had to force her feet to move through it and felt as if she'd lost something dear when it receded completely. She brushed it off and continued.

As they drew closer to the stage, Kristina noticed something she wasn't prepared to see. The band was dressed up as clowns. The man or woman, she couldn't tell which it was, seated at the calliope wore the long coattails of a maestro, the fabric nearly brushing the ground, except in lime green. The person had cartoonish white gloves, and the shoes looked to be at least two feet long. The ballooned pants were black with pink polka dots. The face paint was white in typical clown form with a broad red grin and a big bulbous nose. Blue circles made rings around each eye, designed to make the clown look like he wore a perpetual grin. There were eyebrows drawn unnaturally high on the forehead under a bald head with tufts of green hair around the skull base. A tiny hat with a flower sticking out sat high on his head. The other clowns were dressed in similar patterns, all with different face paint, hairstyles, and hats.

Kristina's feet refused to go any further. She felt her heels sinking into the grassy earth but didn't move to pull them free. Her legs turned to stone, her feet cement blocks weighing her body to where she stood. She couldn't tear her eyes off the musical entities strumming a guitar, banging on a drum, pressing the keys on the calliope. She wondered how they managed to make themselves look so innocent, so unassuming.

Jason continued to walk. As if he'd said something to her and didn't get a response, he turned, didn't see her, and did a circle before he realized she was about ten paces back, frozen in place. He looked back at the band and then to her, his confusion replaced by a softer expression.

A drop of sweat ran between Kristina's breasts. Her mouth tasted like it was full of cotton balls, or maybe cotton-candy, just not as sweet. When Jason returned to her side, she couldn't look him in the face. She couldn't tear her eyes off the creatures before her.

"No one told me they would be in costume," she whispered.

"Kristina, you knew people would be here in costumes," Jason reminded her in a gentle voice.

"I didn't know anyone I'd have to talk to would be dressed up. I thought everyone who was involved in the event would be dressed professionally."

Jason stepped in front of her, cutting off her view of the clowns. "It's just paint, Kris. There are just ordinary people under those white faces and red noses. They're no different from you and me when they wipe it off." His words made so much sense, but she couldn't get her brain to buy it. Her mind told her to run as fast as she could, get in the car, drive away, and don't look back. The thoughts swirling through her told her to flee the danger, her life was at stake, and pain was imminent.

"Can you take the pictures?" She looked deeply into his eyes, praying he could handle the simple task. "I can't do it, Jason."

"Sure, Kris." He brushed a stray hair off her cheek and tucked it behind her ear. "What do you want me to do?"

"Just take the camera and try to get some good shots."

"I can do that." Jason smiled, trying to reassure her. "I'll be right back. Stay right here."

Kristina nodded, thinking she couldn't have moved if she wanted to, but didn't voice that out loud. She watched him walk away, praying they wouldn't hurt him or demand to speak to her. She sweated more profusely than ever, and it had nothing to do with the eighty-degree weather of June in Illinois. It was a cold, scentless sweat—the kind generated by terror.

The conductor turned when Jason approached and shook his hand happily. As she watched, the clown nodded as Jason spoke and then leaned to the side and looked at her, passed the other man. When his eyes met hers, it was as if he spoke to her telepathically. *I see you over there. You can't hide from us. We can always find you. We will find you. There's no escaping us.*

The clown leaned towards Jason, took his average-sized hand in his exaggerated glove, and turned around to his band. Pulling the black bag from his shoulder, Jason dropped to one knee and began snapping pictures as the clowns posed for him. He got up, moved to the side, and continued.

Finally, her friend stood in front of her again. He looked fine; his hand wasn't melting off from where he'd touched the clown. She didn't see any blood and he didn't seem to be in any pain.

"Did you get the shots?" Kristina didn't recognize the broken voice that passed her lips. She cleared her throat and swallowed.

"Yup, and they really hammed it up for me. The conductor's name is Jimmy, and he said to thank you for including him in the spread. Who knew clowns loved to have their pictures taken?"

That's not all he said. Kristina cleared her throat a second time and looked around Jason to the clown named Jimmy. His back was to her, and the other clowns followed his lead on their instruments.

BEEP!

Kristina jumped from where she was rooted to the ground and found herself under Jason's arm. Turning back, she saw another clown on a unicycle, pedaling around the field with a bicycle horn, honking it at each person he came to. He giggled as they jumped and moved on to the next. Kristina breathed like she'd just completed a marathon; her blood pounded in her ears. This place was going to give her a heart attack.

CHAPTER FIVE

June 22ND, 1918

Having completed the set of shows in Chicago, the Hagenbeck-Wallace circus was headed to Hammond, Indiana. It would arrive in the early hours of the morning. The night was warm and clear, and stars shined in the heavens above from a cloudless sky. The train ambled along the track at a slow, steady pace. The cars were old, made entirely of wood planks and steel for the wheels, lighted only by kerosene lanterns. The train was more than a little creaky as each board rubbed against each other while the cars moved.

Inside, the performers slept peacefully. The last four cars before the caboose were sleeper cars. They were outfitted with enough beds for everyone to comfortably slumber while they crossed the night terrain on rickety wheels that knew the way. The beds lined the walls in bunk style with a pathway down the center. Gentle snores and heavy breathing came from each rack.

Around midnight, the train came to a gentle stop. A hotbox on one of the flatcars malfunctioned, and the brake seized. It needed repairing before they could continue. A brakeman disconnected the front half of the train carrying the animals, and the engine pulled away, leaving the sleeper cars of the back end behind so the brakeman could fix the issue. No one minded the delay. Those sleeping inside probably never noticed they'd stopped. The younger flagman posted automatic signals to alert any oncoming trains of the stationary cars on the track while the more experienced gentleman set to repair the damaged hotbox.

"Fine night to be stranded." The clang of metal on metal as the brakeman hammered on the brake to loosen the bearings echoed through the silent night.

The flagman held the lantern high, aiding the man working between the wheels. "I didn't know any night was a good one for being stranded."

"Could be worse, you know?" The dirty-faced man paused his hammering so the other man could hear him better. "It could be raining, or we could have a cyclone or an earthquake, or God forbid, a train wreck. Instead, it's just one lousy hotbox on an overused bearing giving us trouble."

The flagman lowered his light and glowered in the older man's direction. "You shouldn't say things like that, Ralph. You know it's bad luck even to mention it."

"Mention what? A train wreck?" Laughing, Ralph pulled himself back under the car, his back pressed to the wooden cross ties and ballast rocks surrounding them. "Don't you go soft on me, Edgar. If I wanted something soft out here with me, I would've brought me a woman. That's just an old wives tale, kid—no truth to that kind of thing. You can say whatever you please. Your words won't cause anything to happen that the Almighty hadn't already planned."

"If you say so," Edgar lifted the light back to shoulder height. The kerosene lantern hanging from his fist cast an eerie yellow glow on the side of the Pullman car. "I don't like it, though. It makes me nervous."

"Can you pull that light down here? I can't tell my fingers from my balls."

Complying instantly, Edgar dropped to his knees in his worn-out overalls and positioned his body halfway under the car so the light would shine where Ralph worked. "That's more like it, son. Just like that. Hold'er steady now."

Edgar beamed with pride, hearing the older man's compliment.

"She's stuck and won't come loose, goddamn her!" Ralph pounded on the bearing to no avail. "This train shan't be moving anytime soon until this beast releases her grip on the poor brake." The hammering continued. Sweat and black soot coated Ralph's face. Only the man's eyes and teeth were readily visible in the low light.

"What should we do?" Edgar implored, getting closer to the thing that was causing so many problems for his friend. He didn't understand all the train's moving pieces, but his position as a flagman guaranteed he would learn everything there was to know. At the ripe age of seventeen, he was the man of his family, but scarcely more than a child compared to the older men in the field.

"Beat this bitch senseless. She'll give up eventually." Ralph hit the piece of metal again for good measure. His hammer dinged, and a spark flew from the contact. He grinned at the boy squatted on the iron piece of rail beneath the soles of his shoes.

"Do you feel that?" Edgar set the lantern on the wood plank, making sure it wouldn't fall over, and placed his palm flat on the rail. "There's a vibration."

"Don't you start with, *there's a vibration*!" Ralph bellowed from below. "You hold that light up and help me finish this! Stop falling for tricks of the imagination. What time is it, boy?"

Edgar pulled his pocket watch, a gift from his father, from his breeches, and trained his young eyes on the face. "Nearly four in the morning, sir." Returning the trinket to his pocket, he lifted the lantern anew so as not to get a stern word from the brakeman.

"We've been pounding on this old girl for four hours!" Ralph gripped the wheel and pulled himself out from under the hotbox and stretched, popping the bones down his back in one movement. "I'm getting too old for this kind of work. Maybe it's time I found myself a misses and settled down somewhere. Preferably somewhere with no trains whistling through the night."

Clouds drifted over the waning moon. The night that began so clear grew darker, each star extinguished by an angry being, pulling a blanket of black over the already low light. The lanterns did little to light the surrounding area, giving enough lumens for perhaps three or four feet into each direction before tapering off into an unknown abyss. Edgar began to feel uneasy, his gut clenching with the feeling of impending doom.

He put his hand on the track again. "You really don't feel that, Ralph?" The thrum of movement under his fingertips was undeniable. His skin tingled where it met the iron rails.

"For the last bloody time, there ain't no vibration! It's all in that stupid head of yours!" Ralph turned toward the rear of the train, wiping his greasy hands on a rag tucked into the hem of his pants. The threadbare cloth did nothing but smear the mess. His arms dropped to his sides and he froze, the towel fluttering to the ground from fingers that no longer held it tight. His eyes grew wide, his pupils lit by the flicker of the lantern, dilated to black pools reflecting the sudden fear overtaking him. His toothy grin vanished, fear spreading across his dirty features. "Run, boy, run!"

Edgar whipped around, focusing his eyes further down the track. A plume of black smoke, barely distinguishable against the night sky, and a ball of yellow light from an oncoming train was visible not a quarter mile out from where the two men stood. It was a Michigan Troop Train, and it barreled straight towards the circus train and the helpless sleepers onboard. It wasn't slowing.

The crash was deafening as the six-ton steam locomotive plowed into the caboose and the four rear wooden sleeping cars of the circus train at the rail crossing known as Ivanhoe Interlocking. It was going approximately thirty-five miles per hour with no indication of a brake application. Steam wasn't let off. No whistle sounded to warn the stationary train of some kind of malfunction. The noise that followed sounded like dynamite blowing through rock, the devastated, twisted metal from the undercarriage of the broken-down train was bent and broken like twigs from a tree.

Lamps filled with kerosene inside the wreckage ignited the wooden cars, and the fire spread quickly like a wave of molten lava. It was as if hell itself rose through the layers of earth and spewed death and brimstone upon all who were present.

The brakeman and flagman, Ralph and young Edgar, couldn't outrun the calamity. Their bodies remained among the missing.

Most of the eighty-six people killed in the wreck perished within half a minute of the collision. The flames ignited those who survived the initial impact; their bodies burnt so severely; identification was rendered impossible.

Two men stationed at the Ivanhoe Signal Tower, roughly one-hundred feet from the accident, witnessed the disaster. Taking up the phone, they dialed the operator to try to get help for the victims.

"Pick up, you Bastard!" Steven Brasso screamed into the receiver, waiting for someone to take the call.

"Sir, your party isn't responding. Would you like to wait a bit longer or make another call?" The operator's voice trembled, responding to his fear.

"Just wait, goddamn it!"

"Yes, sir." The woman's voice left the line, and Steven continued his prayer that someone would hear the ring.

"Steve! The whole thing is burning! We need help!" Philip leaned over the railing towards the cloud of black smoke. There were pieces of train littering the landscape, moans from victims the men couldn't see rose from the ground. The night was a roar with the screams of those dying and the blaze consuming the wreckage. Philip's ears still rang from the deafening explosion that awoke him from a dead sleep.

"I know, you idiot! What do you think I'm doing? Calling my mother?" Steven glared at the other man, his face equal parts fear and anger. "Yes! Hello! Sir, there's been a crash at Ivanhoe Interlocking. Send help immediately!"

He paused while the person on the other end responded. "I don't bloody care if it's after four in the morning. People are dying out here, you twit!"

"What's he saying?" Philip demanded. "Tell him everything's on fire!"

"The whole bloody thing's up in flames, sir. We need the fire department and as much medical personnel as you can rouse." Steven watched a flatcar collapse in on itself, the wood clattering against the ground where it continued to burn. "It was a train crash! A steam engine ran right into the stopped circus train, sir, it didn't even try to stop!"

Another pause.

"Are they coming?" Philip screamed.

Steven put a hand up, silencing him. "I don't know how many souls were on board, sir, but I can hear them dying. Some are screaming for help. They won't last long."

Philip edged closer to Steven both to hear the conversation and for comfort. The man couldn't fathom how something like this could've happened. He saw the flames reflecting in his coworker's eyes, and it shook him to the core. *Lord help us all.*

Slamming the telephone down, Steven turned to the other man. "They're coming! Help's on the way!"

"Thank Christ," Philip exclaimed.

Gary, Indiana's mayor, William Hodges, was the first on the scene. With him was the fire chief. Before arriving, he pounded on the doors of every doctor and nurse employed in the city to come and assist the victims. Little by little, the sleepy townspeople began to arrive bringing supplies for the wounded. A tangled mess of steel greeted them along with an out-of-control blaze and more dead than they could handle.

"God almighty, how could this happen?" Mayor Hodges exclaimed as he surveyed the destruction.

Men lugging heavy buckets of water from a nearby spigot desperately tried to assist the firefighters who sprayed the blaze from a hose attached to their truck connected to a large tank taking up most of the back end. They would need several more of the trucks to complete the job and the one they had needed to refill multiple times. The hose was heavy and unruly, needing four men to handle the twisting snake to keep it aimed where it should be. The buckets were next to useless.

The doctors, nurses, and other onlookers didn't wait for the inferno to burn out. They began rushing in and out of the wreck dragging burned corpses and those still alive away from the blaze. Their charred bodies were nearly unrecognizable under the black flesh. Melted hair, lips burned away, leaving all the teeth visible, and eyes shriveled in the skull were all that remained. These were the best of circumstances for a great deal of the bodies. Others were in the fire so long they were crispy, a brick of charcoal that came apart in their rescuer's hands.

"How many have been recovered so far?" Mayor Hodges's skin looked pallid, coated in a thick film of sweat. His hands shook, and his voice sounded gravelly from inhaling smoke. When the chief didn't readily respond, Hodges coughed, cleared his throat, and asked the man again louder so the gentleman might hear the question.

"Forty so far, sir. They're laying the bodies on the west embankment, hoping the survivors might identify some of them. I don't think there's much hope of that, though. The men think most of the deceased are the black porter boys. All of the bodies are black." The fire chief wheezed from the smoke, out of breath. His heavy yellow jacket had black soot covering it.

The mayor imagined the other man smelled like fire and ash, although he couldn't tell from where they stood. They would all smell that way for days. *Why are you thinking of these things right now?*

The chief bent forward, looking him in the face. "Sir, I think maybe you should sit down. You're not looking so good."

The mayor only nodded but didn't move to take the advice. All he could see was the fire and the husks of the people who died inside.

A man rushed toward them. "Mayor Hodges! The operator of the troop train! He survived! He's banged up a little, but he climbed out of that engine himself. The nurses are tending to his injuries."

Mayor Hodges turned to the man and scowled.

"After his wounds have been properly dressed, have him taken into custody. Tonight, that man became a murderer." He turned back to the fire chief with a grave expression. "Please get me an updated count, Christopher. The chief nodded and rushed away.

The flames were mostly out now, replaced by more thick smoke and glowing embers. The responders were nearly as black as those they'd pulled from the wreckage of the train, hair singed and coughing hard. The dead were on one side of the carnage, those who survived on the other. Many milled about, asking about those they didn't see among them. The attending nurses didn't know what to say.

As dawn arrived and the sun began to chase the darkness away, the real horror of what occurred began to take shape. Operating on little sleep, the chief returned to the mayor with grim news.

"Sir, we've searched everywhere, under every smoldering board.

Among the dead are eighty-six souls, and I dare say there may be more we couldn't locate. Another one-hundred and twenty-seven taken by ambulance to St. Margaret's Hospital in Hammond to have their injuries treated. God save them." The chief removed his hat and looked towards the heavens in prayer.

"Who was the engineer who caused this? What's his name?" Mayor Hodges also removed his hat out of respect. "I want him tried, and if a court of his peers finds him guilty, hanged."

"His name's Alonzo Sargent, sir. The fellow told the officers he fell asleep at the throttle. He didn't know what happened until he hit the circus train."

The mayor's lips flattened into a straight line, turning white from the effort to control his temper. "He fell asleep. His negligence took eighty-six lives tonight. That's a piss poor excuse if I've ever heard one. I'll personally petition for his execution when they bring him to trial."

"I wouldn't expect anything less from you, sir," the chief agreed. "Nothing less at all."

CHAPTER SIX

May 5th, 2018

Kristina ran her hand through her long hair as she scrolled through the photos they'd taken during the memorial. Between the two of them, there were over two-hundred little glimpses into the lives of the people directly or indirectly affected by the Hagenbeck-Wallace circus train crash. They'd met family members and friends, other performers who'd merely heard about the accident and wanted to pay their respects, as well as people who had nothing to do with the circus at all but were interested in the story.

After they'd left the cemetery, Kristina was finally able to breathe again. She'd gotten herself back into the game and began to think about what needed to be done next. Jason wasn't good at making selections when it came to which photos to submit to the editor and which ones were garbage. There was also some editing to be done, fixing lighting, and resizing. She always tried to keep the pictures she took mostly organic without too much manipulation.

Jason wanted to stay to see how she went about everything. But the day had been too stressful, and she needed some time by herself. This part of the job was cathartic. Still frames of mourners, happy children, and people delivering speeches filled her screen in gray scales and full color, and she gave each one the love and attention they deserved while deleting blurry and repetitive shots.

She would go through what she did with Jason tomorrow when her nerves weren't on edge.

Her office room was bathed in blue light from the computer monitor. The rest of the apartment was silent as the grave. Before he'd left, Jason insisted on checking every nook and cranny to make sure she was safe after the scare they'd had when he picked her up. They found nothing. Everything was in its place, and the door remained bolted.

Jason made sure to poke fun at her before she shoved him out the door and locked it behind him.

Now she was alone with nothing but her thoughts and the work to sort through.

So far, pictures of stone elephants with trinkets at their feet were all she'd gotten through. Little statues of porcelain clowns with happy faces, miniature lions and tigers, and a plethora of pocket change covered the ledge the elephants stood on. Kristina was amazed the coins weren't stolen, and it was apparent many of them had been there for years. The copper pennies turned green from oxidation, sticking to one another and the stone itself. It all belonged to those buried within the gates, the ones the elephants guarded.

A chill ran down Kristina's spine. She could almost hear the trumpeting of those animals, the whips coming down on their backs as they were forced to balance on small platforms and lift acrobats in the air.

She paused to get a glass of water from the kitchen.

There wasn't any need to bother with the lights. The streetlight outside the living room window was ample enough for her to see where she was going. The kitchen was orderly, and everything was in its place. It wasn't difficult to locate a glass and get it under the ice maker on the front of the fridge. The water made a rushing sound as it burst forth from the little nozzle beside the ice shoot. Kristina stood barefoot, taking a greedy gulp before refilling the glass to take back with her.

In the darkness, her foot came down on something squishy. The object collapsed in on itself beneath her toes before she could react and pull away. Kristina fumbled for the light switch, careful not to spill the water. Harsh, bright light illuminated the room instantly, and she blinked to adjust her eyes. Lying on the floor just outside the kitchen was a clown's bright red nose.

The glass of water Kristina had been holding slipped from her unsteady hand and shattered at her feet. Water and ice careened across the tiled floor, encircling the bulbous monstrosity but not touching it as if the water was afraid of the thing too.

The hair on the back of her neck rose with the electrical charge that came when you knew you were watched. Kristina felt exposed, violated, as if someone was just behind her, standing too close for comfort within her personal space. Turning quickly, she flinched, expecting another person to be there, but she was still alone. She took a step backward, one hand on her chest, against her beating heart.

Pain shot through her foot and up her leg, taking her by surprise. Leaping forward, Kristina lifted her right foot, balancing on the left, and looked down at the floor. Blood droplets fell from her suspended appendage, where a long sliver of glass penetrated her skin.

"Goddammit!" She shrieked, hobbling to the island and pulling her body up so she could sit on the edge. She lifted her foot into her lap and surveyed the damage. Dangling it over the sink, she held it steady with her left hand and gingerly removed the glass with her right. The wound felt red hot and bled freely once the alien body was removed.

"I'm going to kill Jason for that." Kristina eyed the red nose lying innocently on the floor and thought about her friend. What a great guy he was. He knew she was losing her shit all day over clowns, and he plants that on the floor right where he knows she would step on it. Kristina searched the counter for her phone before remembering she'd left it lying beside the computer. "Perfect, just perfect."

Leaning over as far as she could, her fingers barely brushed the paper towel holder on the far side of the sink. Stretching her fingers out, she caught the edge of the roll and tore a long section off, and pressed it to her wound. The puncture wasn't exceptionally deep, but it was a bleeder. She would need to put a compression bandage on it to get it to stop.

"You just wait, buddy. I bet you're sitting at home laughing, waiting for me to call and tell you I found your little prank." Kristina wasn't sure why she spoke out loud to herself, but it broke up the silence and made her a little less afraid. "You'll think it's hilarious when I spill a drink all over your car." *Okay, that's going too far; property damage is never the answer.* "I can't wait until you leave your Facebook open on my computer. You're going to love the post I make telling everyone you're gay and asking the ladies to please stop calling you." Kristina grinned wickedly from ear to ear. That was definitely the way to handle this. Besides, a little public humiliation never hurt anyone, especially a major playboy who prided himself on how much attention he got from the opposite sex.

Kristina hopped into the bathroom with the paper towels wrapped around her injured foot. By the time she plopped her butt down on the closed lid of the toilet, she'd bled through, and a little trail of red dots led back the way she came. The compression bandage was in the bottom drawer of her vanity. She grabbed a bottle of peroxide from under the sink and a clean washcloth and cleaned the wound thoroughly before wrapping it tightly.

The puncture pulsed angrily under the sleeve, and Kristina pondered whether she should call Jason and ask him to take her to the hospital for stitches. She cursed herself that she hadn't taken the time to get another vehicle and left herself at the mercy of others to be available when she needed them.

Her phone was only across the hall on the desk. She could make it there in a couple of hops. Deciding to try, Kristina steeled herself against the pain, gritted her teeth, and held her foot high while bouncing on the left foot to the other room. She sighed in relief when she reached the rolling leather chair. Catching her breath, Kristina looked up at the computer screen.

The clown posse band was featured in high definition, with the picture zoomed in on the conductor's face right as he'd looked around Jason at her. There was no way this picture could've existed. Jason's back was clearly visible to the side of the clown. He'd had her camera in his hands. The only way someone could've taken this, was if they'd been standing right beside Kristina, but she'd been alone in that moment, and it was on the same memory card as all the others, but she could see the Nikon dangling from Jason's grasp.

Fumbling for her cell phone, Kristina located Jason's number with shaking fingers. She listened to the ring while she stared into the clown's face. His eyes fixed on her just as they'd been earlier in the day. It struck her that the makeup the thing wore was eerily similar to what the clown she'd imagined in her apartment had on. He could have been a perfect twin to the figure who stood in the middle of the street waving to her as Jason pulled away from the curb.

"Hey, Kristina," Jason picked up. "You change your mind about getting a drink? I'm already naked, but I'll come right over."

"Shut up." Kristina exited the folder holding the pictures from the day. "Why did you do it, Jason? I know you like to pull pranks, but wasn't the flower enough? Why did you have to take it this far?"

Jason didn't respond for a few seconds. "Kristina, I'm not sure what you're talking about. Did something happen?"

"Please don't play dumb. I can't take much more of this today."

Hot tears welled up in Kristina's eyes. She blinked, trying to clear them, and cleared her throat. She couldn't stand Jason knowing she was crying.

"Kris, seriously. I didn't do anything." His voice was low and caring, not the smug tone of voice he would take when he knew he was guilty of something. A fresh wave of fear washed over her as she realized she hadn't been wrong when she saw the clown through her window. It wasn't a hallucination from the stress of the job. He was real, and there was a good chance he was back. The nose wasn't there when they'd done the walk through upon returning from Showmen's Rest. If Jason hadn't put it there, then where did it come from?

"Can you come over? Right now? I don't think I'm safe here, and I'm injured." Kristina's heart thudded against her ribs like the pistons in an engine. "I might need stitches."

"Stitches? What the hell happened after I left? I'm putting on my shoes. I'll be right over."

She could hear the commotion on the other end of the line as her friend rushed to get out the door. Guilt that she'd been convinced he was behind the nose nagged at her. Why would she think he would do something like that? Jason liked playing jokes, but he wasn't malicious. Her foot pulsed with pain, and the rest of her body quaked.

"I stepped on some broken glass. Please stay on the phone with me, Jason. I'm afraid to be alone."

"I'm not going to leave you alone." A door slammed on Jason's end. "I'm already headed to the car. I'll be there in five minutes."

CHAPTER SEVEN

J une 22nd, 1918

Alonzo Sargent and his fireman, Gustav Klauss, were arrested following the retrieval of the bodies from the accident. Both men were very shaken but weren't injured more than a few bumps and bruises from the impact. Sitting under the awning of the signal tower with heavy woolen blankets over their shoulders, the men waited in shackles to be taken away.

"What were you doing in there that you didn't see a whole train sitting on the track!" Gustav demanded answers from the man who'd been at the throttle all evening. "Hitting a cat, I can understand. Hell, I wouldn't give it a second thought if you hit a cow, but a whole goddamned train, Alonzo!"

"You're just as much to blame." Alonzo snapped at the fireman, glaring at him menacingly through heavily lidded eyes.

"How do you figure? I'm not the engineer of this train, sir."

Alonzo sneered. "No, but you're supposed to take over for me if I'm too tired to operate the beast properly, aren't you? You knew I hadn't slept in some forty or so hours, where were you? As I recall, you were in an empty Pullman car behind the engine having some vodka straight from the bottle."

Gustav shook free of his blanket and tilted his body towards his boss. "You want to settle this right here as men, Sargent? I'll have no trouble knocking your block off. I doubt anyone would stop me under the circumstances."

"How are you going to manage that with those nice bracelets you're wearing?" Alonzo caught the eye of the officer keeping watch over them. "If you're so innocent, then why are they arresting you?"

Shrinking against the wooden beam at his back, Gustav sighed and surveyed the carnage before them. "I can't go to jail for this. I have a wife and son to think about. We'll go to the gallows for sure. There's no mistaking that. Can't you just say it was all you and spare my family the pain? You don't have anyone waiting for you. You won't be missed. There's no sense in both of us hanging."

"How dare you, you blasphemous old fool!" Alonzo tried to get to his feet, but the shackles at his wrists made it impossible for the heavy-set man to get any traction. "You think I give a rats ass about your whorish wife? Plucked her right off the streets in Boston, didn't you? That boy of yours doesn't look a thing like you either. You can't tell me you believe you sired a faired-haired boy when you and her both have dark hair and eyes?"

"My mother was fair," Gustav protested.

"And my mother was goddamned Queen Victoria."

The officer had enough of their bickering and kicked Alonzo in the shoulder, pushing him into the other man, effectively ending any discussion. "Can't you see what's happening in front of you men? You see those bundles with blankets over them? Those are the people you killed tonight. None of them get to go home to their families, so why should you? If you have any wits about you, you'll sit there and shut those holes in your faces while your mess is cleaned up and take whatever fate God sees fit for you."

Alonzo straightened his body the best he could without the use of his hands. "They're just carnies. It was more a loss for the train to be destroyed. None of them were worth two cents anyway."

"Who knows how many crimes we prevented by ending their

miserable existence?" Gustav added, finally on the same page as the engineer.

"God have mercy on both your souls." The young officer turned away from the men, preferring the sight of smoke and death than to look at them any longer. His mouth was set in a thin line of disgust. Nothing in the five years he'd served on the force prepared him for a night like this.

The bodies were loaded onto carts. There were so many of them that they had to be stacked one on top of the other until the wagons themselves sagged in the middle under the weight. The sight reminded Mayor Hodges of pictures he'd seen growing up of the plagues in Europe when the undertaker would go from house to house collecting the dead. The smell would be different, though. Here, the air was filled with the stench of burnt flesh and hair, a pungent odor that drove the man to pull his shirt over his nose and mouth. Still, the air stung his nostrils, and his eyes watered profusely. He imagined the plague times carried a haughtier smell of disease and decay. Right now, he couldn't decide which was worse.

Mayor Hodges scanned the area and found the two men responsible being held beneath Ivanhoe Tower, out of the way of the responders. The whole area filled with people who heard the crash and those who heard of the crash from others. There had to be over a hundred people milling about, pulling at debris, and talking amongst each other while quietly pointing.

Whistling through his fingers, the Mayor summoned the officer keeping watch over Sargent and Klauss and motioned him over.

"Sir," The young man stood at attention as a soldier would have.

"There's too many looky-loos here. Pretty soon this place is going to turn into a zoo. Get those two out of here before the press shows up." Out of the corner of his eye, Mayor Hodges saw another man raise a heavy camera and snap a photo. The flash was only a blip against a backdrop of thick smoke, and the Mayor's eyes were too scorched to make out the photographer's face. "Fuck, they're already here. Get them out of here as discreetly as you can manage. I don't want to see them in the papers until a formal report is written."

"Yes, sir." The officer hurried back to where the men were sitting

THE SHOWMAN'S GHOST | 57

and began to pull them to their feet. The blankets stayed wrapped around them, and their shackles lay hidden by the material. The press agent didn't seem to notice them.

The wagons pulled away, taking the smoldering corpses with them. It was a good old fashioned draft horse pulling the heavy burden off the tracks. They couldn't have gotten an automobile back here through the trees. Someone wrapped a white cloth over the horse's eyes and nose. Hodges wondered if it was to keep the animal calm or to keep it from breathing in the smoke. Either way, it did the job it was meant for. The mortuary wouldn't have the space for this many people at once. There were already murmurs going through the crowd that they should be taken elsewhere, that perhaps the circus performers weren't of good enough stock to be attended to by the same man who dressed their dead.

A queasy feeling started in Hodges's belly. There was a good chance the bodies taken from the crash would never see a mortician. A good number of them wouldn't be claimed, and the Mayor wasn't sure what would become of the bodies if that happened. The city wouldn't pay to bury them, that was for sure.

The respect and care given to ordinary citizens wouldn't be extended to these men and women who'd just been passing through.

Mayor Hodges turned to leave the crash site. The fire was out, and there wasn't anything left to see but the clean-up, and he wasn't interested in that. He'd done his job, and no one could say anything negative about the way he'd handled it in the damned newspaper. He'd done his best to look grief-stricken and worried. He would be able to use this for his re-election campaign in the fall.

Standing in the tree line, just past the plume of smoke, was a man as big around as he was tall stood. His face was painted in the colors of a circus clown. His clothes were singed and black. Mayor Hodges squinted to see the man more clearly, but the harder he looked, the harder he was to make out. His eyes were the only things standing out clearly. He was angry; his stance was set in a determined pose, eyebrows low over the radiant, white-blue irises surrounded by blue paint. He seemed to be glaring at the mayor like he knew what he really thought. The clown knew there would never be peace for those who fell; no one would care to make sure they were at rest. Mayor Hodges felt the intrusion of thoughts into his brain as if he were screamed at.

I'll never rest until justice is served. An eye for an eye, a soul for a soul, the guilty will reap what they sow.

Hodges rubbed his eyes with the backs of his hands and then blinked into the early morning sunlight. He skimmed the trees for the man he'd seen standing there, but he was gone.

CHAPTER EIGHT

May 5th, 2018

True to his word, the bumblebee yellow Mustang was in front of the apartment complex and halfway on the curb in five minutes flat. Kristina watched from the living room window as a frazzled Jason ground his black rims against the concrete in his haste to get to her. He didn't even glance at the damage as he sprinted to the door and took the steps three at a time. Even from where she stood with the sheer blinds clenched in her trembling fingers, she could see the ravaged metal that had been perfect before his visit.

The doorknob turned frantically. "Kristina! Open the door!" Jason twisted and pulled from the outside trying to gain access to her.

Kristina's feet felt rooted to the floor. She knew she needed to cross the room but there was so much space. Anything could happen between here and there; evil things could be waiting to grab her from the shadows. The cut on her foot pulsed with pain. She balanced the appendage on her toes so as not to put pressure on the wound.

"Kristina, if you don't open the goddamn door, I'll kick it open!"

Move! Get to the door! Get to Jason!

"Jason! I'm scared!" Kristina took a step, still grasping the gauzy, white curtain panels and pulled her foot back quickly when a white hand shot out, groping for her, from under the couch. Mechanical, creepy laughter came from the piece of furniture. "He's in here, Jason! I can't get to you!" Kristina panicked, throwing her form against the window ledge, trying to pull her whole body onto the small lip adjacent to the glass. It wasn't big enough to support her, but she continued to try. A cracking noise sounded from where her back rested against the window. If she put any more weight on it, she would tumble to the street a full story below.

"Kristina, I'm breaking the door! Stay away from it so I don't hurt you!"

The white hand slithered back where it came from. Heavy footfalls filled the apartment from Jason's kicks. The door jumped under each strike, groaning against the hinges. The frame began to splinter. It was coming loose now, inching past the casing, until the jamb gave, and the door slammed against the wall with a loud thud.

Jason fell into the room, landing on his hands and knees. His face was scanning, looking for the danger.

Kristina knew how it must look. She was alone, cramming herself on a window ledge, trying to escape an invisible assailant. There was still glass and blood on the kitchen floor leading to the bath—her own blood. From where she cowered, she could see the red nose was gone. Or maybe it had never been there to begin with. She began to cry. Inching her body onto the floor, she wrapped her arms around her knees and sobbed. Fingernails dug into her flesh under her thin pants. She buried her face in her arms, not wanting to see the confusion on Jason's face.

Jason rushed to the apartment to save her. But from what? Was any of this real? Or was she losing it?

Kristina jumped when his hand touched her back. The touch was soft and gentle. She flinched beneath his fingers and tried to pull away, but he enveloped his arms around her quaking body, pulling her in close against his chest.

"Tell me what happened, sweetheart. Who's trying to hurt you? Who was in your apartment?" His fingers ran up and down her spine, consoling her the way she needed. "You said you're injured, honey. Where? Show me."

Losing his balance, Jason fell backward on his butt, taking Kristina with him. She eyed the couch wearily when his hand landed beside it. How had she thought something was under there? There was only about three inches of space. An animal couldn't fit beneath it, let alone a human. She squeezed her eyes tight, trying to get a grasp on reality.

One. Two. Three…

Kristina counted in her head, willing her heart to stop beating so fast. She imagined her limbs steady and unmoving, forcing them to stop shivering. Taking a deep breath, she held it, counted again, and released it slowly, in through her nose out through her mouth.

"Kristina?"

She met his eyes slowly. His pupils darted back and forth from each of hers.

"It's my foot. I dropped a glass in the kitchen while the light was off. I stepped on the shards. I thought I saw… something." Holding up the injured foot, Kristina turned her gaze back to the kitchen where it all started. There was still nothing there but her own mess. *Should've just turned the stupid light on. No wonder you saw things that weren't there.*

"That's a lot of blood seeping through. Can I unwrap it? I took a first aid class in college. I'll be able to tell if it needs stitches or not."

Kristina nodded, permitting him to remove the compression bandage. He took his shirt off and laid it over the carpet to protect it from any fluids. The breath caught in Kristina's throat. It was the first time she'd ever seen him without a shirt. Despite her fear and pain, she couldn't help but think he looked like one of those models on the cover of a raunchy romance book.

"I'm sorry, did I hurt you?" His fingers paused where he worked on her.

"What?"

Jason cupped her ankle in his hand for more support. "You gasped. Did it hurt when I pulled on the bandage?"

"A little." It was all she could manage to say. Her lips felt numb, her tongue swollen in her mouth like a bee got in there and used his stinger everywhere it mattered. To her, the words escaping the hole in her face sounded garbled, nearly incoherent. Jason didn't seem to notice.

"It's not bleeding much now. I don't think stitches are necessary." He was so calm. Kristina's eyes flitted to the door he'd kicked open a few moments before. She hated to bring it up when he seemed to have forgotten what transpired moments before, but she needed him to know she wasn't losing it. Although, to be honest, she wasn't entirely sure she wasn't.

"Jason," she started with a sizable amount of apprehension coating her mouth. "I'm sorry you had to rush over. I know I've been a lot to handle since we took the circus job. I saw something in the kitchen when the lights were off, and I freaked out." She didn't mention the strange photo on the hard drive or the hand she saw coming out from under her couch. There wasn't any explaining either of those things except to conclude she was a certifiable nutcase, and she wasn't ready to take that leap yet.

"Hey, don't worry about it." He rewrapped her foot with gentle, knowing fingers and gingerly set it on the floor with her toes pointed in the air. "Everyone's brain gets away from them occasionally. You've been stressed out to the max. It's not your fault." He followed her line of vision and settled his gaze on the busted door. "We're going to have to fix that tomorrow. Sorry I broke it."

"It's my fault. I can't ask you to fix it."

Jason shifted, settling his weight back against the wall, a hair's breadth from where the hand appeared. "You want to tell me what you saw?"

Kristina hesitated, scooting her body a bit farther away from him. She didn't want to tell him anything. It wasn't that she didn't trust him or thought he wouldn't want to be her friend anymore. It was nothing like that. She was embarrassed to admit to the things her brain made her think. Grown adults didn't see monsters in the darkness. That was something kids did before they knew the difference between what was real and what wasn't. Kristina wasn't a child.

Chewing on the inside of her lip, Kristina brought her eyes to Jason's lavender ones slowly. "You wouldn't believe me if I told you. It wasn't real. Any of it. I—"

Jason grabbed her hands as she swung them wildly through the air while she spoke.

"Try me." His silky-smooth voice cut through the excuses she made for herself. "You don't have to be embarrassed or scared that I'll laugh at you, Kris. I got you."

Kristina swallowed hard and weighed her options. As far as she could see it, he would either think she was crazy or a bad liar, and neither of those options appealed to her. Knowing Jason, he would think the whole thing was an excuse to get him to come back over and do God knows what.

"A red nose." The words slipped out before she could stop them. "There was a clown nose on the floor in the kitchen. I thought you put it there to scare me."

"I didn't do that." Jason craned his neck around to see the floor in the other room—the floor that was magically devoid of any parts of a clown costume. "I don't see anything."

"I know." Kristina dropped her gaze, feeling the heat seep back into her skin from a blush that took her by storm. "That's because I imagined the whole thing. I scared myself, dropped my glass and stepped on the pieces like an idiot. Then I hobbled into my office to call you to tell you how mad I was, and I saw the strange picture on the hard drive."

Jason blinked and tilted his head at her. "Strange picture?"

"Yeah." Kristina wiped away the stray tear rolling out of one eye before she could rein in the emotion. She took a deep breath and banished any more from falling. She wouldn't allow herself to cry. "There was a picture of you holding the camera while the clown conductor looked at me."

"Kris, that's not possible. I had the only camera. I couldn't take a picture of me holding it."

"Don't you think I know that?" Kristina got to her feet, momentarily forgetting about the gash beneath her toes. At this height, she could see the crack in the window where she'd pressed her body trying to escape the creature climbing from under the couch. Out of instinct, her eyes went back to that spot, searching for anything to verify that horrendous vision had been there and make her feel sane. She sighed and looked away, realizing that like the nose, there was nothing there. The tears threatened to come again. "Jason, I'm sorry. I didn't mean to yell at you."

He shrugged. "Why do you keep looking at the couch?"

"What do you mean?"

"Every few seconds, you look at the couch like there's a big spider you're trying not to look at." As he mentioned it, she felt her eyes going there once more. All she saw were leather cushions, white throw pillows, and a blanket draped over one arm. Nothing nefarious.

Not a spider, something worse. Something alive and evil.

"I don't know. I didn't realize I was doing it."

Jason grunted and pushed himself off the floor. He walked over to the item in question and sat down, smashing one of the pillows in the process. Kristina sucked in a breath, imagining him sinking into the seat, pulled down until there was nothing left. In her mind, she saw the white gloved hands grasping his body, taking him hostage, and the accompanying evil laughter. She shivered and ran her hands up and down her goosebump covered flesh.

"Are you going to be okay?" His words snapped her back to reality, the nightmare vision melting away until it ceased to exist. "Kris?" He said her name again when she didn't respond.

"I don't know. I don't know what's wrong with me."

He nodded to himself as if he'd just made up his mind about something. "I'm going to stay here with you tonight. We can fix the door tomorrow. I don't know if you know this, but I'm pretty handy with a credit card. Your apartment manager won't be able to tell it was ever broken when I'm done."

"Jason, if this is a halfcocked plan to get me to sleep with you—"

"I'll sleep right here on the couch." He patted the cushion beside him and grinned. "You won't even know I'm here. And if anyone comes through that door, it'll be the last thing they ever do."

Kristina couldn't shake the sudden queasy feeling she experienced.

The thought of him out here all night when she'd seen that thing under there, made her feel sick.

"Sleep in the bedroom."

"Oh, Kris, I thought you'd never ask—"

Kristina rolled her eyes. "It's not like that. I just don't want to be alone."

CHAPTER NINE

June 27th, 1918

Gregory Brooks held his hat in his hands while Diane Caster, Henry's widow, executed a perfect bowtie at his throat with shaking fingers. She was pale and drawn, her eyes red and swollen. Gregory didn't know what to say to the woman. She'd taken the first train to Chicago after the telegram arrived informing her of her husband's death. No one mentioned her son, and when she got into town, she was prepared to find two bodies waiting for her. Much to her relief, she found the child alive. He had a large gash on his forehead, bumps and bruises covered his small body, and he wasn't speaking, but everyone said once the shock wore off, he'd be fine.

The second in command didn't know how to tie a proper tie. The one he wore during shows clipped onto the jacket and required no work at all. The only other time he'd worn a tie was when he'd been in the military, and he did everything in his power to erase any memories of that time from his brain. He had a woman then, and she'd stood before him, much the same way Diane did now, and tied that strip of fabric around his throat every time he got into a dress uniform. Then she ran away with his brother. Not long after that, Gregory deserted his post in the middle of the night. He'd been thinking about his wife and feeling down on himself in general and decided to go out into the forest and use his rifle on himself. Instead, he'd come across a circus.

The ringmaster, Charlie, encountered him first. The man stood outside smoking a cigarette at the edge of the trees when the uniformed soldier stepped out, scaring him half to death. Charlie had a way of reading people, and he recognized Gregory's state of mind. He'd ushered him into his tent, got him fresh clothes, and gave him a new life. Ever since that moment, the ex-soldier did everything he could to make the ringmaster proud, becoming his second in command within months.

Charlie kept his secret. No one in the troop knew where he'd come from. There was plenty of speculation, but no one ever knew for sure. Now Charlie was dead.

"There you go, Gregory. You look sharp as a new penny." Mrs. Caster stepped back and dabbed a handkerchief to the sides of her eyes while straightening to her full height. "Charlie would be mighty proud of you. You know he thought of you as his son, right?"

Gregory swallowed hard. "He wasn't nearly old enough to be my father."

"Yeah, but that man knew you still needed some rearing, and he was happy to do it. Henry wrote me and told me when he made you his second. He was so proud of the man you'd become since joining the troupe. Henry respected you immensely as well."

"Henry was a good man." Doing his best not to cry in front of the woman, Gregory cleared his throat and fidgeted with the buttons on his coat. He didn't own nice clothes and had borrowed the ones he wore from one of his mentor's trunks that survived the accident. He figured the man wouldn't mind him taking them under the circumstances. All his own clothes were destroyed, along with the trunk hiding his service uniform in Charlie's train car. It was all gone. Just like the men and women he'd grown to consider family.

"What about your boy?" Gregory nodded to her son, standing close by her skirts. "You going to be my second in command now?" The boy ducked his face into the long folds he clung to and didn't utter a single word.

"Forgive him," Diane said. "He hasn't said a peep since I took him from the hospital."

Gregory got down on the boy's level. "When you're ready to talk about what happened, you come and see me. I'll be here." Smiling at the mother, Gregory took a deep breath, feeling the air fill his lungs, and thought about all the people who would never do that again. A flash of charred, black flesh and the smell of burning hair invaded his brain, and he slammed his eyes closed tightly to fight off the vision. When he opened them again, the boy looked at him curiously. Gregory nodded to him, knowing the boy saw the same terrible things when he closed his own eyes.

"Allow me to escort you both to the cemetery." Gregory extended his arm, allowing Mrs. Caster to slide her petite, gloved hand through the gap. "I'm sure this is hard enough on both of you. Let me offer you some support."

"Do you have no one waiting for you, Mr. Brooks?" Diane gazed up at him through black lashes.

"No, ma'am. Just myself, and I'd be honored to have your company."

The woman looked down demurely. Her black dress billowed around her legs and brushed Gregory's trousers as he walked. It'd been a long time since he walked with a woman, and even under the dire circumstances, it felt nice to have her on his arm. The child crossed to the other side and put his small hand in his, needing support just as badly as his mother. Gregory was happy to oblige.

The walk to Showmen's Rest was a short one from the accommodations the Showmen's League of America had provided the survivors and their families. The streets were crowded with those making their way to the cemetery and well-wishers tipping their hats in sympathy. Performers of every ilk clogged the walkways in the manner of which they worked. Clowns and men on stilts, women in provocative costumes, and animal trainers in coattails made a procession with none of the festivities they normally exuded. Faces were drawn and sad, tears flowed freely, and Gregory tried his best not to succumb to the feelings overtaking him.

"You hold my hand and stay close to me, you hear?" Diane bent at the waist and addressed the child, who seemed nonplussed by the magnitude of the event. After traveling with the circus for most of his young life, he was used to the crowds and strangely dressed people. He nodded his head to his mother, and she continued to look at him as if expecting him to respond orally.

Inside the wrought iron gates, the grounds were even more congested than the streets had been. Greeting the people on either side were two massive stone elephants with one foot raised, resting on a ball and their trunks lowered. It was customary when depicting elephants to have their trunks raised for joyous events and down to signify mourning. Gregory strained to see over the heads of hundreds of men and women to figure out where they were supposed to go. Top hats and feathers got in the way of his view. Mrs. Caster held tight to his arm, relying on him to take care of her.

"Gregory!" A voice sounded from his right, pulling his attention from the path he'd been set on. "Gregory, over here!"

A man stood waving both arms over his head. Gregory could see the beginning of the massive opening in the ground by the man's feet before someone stepped into his line of sight, cutting off his view. "Over there," he lowered his mouth close to the woman's ear so she could hear him over the din of the crowd.

At the far right of the Showmen's section of the cemetery, the survivors from the wreck gathered. It was mostly the workers who set everything up, a few porter boys, and one half of the Flying Wards, the brother. Jenny Ward was among the dead. Making his way through the onlookers, Gregory did his best to shield the woman and her child from being bumped into or harassed by press members looking for a story. When he reached his friends, a flashbulb went off by his face, momentarily blinding him.

"Care to give an account for the paper, sir?" The cameraman asked while adding a new bulb to his large camera.

Grabbing the young man by his vest, Gregory sneered and bared his teeth. "Get the fuck out of here! We're here to say goodbye to our friends, not to get our names in the paper. Show some fucking respect!"

Diane cleared her throat from beside him, and Gregory felt remorse instantly when he remembered the child. The pressman rushed away to find other prospects, not deterred by his outburst in the slightest.

"Those guys are like cockroaches." One of the roustabouts shook his head. "I've never understood why circus folk get such a bad name pinned to them when garbage like that exists in the world." The others nodded, agreeing with him.

"When is this thing supposed to get started?" Gregory asked wearily. They'd departed the hotel almost an hour ago under the assumption that the funeral services would begin at precisely ten o'clock, but a look at his pocket watch informed him that that time had passed. He snapped the face down and dropped the thing into his pocket, sighing at the crowd pushing in around him.

"I don't think they expected so many people to show up." The worker pointed a thick, stained finger towards the center of the space. "Have you seen what they did with them all?"

Gregory shook his head. "No, I've only just arrived."

"They dumped them all in a mass grave. All fifty-seven of them." The older man pursed his lips. "They said it was easier than burying them all separately. Damned disrespectful if you ask me. They don't even know the names of those who departed. I heard they made stones that just say unknown on them for most everyone unless someone came and claimed the bodies. Most of them just looked like human-shaped lumps of coal, though."

Diane started to cry, turning her face toward Gregory's sleeve.

Gregory patted her hand while ignoring her cries.

"Sorry, ma'am, I didn't mean to upset you. But those are my brothers and sisters down in that hole, and they deserved much better than what they got." The man clutched his hat against his chest until his knuckles turned white. He blinked rapidly, trying to hide the tears forming in his eyes."

"Everyone, if we can have your attention, please." The banter filling the yard ended abruptly as everyone turned and headed towards the edge of the massive hole. The Hagenbeck-Wallace survivors stepped carefully through the throng to make a spot for themselves near the burial site.

After gently moving a few people to the side, they all stood, shoulder to shoulder, looking down at fifty-seven donated coffins. The town came together to make sure the bodies at least had their own coffins even though they would be buried together. It was quite the sight to behold. All types of people pushed in around the dead until you couldn't discern a space between them. It felt odd seeing businessmen in expensive black suits standing next to clowns in riotous, colorful costumes and women in full skirts and corsets beside other women in nothing but a leotard. In a normal setting, these opposites would be appalled to be seen near one another, but here, no one blinked an eye.

A pressman on a ladder snapped pictures from above, and Gregory felt a pang of anger ripple through him that the league allowed them here for this, but there wasn't anything he could do about it.

A man with a megaphone pressed to his lips, standing on a large, red and white circus box usually used for elephant stunts, cleared his throat. "Good morning, everyone. I know this is a very sad reason for all of us to have gathered, but it warms my heart to see so many people here showing those who perished were loved. Early this morning, we interred the deceased in coffins paid for by the lovely people of Forest Park, Illinois, and Hammond, Indiana on this land, purchased for all departed Showmen by the Showmen's League of America. Here, no matter what they had in life, performers can be put to rest with respect and dignity."

The old man beside Gregory scoffed. "Guess that's why they put them in there together."

The man with the megaphone continued. "Before you lay fifty-seven of the best men, women, and children you ever could've met—performers who spent their lives trying to make folks smile. While we don't know the names of all those who lay below, we know each of them made their mark on this world, and somewhere, a child thinks of them fondly.

"I know there are family members here as well as those who lived through the tragedy." The man gestured toward the troupe, and the crowd turned their collective gaze on the survivors and families, all huddled together for comfort. "We are eternally grateful the accident didn't claim more lives than it did."

The little boy tugged on Gregory's hand and pulled him down so he could ask a question. "Which box is my daddy in?"

Diane brought her hand to her mouth, hearing the child speak for the first time since she'd returned.

"I don't know, son. They're all closed already. How about you pick the one you like best, and that's the one your daddy will be in." Gregory lifted the boy into his arms so he could see better and watched him scan the caskets. He seemed to zero in on one in particular and squeeze his eyes shut as if communicating to the person inside. He didn't say another word.

"Among the recognized dead are Ringmaster Charlie, who'd overseen the troupe for nearly ten years, Baldy the clown who'd been touring for twice as long as his leader, and his wife Martha, and son, Reginald. Henry Caster perished whilst saving his only son, who is standing over there to say goodbye to his father." All eyes fell on the boy who immediately blushed and hid his face against Gregory's shoulder. Gregory felt fury that the man would single the boy out during this painful time. Diane pulled her arm from his as if not wanting people to see them touching and assume things that weren't true. When everyone turned away from them again, she slid it back through, and Gregory lifted his arm to grant her access. *Fuck what they thought about it.*

By the time the man stopped talking, half the crowd disappeared. They'd seen the open hole in the ground and the coffins all in a row, and that had been enough. All that remained were the real performers, family members, and those from the League overseeing the funeral. It seemed as if the pressmen vacated the area as well, after getting all the candid shots they needed for their news articles that would plaster the pages the following morning.

Diane dropped to her knees, relinquishing her hold on the second in command's arm. "Henry!" she wailed. "Henry, how could you do this to me! To our son! He needs his daddy, Henry. Why did you have to go and die?" Gregory placed a hand on her shoulder and felt her body heaving with her sobs beneath his fingers. The little boy continued to stare into the hole from his perch in the man's arms, his mother's breakdown not reaching his fragile mind. Gregory wondered what he was thinking about.

The only people left in the cemetery were those working and the troupe of the fallen. Sometime during that time, Diane collapsed. The League packed up the box the man had been standing on to speak, and workers began to shovel earth back into the void. Gregory didn't try to move the woman for some time, just letting her cry it out. "This is all my fault," she said from the ground. "When I left, Henry asked if he should leave the circus and come with me. He told me he didn't want to be so far apart, but I told him to stay because I knew how much he loved it. If I'd just said yes and made him leave it all behind, he would still be alive."

Gregory sat down and dangled his feet over the edge, balancing the boy on his knee. "This wasn't your fault, love. This was no one's fault except the conductor who thought a nap would be better than watching where he was going. You don't let that thought play on your conscience for one second. Those are the kinds of thoughts that get people in trouble. What you should do is think of the things that have always made you happy and do those things. Henry is in heaven. He's not suffering, and I'm sure he would want the both of you to be happy, too."

"What's going to happen to the circus?" Diane asked, taking the boy out of Gregory's arms and snuggling him against her chest. "Are you going to disband?"

Gregory looked at the group of men surrounding him and took in all the faces looking back at him. Everyone waited for him to answer the question. "No, ma'am. Us showmen live by a code, and that code is, the show must go on. I'll put out a bulletin to other traveling circuses in the area and see if they have anyone they can spare until we can find more permanent people to join us. We'll likely miss a performance or two, but we're gonna keep on doing what we do, making people happy."

"Good." Diane nodded and kissed her son over the bandages on his head. "I know that's what Henry would want you to do. He always told me, come hell or high water, the circus would come to town. I think you're just the man for the job, Gregory."

"Let me escort you back to your lodgings. Henry would never forgive me if I didn't."

The walk back to the hotel was a solemn one. Even more so than the journey to the graveside had been. A blackness seemed to fall over them, a finality, a conclusion to a journey that wasn't fulfilled. Gregory could hear the cries of the dead in his brain, begging them to return, to help them. He remembered his mentor and the promise he'd made to the man to keep the circus going should anything ever befall him. He meant to keep that promise.

Once Diane and the boy were settled back as comfortably as they could be in their room, Gregory made his way to a tavern on the same street. He spent the remainder of the day there, drinking himself into oblivion. The bartender wouldn't take his money but kept his glass full. It was exactly the kind of medicine he needed to forget the day's events.

When the sun began to set, Gregory stumbled out of the door, barely able to walk, and tried to remember how to get back to his room. He started in what he believed was the right direction, confident in his choice until he stood between the two stone elephants. Somehow, he'd taken himself right back to the cemetery.

Instead of correcting his error, he ventured inside. The hole in the ground was gone, replaced by an expanse of dark brown dirt. There were no stones, but he knew those would come later after the mason had an opportunity to craft them. Making his way to the center, he lay flat on his back over his departed friends and spread his arms and legs out. Tears ran from the corner of each eye, making trails down the sides of his head into his hair. No one was around to see him cry, so he didn't bother to wipe them away.

Closing his eyes, he drifted. He saw the whole crash happening behind his lids as if on repeat. And then he saw Baldy. The clown exited the wreckage unscathed. The smoke didn't mar his pristine white costume.

"Baldy? You're alive?" Asleep, Gregory called out to his friend.

The clown shook his painted face. "Dead as dead can be, my friend.

But I'm not going anywhere. I need your consent to allow me to take care of this. I took care of them in life, I want to take care of them in death. Someone needs to pay for what they did to us. Everyone involved should suffer the consequences. Martha and Reginald are gone. I saw their spirits turn white and float towards an overwhelmingly bright light, but I didn't go. I had to be the one to stay."

Gregory was stunned. "Of course, you have my consent. What are you going to do, Baldy?"

The clown's grin grew too big for his own face. "I'm going to make them suffer as we suffered."

CHAPTER TEN

May 5th, 2018

There were so many bright, strobing colors. Lights shimmered in hues of red and white, and sparklers erupted around a glorious stage like a fourth of July celebration. Kristina never saw anything like it. On the stage, a ringmaster grinned from ear to ear, extending both arms out to his sides while holding a baton in one outstretched hand and a silky black top hat in the other. The buttons trailing down his chest gleamed gold against the red fabric of his waistcoat. Slicked back, black hair barely touched his collar with a red bowtie knotted perfectly at his throat.

His voice boomed, projecting forth from his lungs in a charismatic voice that sent chills down her spine.

Kristina's heart raced. What happens next? She inched herself to the edge of her seat, fixated on the man.

"Ladies and gentlemen, never in the history of the world have so many extraordinary people and animals been under one tent." Small cannons erupted around the stage in a synchronized blast. Smoke twisted and turned toward the ceiling in calculated plumes accentuating the man's frame in long shadows. The spotlight directly above him made his features look exaggerated and the white paint on his face took on a ghastly hue. "What you see this evening will tantalize you. It'll shock and amaze you. No one will be the same person they were before entering my tent—my world."

The man fell silent, his gaze starting at one side of the roll away bleachers and casually moving to the right until he'd connected with every spectator. A smile spread across his face, pulling the skin taut, showing a row of perfectly white teeth. The suspense built to a fever pitch.

"Ladies and gentlemen, welcome to the Hagenback-Wallace circus. The greatest show on earth." The ringmaster executed a perfect backflip, landing on the balls of his feet. Behind him, twin elephants trumpeted with their trunks and front feet in the air, a salute to their circus king.

Kristina grabbed the hand of the person beside her. She could barely contain her excitement. "Look at that!" Her voice leapt from her ribcage as a man thrust a torch down his throat and spewed fire from his mouth like a fire-breathing dragon.

"It's amazing!" Kristina turned to the person and recognized Jason's lavender eyes leveled at her as if she were the one on stage doing fantastical things. As she looked at him, she realized the bleachers had melted away.

Below her, air whistled past at a blistering speed. Jason grasped both her wrists. Kristina in turn, held both of his. His long, muscular thighs and calves gripped a trapeze bar tightly, and they soared through the atmosphere above the rest of the circus.

"Jason!" She screamed to her grinning friend. "I can't do this!"

"You're doing fine!"

She squeezed her eyes closed tight as he threw her. Her body tumbled, doing somersaults in rapid succession until another set of hands caught her from a second swing. Maniacal laughter filled her ears from the stranger whose fingers dug into her wrists. Kristina opened one eye and then the other. White gloved hands held her tightly. A red, billowing costume flowed from the arms attached to the hands as if alive. Her gaze traveled upwards, hesitating before they reached the face she knew would be there.

White face paint, an exaggerated mouth, and rings of blue around icy eyes looked back at her. The clown's diabolical smile stretched to impossible lengths, his face opening until rows of pointed teeth reflected the spotlight's red color.

"No!" Her voice came out as a screech. Her heart slammed against her insides, threatening to break free from the cage that retained it. "Not you!"

The clown's laughter drowned out her voice. It was all she could hear echoing through her brain. He looked down at the ground, and Kristina dreaded to know what he saw. Unable to resist, she followed his gaze. The floor of the circus tent fell away revealing a massive black hole. As she watched, fire erupted, licking the inside of the walls. The voices of burning, writhing souls reached her, mixing with the clown's chortling. They pleaded for help, begged for the fire to be extinguished, agonizing over their pain.

He released one of her arms, holding his hand in the air with his mouth pursed in a perfect circle. Kristina twisted in the air, with only one hand preventing her from plunging to her death.

"Please, don't!"

Lifting her several inches in the air, the clown brought her face level to his. "They all died." His mouth didn't move as he spoke, staying hideously posed in the impossible grin. "Those who should've died survived. The show was blood. The show was fire and twisted metal. It won't end with our deaths. The show must go on. Act two will be revenge, and you'll be in the center ring!"

With the last of the cryptic words, he released her from his grip. Her body contorted like a cat painfully as she tried to slow her fall. The flames grew closer, the heat burning her, and the laughter continued.

"No! No! No!"

"Kristina! Wake up!" Jason shook her violently from the other side of the bed.

Her eyes snapped open. The room remained shrouded in darkness, the only light coming from the bedside clock. Straining, her pupils fought to adjust to see her surroundings more clearly. After blinking a few moments, the black masses looming beyond her vision began to take form into a dresser, a partially opened closet door, and a flat screen TV mounted on the wall. All innocent items that weren't evil clowns trying to kill her.

Kristina rubbed her fists into her eye sockets until it hurt. The explosion of white splotches behind her lids mirrored the spotlights from her nightmare.

Jason rubbed her shoulders as she laid her head against his shoulder. It was more than humiliating for him to see her cry yet again. She'd always held herself to a higher standard. Tears were for the weak, and she was not that. Crying in front of men wasn't something she'd ever allowed herself to do. Not since she got teased as a child for it. Having a brother made her tougher than most girls. But there she was, blubbering like an idiot, face scrunched and wet, eyes blurry, body shaking. Thankfully, Jason knew well enough not to give her shit, at least not now. Tomorrow might be a whole different story.

"I've got you, Kris. It's okay. It was just a dream." Jason rolled his hand across her back in slow circles. "I'm here; you're safe."

Kristina couldn't shake the words the clown said to her before she'd jolted awake. Somehow, she knew it wasn't just a dream—more like an omen of things to come. Jason would never believe her if she told him that. She held her breath and counted to ten, willing the tears to stop, forcing her heart to stop beating at a frantic pace.

"When did you get in the bed?" When Kristina's mind calmed enough to form a coherent thought, she remembered Jason had been on a pile of blankets on the floor beside her. She'd never felt him slide under the blankets and frankly, she felt a bit unnerved knowing he did so without an invitation.

"Don't worry. I didn't get in your bed until you woke me up screaming." Jason didn't relinquish his hold on her, instead, his left arm went around her front until his hands overlapped, and he pulled her in closer against his bare chest. "I couldn't just lay down there and listen to you struggle. You were flailing and kicking at the blankets like something was attacking you."

"Something was." Kristina wrapped her hands around his wrists across her chest and held on. She couldn't stand him seeing her in such a weak moment, but she felt so grateful not to be alone. Somehow, she imagined it would've been way worse if he hadn't woken her.

"You wanna talk about it?"

Kristina sucked in a breath and held it. "Maybe in the morning. It still feels too real right now."

"No problem, babe." Jason laid his cheek on top of her head, nestling his face into her hair. Kristina's belly went tight with the intimate contact. She could feel his warm breath against her scalp.

Don't let things go there. Your friendship will never be the same if you allow this to go further. Jason's a man whore, and he'll never look at you the same way again. Kristina removed Jason's arms and shifted her body away from his. The loss of his heat made her feel frigid even though she knew the room was warm.

"Did I do something wrong?"

"Why are you being so nice to me about this?" Kristina looked at her hands lying in her lap. She was afraid to look into his eyes, fearful of what she'd see there. If it was revulsion or pity, she'd be heartbroken, if it was the same heat she felt building between them, she'd be worried. Mostly because she found him attractive, and she didn't know if she'd be able to stop if he tried to take it further.

"What do you mean? Am I ever not nice to you?"

He attempted to pull her back into his arms. Kristina started to resist, but when his hand slipped around to the nape of her neck, and his fingers trailed through the delicate hairs there, she came undone.

"No." Kristina sighed as his grip worked out the tension beneath her skin.

"No as in, you want me to stop? Or, no, I'm not mean to you?" His voice sounded huskier than usual, taking on a tone Kristina didn't recognize.

Kristina felt a moan escape her mouth before she could clamp her lips shut. "You're not mean to me." His fingers continued to work their magic.

"I'm sorry you're having a hard time right now, but I'm here. I'm not going to leave you to face whatever it is on your own." His left hand came around and grasped her chin softly. He brought her face around until she was looking directly into his eyes. "I don't care how embarrassed you feel when you're afraid. You're not embarrassed with me. You understand? I'm in your corner, Kristina."

Surprising herself, Kristina closed the distance and pressed her lips to his. His hands tightened on her as he pressed their faces closer together and claimed her mouth for himself, nudging her lips open and swirling his tongue around hers. The room melted away beneath them. An inferno blazed to life between her legs, and she clenched her thighs together to try to stifle the flames.

She broke the kiss first. "I'm sorry, I shouldn't have—"

Jason pulled her back to him and sucked her lower lip into his mouth, releasing it quickly after. "You definitely should have."

"It's a clown," Kristina spoke the words just as he went in for another go at her mouth. She leaned back a little to avoid another kiss. She wanted him desperately, but he needed to know what kind of crazy came with her. "I've seen him everywhere, ever since I agreed to do the circus train story. He was the one I saw in my apartment before we went to the cemetery. And I saw him again in the street behind the car as we drove away."

"Why didn't you tell me?" Jason propped himself on his hands, leaning away from her, giving Kristina an ample view of his incredible physique.

"You're always giving me hell." She whispered the words, knowing she'd ruined the moment, and feeling pretty damned let down by it.

"I wouldn't have given you hell about something like that."

He frowned at her, and she couldn't help but think how he looked even sexier when he was mad. But where did that thought come from? Sure, she'd thought he was attractive since the day he'd walked into the paper for the job interview, but she'd never drooled over him. It was like she just now truly noticed him.

"Jason, I'm relatively certain I'm losing my mind. How could you not think I'm nuts if I'm not even sure myself?" She felt the pressure behind her eyes and knew she was dangerously close to crying again. *Get it together, Kristina.*

"Because you're not." He said it in such a matter-of-fact way, she almost believed it herself.

"Oh yeah? You want to know what really happened tonight? Other than finding the clown nose on the floor and the weird picture on the computer that can't be explained?" Kristina felt herself getting angry, and she wasn't sure why. All he'd done was try to make her feel better, and she was jumping his ass for some reason. "Hands came out from under my couch. Not like normal ones either. White gloves, frilly sleeves, and a clown's stupid laugh. They reached for me, trying to pull me under. That's why I kept looking at the stupid thing. You sat on the floor right beside it, and I expected those—those things to come back out and snatch you up."

The disbelief in Jason's eyes was hard to miss. He didn't believe her, and how in the hell could she blame him?

"The same stupid clown was in my nightmare. We swung from the trapeze in a circus, and he held both of my wrists. The floor opened under us, and it was hell, Jason. Fire and screaming souls twisting and burning inside the flames. And then he dropped me. You woke me up just before I fell inside. And the clown was high above just laughing away."

"Kristina, you're just overwhelmed by work. We're done with that job now. Everything can start going back to normal."

"We aren't even close to done. All the pictures still need to be edited. That's going to take another week at least. I don't know if I can take another week of this." She hesitated to tell him what was said to her in the nightmare, ultimately deciding, what the hell? What was one more thing to make her look insane? "When we were in the air, he spoke to me."

"It was just a dream, Kristina. None of it was real, I promise you—"

"He said, 'They all died. Those who should've died survived. The show was blood. The show was fire and twisted metal. It won't end with our deaths. The show must go on. Act two will be revenge, and you'll be in the center ring.' He never even moved his mouth. It was like his voice was inside my skull."

Jason pushed past her stony exterior and drug her body back to his chest. "Kris, we covered a train wreck. People burned to death, and the train was a heap of scrap metal and wood embers after. So many people died, and the conductor who hit them lived. Babe, this is your subconscious processing that. Why would anyone want revenge against you? You weren't there. You didn't know anyone there."

Kristina curled her legs in tight against her chest, allowing him to cradle her. "You should think I'm crazy. You should run for the hills. I've seen you scared off from other women for way less."

"That's because those other women weren't you."

The lump of muscle behind her ribs skipped a beat and started beating erratically in her chest. "What do you mean?"

"I'm surprised you don't know. You always seem to know everything." Running his palms down her thighs, Jason didn't seem to want to stop touching her. "Kristina, I've been trying to get your attention since day one. I only took the job at the newspaper to talk to you. You did a job at Lake Michigan. The one about conservation of indigenous species? I was there. You took pictures of my father for that shoot. His name is John Asher. Do you remember him?"

Kristina's mind went back to the job she'd completed the previous year, and she stifled a gasp. "John Asher is your father? How come you never said anything?"

Jason shrugged. "You never asked, and I didn't want you to think I was stalking you or something."

"But you're like, a trust fund baby or something. That guy funded the whole damn project!"

Jason ran his hand through his hair and averted his gaze. "Yeah, I know."

"You don't even need the job at the paper." Clowns be damned, this was far too interesting to be hung up on a nightmare.

"Nope." Jason looked sheepish. "But how else was I going to get the chance to talk to you?"

"I guess that explains why you're so terrible at this job."

"And how I got paired up with you," he admitted. "You're the best photographer on their team. There was no way they would have just let me work with you. You're way out of my league. I went to your boss and offered a large donation to the paper if he gave me a job and promised to let me work with you, and he took it. I didn't really have an interview. It was more like me saying, here's some money, this is what I want from you."

Kristina bit her lip. "How much?"

"How much what?"

"How much did you buy me for?" Kristina didn't know if she should be mad or flattered. But she wanted to know what the going rate was before she kicked him out of her apartment and gave her boss a piece of her mind.

"One million."

"Dollars?" she exclaimed.

"My dad approved the transaction. He thinks it'll make him look better with all the other rich assholes." He struggled to hold onto her as she tried to wiggle out of his arms. "I could care less about the money. All I wanted was a chance to meet you, I swear. That's why I didn't tell you who my dad was or how much he's worth. I wanted you to like me for me."

"That's why you went through all those other women then? That didn't really impress me, Jason Asher."

"I got frustrated because you didn't seem to have any interest in me other than a friend and coworker."

Kristina sighed. "I didn't have any interest because I thought you were a whore."

"Ouch. Well, I guess we were both wrong." Jason smirked.

"Oh no, you're still a whore."

Jason threw his body weight forward, pushing her back against the bed. His arms came down on either side of her shoulders, pressing the bed down around her. Intense lavender eyes burned into hers with a promise he meant to keep. "Now that we know exactly who we both are, why don't you let this whore show you what I can do."

Kristina's breath caught in her throat. The fire reignited instantly. When he lowered himself on his arms, his biceps straining, Kristina didn't try to stop him from finding her mouth once more.

CHAPTER ELEVEN

September 30th, 1918

In Lake County, Indiana, the birds chirped without a care in the world. Clouds obscuring the sky during the unseasonably hot night had dissipated to nothingness, leaving a vast blue blanket above. In a few months' time, the area would be reduced to blinding white swells of snow and freezing winds. But for now, the summer held on with an unrelenting death grip.

Inside the small two-story courthouse, Alonzo Sargent sat silently. His fireman, Gustave Klauss sat nearby, and neither man had anything to say. Tight lipped and stoic, they listened to their counsel plead their case and cringed as the prosecution attempted to tear it all down around them. It was a full house, every folding chair occupied by someone who either believed them to be innocent or wanted to see them hanged. The overwhelming majority shifted angry eyes in their direction and nodded enthusiastically when evidence was presented against them.

Sargent felt the heat of the hate in the room.

"Hey." The man's lawyer leaned towards him, laying a slender hand on the wooden table before them. "Don't worry about any of this. We have a solid case and whatever you hear, just remember this whole thing was an accident. No court can find you guilty of something that was in no way your fault. All the people here, they're just looking for some kind of justice, and they don't care who they get it from. You're not the man responsible for this, though." The lawyer in a tidy waistcoat and tie smiled warmly, offering as much reassurance as he could without making a promise he couldn't keep.

Gustave's lawyer wasn't as pleasant. The man hadn't said two words to his client since the hearings began, and Gustave looked more than worried.

"What about him?" Sargent nodded towards his cohort in a hushed voice.

"I don't represent him. If I must shift the blame in his direction to make sure you walk free, that's what I'll do. I don't think that'll be necessary, though. Like I said before, it's a pretty solid case."

The judge cleared his throat, looking directly at Sargent and his counsel. "Are you two quite done?"

"Yes, Your Honor." The lawyer tugged at his collar as if it had become a bit too tight. "I was merely conferring with my client about a sensitive manner. I apologize."

The judge didn't look impressed or moved by his apology. He held the gavel grasped tightly in his weathered hand, ready to call order for the disturbance. "Mr. Long, it would do you well to remember this is my courtroom, and you'll adhere to my rules. If you wish to speak to Mr. Sargent, sensitive matters or not, you'll wait until an appropriate time to do so. Do I make myself clear?"

"Crystal clear, sir."

The prosecuting attorney cleared his throat, throwing a nasty glance at the young lawyer on the other side of the room.

"Mr. Powers, you may proceed." Judge Stanley settled back into the big chair he occupied above the rest of the courtroom and folded his hands in his lap over his black robes.

"As I was saying, the evidence doesn't lie in this matter. The fact remains that Mr. Sargent was fully negligent for the death and injury incurred due to the crash. If he'd not fallen asleep while at the throttle, he would've seen the flares set out by the circus train." When he mentioned the death and injury, he looked at the jury pointedly, reminding them how important their jobs were to bring the guilty party to justice.

A woman sobbed in the gallery, holding a kerchief to red, swollen eyes. A small child with a bandage over his head clung to her skirts.

"Who's that woman?" Sargent didn't recognize the blonde who scowled at him through her tears.

"Hush, I'll tell you when the judge calls for a recess." Long whispered without looking in his direction. The judge didn't notice.

Mr. Powers went on. "The Michigan Troop Train Mr. Sargent operated didn't reduce speed, didn't apply a brake, and didn't heed any warnings, even though they'd been aware the slower moving train occupied the tracks not miles in front of them. In fact, Mr. Sargent and Mr. Klauss were forced to slow several times before the collision to account for the other train's slower speed. They were well aware of the mechanical issues plaguing the other. Therefore, the pair should've been hyper vigilant the night in question."

Sargent felt like his neck ache from the sudden tightness of his tie. His windpipe felt obstructed, and he opened his mouth to take a large gulp of air. He could already feel the rope pulled snuggly around his neck, could hear the crowd jeering, demanding a pound of flesh for his crimes. He squeezed his eyes shut, trying to drown out the words from the other lawyer.

Mr. Long slid a glass of water across the table with the back of his hand. Behind his closed eyes, Sargent heard it scrape against the rough wood and stop in front of him. Gratefully, the accused brought the liquid to his parched lips and felt it cool the scratching in his esophagus. He liked the lawyer. If anyone would get him out of this mess, it would be Long. God knew his fee was high enough. Sargent was lucky he'd been saving a bit of each paycheck for years. He'd hoped to use the money to go to a holiday someplace warm, but saving his life was just as important, he decided.

"Thank you." Powers took a seat at a table by himself and grinned at the defense attorney. His eyes said, *"Good luck countering any of that. You're screwed."*

Sargent swallowed back a lump and waited to see what happened next.

Judge Stanley made some notes on a pad of paper beneath his palm. "Counsel, does your client wish to take the stand in his own defense?"

The train operator opened his mouth to say yes, but the lawyer cut him off.

"No, your Honor."

Sargent looked at the man in disbelief. "At least let me tell them what happened. They all think I'm a murderer! I have to defend myself."

The young lawyer patted Sargent's arm. "I have your statement. Let me tell them your side. They think you're guilty, and they'll tear you apart if I put you on the stand. It won't help your case, trust me." Long cleared his throat, straightened his tie, and stood. "Your Honor, I have my client's statement of events as given to the officials of the railroad company shortly after the collision. I would like to read some of that to you now."

"Very well, Mr. Long." The judge settled back into his chair again. The prosecuting attorney, Mr. Powers, mimicked his posture.

The woman continued to cry.

Long positioned his body in a sideways stance so he faced the judge and jury simultaneously. His back was to the opposition in a display that seemed to undermine the other man completely. If Powers felt slighted, he didn't show it. "Mr. Alonzo Sargent has been a respected conductor for the New York Central Railroad for over twenty years. In those years of faithful service, he'd never been involved in any kind of investigation against him. He was called in shortly after eight in the evening for a deadhead trip, that's an overnight haul, from Kalamazoo, Michigan, having just come off another deadhead the previous evening. My client had very little sleep in between both hauls."

Sargent was impressed by how Long portrayed him as a hardworking man who did everything asked of him. He painted a picture of a respectable man who didn't have a choice in the hours he kept. He found himself enthralled by the younger man's words.

Long gestured towards the man sitting at the table in prison colors with a frown. "Mr. Sargent indulged in a few heavy meals that day, having no idea when he would eat again, knowing the strenuous schedule he would be keeping to. People of the jury, can you imagine yourselves running a steam locomotive through the night, taking a few hours respite for a nap and food, and then having to do it all over again? My client was exhausted, overworked, and, due to a bad kidney, he'd been on medication making him perpetually tired. Medication that his employers were aware of but took no pause over." Long paused, allowing the jury to nod in understanding. Hoping they would feel sorry for his poor client.

The judge sighed as if he were bored.

"It was a series of stops and goes through the night with the slower train traveling ahead of them experiencing mechanical issues constantly. The towers overlooking the trains should've done the right thing and made the circus train pull off the mainline near East Gary, Indiana, where they could've safely repaired the damage without fear of other traffic. But they were overlooked. If the tower had done their jobs, we wouldn't be here today."

Sargent nodded enthusiastically, looking at his fireman, Klauss, who was sitting on the edge of his seat beside his own attorney.

Long smiled at his client. The jury was engaged by his story of a man being in the wrong place at the wrong time. "Sometime around four in the morning, just east of Ivanhoe, there was another signal of caution ahead. My client saw no need to slow since he couldn't see the other train, and at every other caution, the train was cleared before the troop train arrived.

"The wind blew hard through the small window on my client's side of the engine, causing him to develop a pain in his ear. Not wanting to fall ill, he closed the window and continued. The cab grew steadily warmer, and the combination of no sleep, heavy meals, and the medication for his bad kidney caused Mr. Sargent to doze at the throttle. This was through no fault of his own. His employers should've offered him paid time off while he recuperated from his impairment, and under no circumstances should they have asked one of their engineers to do two deadheads in a row. Their unethical business practice was the culminating factor to the calamity that followed."

Sargent looked at the jury who all looked back at him. He tried his best to look sad, afraid, even ill after the mention of his kidneys. If he could force his skin to pale, he would've.

"Mr. Sargent shouldn't have been left to his own devices in such a state. Mr. Klauss was on board just for this reason. As second in command, when my client began to feel fatigued, his fireman should've taken over for him. But this didn't happen. From what I've been told, Mr. Klauss was in a wholly different car with a bottle of liquor when he should've been ensuring the safety of the train—"

"Objection!" Klauss's lawyer leapt from his seat, pointing his finger in Long's direction.

"Overruled." The judge didn't lift his pen from the notepad he furiously scribbled on. Bringing his eyes to the angry gentleman, he spoke in a gruff, unmoving voice. "You'll get your turn to defend your client anyway you see fit, counsel."

The man took his seat in the hard backed chair, his lip curled in frustration.

Sargent looked at the man who used to be his closest friend and saw only animosity. It was clear to both parties where the finger of blame would land.

Long continued. "If Gustave Klauss took his position seriously, Alonzo Sargent would've been relieved from his post when he started showing signs of fatigue. This tragedy wouldn't have occurred if not for his lack of a sense of duty."

Sargent hung his head, mustering as much guilt as he could to gain sympathy. He heard Klauss scoff from off to his side. If the man took the stand, he could paint him in a whole different light. Sargent hoped the other man's attorney would keep him off the stand as well.

"My client helped pull the injured out of the wreckage for hours before being detained at the crash site and made to sit and watch with Mr. Klauss as the bodies of the dead were laid out before them. The mayor felt it more necessary to make them see the damage done than to allow the men to help with the rescue. If the mayor had a bit more humility, there's a chance more people could've been saved, and we wouldn't be looking at a death toll of eighty-six souls." Long got away with this statement because the mayor chose not to be present for the proceedings.

Gasps went out through the gallery. The woman who sobbed through the entire hearing looked at the young attorney in shock. Sargent knew his lawyer had hit a home run.

Long thanked the jury for their time and took his seat beside Sargent. Klauss's attorney was up next, and he took the easy way out, piggybacking off the testimony made before him, offering nothing new, to Sargent's relief. Klauss looked totally put off with his thick arms crossed over his chest.

"Don't worry. We have this. The jury has been totally won over to our side." Long tapped the table again.

"The jury will be sequestered for deliberation. Foreman, please advise us when you've come to a decision." The judge struck his gavel and stepped out of the judge's box, retreating to a private room beyond.

The bailiff collected both prisoners and escorted them to a holding cell.

The room was tiny, damp, and made entirely of concrete with a wall of bars at the front. It was the same room the two men occupied since their arrest. At night, rats crawled across the floor, searching for crumbs from the trays of food brought to them at mealtimes. Rats terrified Alonzo more than the idea of hanging. There was something about those whiskers and the beady eyes. They unnerved him like nothing else did.

"How long do you think they'll keep us here?" Klauss broke the silence he'd imposed ever since Mr. Long attempted to turn the blame on him.

Alonzo shrugged his heavy shoulders and picked at the paint peeling on the wall close to his hip. "How should I know?"

"That lawyer of yours was a lot better than mine. You'll probably go free, not me. I'll hang for sure. That twit didn't even try to defend me. It was all, *'nothing further, your Honor.'*"

"He threw a bit of a fit when my attorney said you were at fault." A long strip of paint came free, and Alonzo smiled at it, satisfied.

"He did too, though, didn't he? Otherwise, I could've appealed for having ineffectual counsel." Klauss propped his feet against the bars and stretched his body on the concrete floor. This was how they usually passed the time—one on the stone bench and one on the floor.

Alonzo rolled his eyes. "I think the word you're looking for is ineffective."

"Same difference." Klauss shrugged his shoulders from where he lay.

The sound of a heavy key in an old lock silenced the men. Footsteps echoed down the hallway.

"Someone's coming." Klauss got to his feet, gripping the bars in each hand.

"Oh, good. Now we'll know when to expect to be hung." Alonzo wasn't optimistic about the outcome of the trial.

The bailiff returned and shackled each man before escorting them both back to the courtroom. He seated them at their respective tables with the grim-faced attorneys.

The crying woman was back, dabbing her eyes with a fresh kerchief. The bandaged boy still clung to her like a life raft. As he looked at her, Alonzo recalled his attorney never told him her identity. He made a mental note to remind him. She was the only person present who interested him. Everyone else could go to hell as far as he was concerned. It wasn't like any of the people who died mattered. Circus folk were nothing but rapists, murderers, and thieves anyway. Hell, he probably did the world a favor by running into that train. He knew Klauss felt the same way. Neither man would dare to say so now, though—not when their necks were on the line. But the woman didn't look like any of those things. She was dressed like a proper lady with a large hat pinned to her head. The boy she held close to her was in what looked to be a brand-new suit. It must've been purchased for the trial.

"Stand up." Long elbowed Sargent in the ribs.

"Foreperson, have you reached a verdict?" Judge Stanley spoke to the jury as a man on the end stood and cleared his throat.

A deep baritone voice projected across the courtroom. "No, your Honor. A unanimous decision couldn't be reached by this group of men and women. It's a mistrial, sir."

A collective gasp went out through the onlookers. The woman buried her face in her hands and wept harder than she had before. The little boy at her side threw himself across her lap, grasping her hands in his, trying to console her. If Alonzo Sargent cared at all about the damage he'd done, he would've found the scene heart wrenching. Instead, it was simply mildly intriguing.

The judge went on to ask each member of the jury if they agreed with the conclusion the foreperson suggested. They all did. And with that, they were dismissed, each jury member leaving their seats with a look of relief upon their faces.

"What happens now?" Sargent asked his lawyer in a hushed tone.

Long put a finger to his lips, much to Sargent's chagrin.

"Mr. Powers, do you wish to schedule a retrial at this time?" Judge Stanley looked at the defense attorney inquisitively.

"No, your Honor. The state wishes to move to drop all charges forthcoming against Mr. Alonzo Sargent and Mr. Gustave Klauss."

The crying woman fainted.

Alonzo jumped from his chair and flinched when he tried to throw his hands over his head and the shackles caught his skin painfully. Long tugged on his jacket, and he fell to his seat. Klauss uttered prayers beside him.

"Bailiff, would you please remove the cuffs from both men so they may go?" The Judge no longer looked interested in what happened. It was clear this was a turn he hadn't seen coming, and he didn't care much for it. Standing with a groan, he tapped his gavel three times, warning the people in the gallery to calm down so he could speak.

"Yes, your Honor."

"People of the court, these men haven't been found innocent. They have also not been found guilty. Both sides fought their battle diligently, and so, no verdict could be reached on the matter. There was a lot of fault to be had, and I don't believe the blame can be pointed in any direction more than the next." The judge paused, leaning on his palms. "However, while my jury didn't find the defendants guilty of murder, that doesn't mean those are my views. There were many things that could have been done differently to produce a different outcome, but I'm of the mindset that the biggest factor of the evening was the negligence apparent by the two of you." The judge pointed a long finger at Sargent and Klauss. "If it were up to me alone, I would've seen you both hanged. This accident was caused by Engine-man Sargent being asleep, and from this cause, failing to observe the stop indication of automatic signal 2581, and the warnings of the flagman of the circus train, and to be governed by them."

Everyone in the room listened to the speech intently.

"Further, the great loss of life and injuries sustained to those who survived were caused in part by the circus's own negligence for using the outdated, wooden cars and oil lamps which ignited the fire directly following the crash. Both parties should feel immensely guilty for their contributions."

Alonzo swallowed hard. Klauss cursed the man under his breath.

The judge retreated to his chambers, having said all he cared to say on the matter.

The cuffs were removed from the men's wrists shortly after. "So, we can go? We're free?" Sargent asked.

"Yes, you're free to go." The young lawyer smirked.

Sargent hesitated. "Can you tell me who the woman was now?" As he spoke, he watched the person in question and her child exit the courtroom, her leaning heavily on the boy's bony shoulder. She looked as if she might collapse without his help.

"That was Mrs. Diane Caster. Her husband was Henry Caster. He trained the elephants for the Hagenbeck-Wallace circus. The boy was their son, Allen. Henry threw him off the train before the whole thing went up in flames, but he didn't make it off himself. He died saving his boy." Long shook his head sadly. "He and his wife were estranged, but from what I heard, still in love. She just didn't enjoy the circus life like he did. She came back from wherever she was for the boy when telegraphed."

"So, she's single now, eh?" Sargent grinned at his lawyer with an impish smile.

Long blanched and looked at the ceiling.

"I'm just kidding." Sargent punched his shoulder lightly. "I'm a free man now, though. My life savings are gone—used it all to pay you. I don't have a job anymore. I have to find some way to enjoy all this free time I'm about to have."

"Mr. Sargent, while I represented you in this court, please don't assume that means I believe you're an innocent man. It was my job to provide you with an adequate defense, and I did so." Long moved to shake his client's hand.

Sargent declined, putting both his fists behind his back. "That you did, Mr. Long. I suppose that ends our professional relationship with one another."

"It does. I wish you success in your future and a job that won't hurt others if you should have another bout of drowsiness." The lawyer turned and walked toward the exit before Sargent could come up with a witty response.

"Let's get out of here before they change their minds, eh?" Klauss grabbed Alonzo's arm, all but pulling him from the room.

While they waited for a car to take them both to temporary lodgings, Klauss yammered away about how God was looking out for them. Sargent didn't believe in God. It was all bullshit as far as he was concerned.

A cab came up alongside the men, and they both got inside. Sargent took one last look at the courthouse before they pulled away. On the top stair sat a large man, almost as round as he was tall. He wore a top hat pulled low over his face. White gloves adorned his hands, and he was clothed in a clown's costume. Sargent slapped his friend's arm. "Look! It's one of those freaks from the circus. Those fuckers are like ants. You can never get them all."

Klauss leaned over his friend and peered out the window. "Have you started drinking without me? There isn't anyone there."

"He's right there on the top step, you idiot. He's staring right at us." Sargent pointed at the man pulling his hat up. The mouth painted in a whorish red became visible, along with the stark white paint covering the rest of his flesh. Blue circles ringed his eyes. As Sargent watched, the paint changed from loping circles and smooth lines to jagged edges. The blue circles became severe triangles, and the soft eyes turned hard. "Oh, shit! Did you see that?"

Klauss shook his hand. "You've gone bat shit, my friend. Positively, bat shit."

CHAPTER TWELVE

May 6th, 2018

The bedroom illuminated with a flash of lightning behind the sheer silk blinds. Kristina lazily opened one eye and looked at the bedside clock. It was only six in the morning. She could sleep a solid two more hours before she would need to get up. Thunder crashed as she pulled a pillow over her head, rattling the walls around her. Throwing the blanket back, she stared at the ceiling, annoyed she couldn't just relax while she had the time. Taking a deep breath, she exhaled slowly, wiped the sleep out of her eyes, and yawned.

"You can't sleep either, huh?"

The hairs on Kristina's arms stood at attention, and electricity shot through her nerve endings as if the lightning entered her body. "Jesus Christ, I forgot you were in the bed!"

Jason laughed and stretched his long naked body beside her. "I didn't realize I was so forgettable. Guess I'll have to try harder next time."

Kristina felt the blush creep across her cheeks and was grateful the room was still bathed in enough darkness that he couldn't see whatever shade of red she'd turned. Grabbing the robe from the back of her bedroom door, she quickly slid her arms into the holes and tied the sash around her waist. She flipped the switch on the bedside lamp so her bedmate would have some light to find his clothes. Jason made no move to cover his body. He kicked the blankets off his legs and crossed them at the ankles, laying his intertwined hands upon his chest. His manhood, although flaccid, stood out prominently nestled in a soft bed of hair. Kristina's tongue grew thick in her mouth, and Jason's eyes twinkled when he saw her looking.

"It's early. Why don't you come lie back down?"

Kristina wasn't sure she should've ever been in bed with him in the first place. "I need to take a shower."

"I could join you?"

Reaching behind her for the doorknob, Kristina tried to make a hasty retreat. "Jason, no offense, but I need a minute to myself. Last night was great—really great—but I need to think about this. It's all a bit crazy to wrap my brain around." The door opened, and she stepped through—almost free.

"Hey, I get it. I lied to you about who I was and my affiliations. I'm sorry about that." He sat up with his back to her to retrieve his pants from the floor. The corded muscle rippled down his spine as he reached for the clothing, and Kristina's mouth dropped open involuntarily. His ass was perfectly formed, round, and puckered at the sides where it joined his hips. It was no wonder women fell over themselves for a date with him. *And he wants me.*

Kristina cleared her throat, turning towards the hallway. "There's the whole money issue too. You pretty much bought me from my boss like I was a prized mare or something instead of a human being."

"Would you've given me the time of day if I'd just walked up to you at the lake shoot and asked for your number?"

"No."

Jason grinned, zipping the fly on his jeans. "Then do you blame me? Go take a shower, I'll work on the photos for a bit until you're done." He didn't bother with the t-shirt, leaving it where he'd thrown it the night before, in front of her dresser. Padding barefoot to the door where she stood frozen, he squeezed past, making sure to rub his body against hers as he did so. "I'll check the bathroom for clown cars and any other goofy shit that might magically appear."

"Don't make me throw you out of my apartment only half-dressed, Jason Asher."

"Baby, I'd love to see you try."

THE WATER FELT GLORIOUS CASCADING DOWN HER BODY. THE SENSUOUS heat mixed with the sound roaring in her ears moved her towards relaxation within minutes. She stood with her head pressed against the cold stone of the walls with the warmth pummeling her back, not moving for what seemed like forever.

How had she allowed herself to be intimate with Jason? That was a dumb question. She knew exactly how. It was his mouth, his plump button lip that looked so kissable—was so kissable. It was also those eyes. No man on earth had eyes the same shade as his, and she couldn't resist them any more than any other woman could.

Her train of thought reminded her she was just another number on his long list of conquests. He could say all he wanted about waiting for her and only wanting her, but she wouldn't be another dumb girl who fell for his lines. Kristina wasn't a teenager. She knew men would say anything to get a girl in bed, and it would be a cold day in hell before she let him back into hers until she knew he meant what he said. Jason was going to have some proving to do.

Washing her hair and body quickly, taking care with her wounded foot, Kristina rinsed the remaining soap from her skin. She started to turn the taps but thought better of it, took her razor, and shaved all the important places. Just in case he proved himself quicker than she anticipated—or if she found her will weaker than she expected. She hoped it would be the first reason.

Silky smooth and clean, she stepped out of the free-standing shower stall, and towel dried her body. The bathroom was smoky and humid, the mirror a hazy shade of gray with no reflection on its face. Using her hand, she wiped the condensation from the glass, watching water droplets form behind her fingers.

A shape materialized in the mist behind her.

Kristina screamed at the top of her lungs. The sound was feral and wild. It wasn't a sound she'd ever heard herself make. Turning to face her attacker, she was stunned to see no one was in the room. With a racing heart, she stood stock still, knowing what would be in the glass when she looked back.

"Kris!" Jason was on the other side of the bathroom door. "Are you okay? I heard you scream."

A hot breath slid across Kristina's cheek, pushing her hair forward.

"Jason! He's in here!" Adrenaline surged through her limbs. The breath came again, followed by the tip of a tongue, moving from her neck to her earlobe. "Don't touch me, you freak!" Kristina spun with her hands up, swinging when she faced the rear.

Jason ripped the door open just as her hand smashed the mirror. Shards of glass exploded from the wall, embedding in the flesh of her knuckles. Putting a hand across her face to shield her eyes, the last thing she saw before the surface splintered was the clown's grinning face from inside.

"Oh my God, your hand!" Jason lunged for her, sweeping her into his arms before she could cut her feet again. He settled her back on her legs in the hall, pulling the bathroom door closed behind her. "What happened? Why did you hit the mirror? Who were you yelling at?"

Kristina stared at the closed door. Her body twitched with the need to run. Jason wrapped a blanket from her bed around her wet body. She pushed him away absently, without comprehending she was naked, wet, and bleeding. "He was there, in the mirror. I saw him. He —he licked me."

Jason remained silent.

"He wasn't in the room, Jason. He was only in the mirror. When my back was to him, I could feel him breathing on me. I can't escape him. Every time I'm on my own, there he is. What am I going to do?"

Jason didn't look shocked. "Kris, there's something I need to show you. But first, let's wrap your hand up."

Kristina turned back to Jason. "You believe me, don't you?"

He didn't answer her question. "Come on. Let me take care of you." Jason opened the door and ducked inside the dreaded room just long enough to grab antiseptic, gauze, and tape and closed it again behind him. Her hand was a mess of cuts and blood.

Leading her to the kitchen, he turned on the water and cleaned the wound, ensuring no glass remained in her skin before using the antibiotic and wrapping it up tightly. Kristina was starting to look like a mummy with all the gauze on her body. She'd forgotten to remove the strip on her foot, and it was soaking wet, but she didn't care, and he didn't seem to think about it. Kristina struggled to hold the blanket around herself as he took her uninjured hand.

In the bedroom, he opened drawers finding her panties, bras, and socks. Kristina sat on the edge of the bed and allowed him to put each article of clothing on her body as if in a trance. His fingers were so gentle, so careful. When her undergarments were on, he nudged her to lift her feet and slid a pair of sweatpants onto her legs, prompting her to lift her butt to pull them the rest of the way. A t-shirt went over her head, and she had the presence of mind to put her arms through the holes as he held them out to her. No one had ever taken care of her like that before, and even though her mind wandered, trying desperately not to think about the creature in her bathroom, mentally she took note of how he treated her.

"I got through a lot of the editing while you were in the shower." Taking her by the hand, Jason led Kristina into the office where pictures from the cemetery were on the screen in all their colorful glory.

Remembering the picture of the clown looking around Jason to see her, Kristina's stomach flipped, and acid flooded her mouth. "I need water," she choked out, squeezing his hand.

"Here." Jason grabbed a bottle from the floor beside the desk. "I brought two in here with me."

Kristina loosened the cap and tilted the plastic container to her mouth. The ice-cold liquid felt so good on her throat. Pulling it away and gasping for a breath, she wiped her mouth on the back of her hand and took a deep breath. "What did you need to show me, and if it's got anything to do with that clown, I don't want to know."

Jason's mouth flattened into a straight line. "I wanted to know what happened to the guy who hit the train."

"Alonzo Sargent?"

"Yeah, him." Jason opened the browser on the computer where he had multiple tabs open. "From what I could find, he walked away from the accident without a scratch on him. He and his fireman, Gustave Klauss, were charged and tried for their actions resulting in the accident, but the jury couldn't reach a verdict, and they let them go." He clicked through a few of his tabs until he could find the one he referenced. "No one ever paid for the deaths that accrued."

"We already knew that though—"

Jason put a finger up. "See, that's where it starts to get interesting. I found this article by a guy named Collin Stevenson, who claimed his grandfather was really the one who caused the accident. The train definitively hit them, but according to this other guy, his grandpa Maurice Stevenson did something to the circus train before they got underway that night to sabotage them. The ringmaster's second in command fired him and some other guy, and it made him mad. Whatever he did caused the train to be stuck on the tracks in the first place."

"Maurice Stevenson," Kristina whispered the name to herself. She'd never heard the name before now. "That's interesting, but I don't know what this has to do with anything that's happening."

Jason opened yet another tab. "This is an account of a Mr. Gregory Brooks. Do you know his name?"

"No. Should I?"

Jason grinned. "Mr. Brooks was the ringmaster's second, the one who fired the other two men. He survived the accident and later died of a heart attack when he was quite old. But before he died, he wrote a memoir of sorts. He never published it, but his son, Scott, put it online for anyone interested in the history of the wreck."

A full screen picture of the accident filled the high-definition screen of the computer.

"How did you manage to edit most of the pictures and comb through all of this in the time I was in the shower?" Kristina's mind swam with data overload. It would've taken her hours to do the photos without getting sidetracked on worthless information.

Jason looked away sheepishly. "Okay, I started on the pictures, but I got sucked into an internet black hole. I'm sorry. I don't think I'm cut out for photography."

Kristina already knew that, but she wasn't going to say so. "What's so interesting about the Brooks guy." Listening to him talk was far better than thinking about what happened in the bathroom.

"I'm glad you asked that question because the answer will blow you away." Jason enlarged the picture and zoomed in on a man sitting on the far side of the wreck. "That's him there, or at least whoever took the picture claims it's him. Mr. Brooks told his son, on the day of the funeral for all the people killed in the train wreck, he got insanely drunk and accidentally went back to the graveyard instead of his hotel.

"He claimed he passed out right on top of where they buried all the bodies and was visited by his good friend, Baldy the clown."

Kristina's breath hitched. At the mention of the clown, it felt like the air left the room, leaving an icy nothingness behind that suffocated her. "Visited?" She whispered the word, her voice refusing to go any louder.

"Yeah. He says the clown told him to let everyone who survived know that he was going to take care of the people who caused the accident as long as they would all give him permission to do so."

Kristina's whole body shook. She felt like she was freezing, and it made no sense to her why she couldn't see her breath, and Jason looked perfectly composed with no shirt on. Forcing air into her lungs, she licked her lips and attempted to speak. "What happened to them?"

"The survivors?"

It was in that moment Kristina remembered how exasperating Jason could be. "The men responsible."

"It's kind of gruesome."

The world started to spin around her, and Kristina grabbed the side of the desk to keep from hitting the ground. Jason jumped from the chair and grabbed her by the elbows to help stabilize her. He planted her in the chair and squatted beside her. "Tell me." She looked into his eyes, imploring him to continue.

"Alonzo Sargent clawed his own eyes out and was admitted to a psychiatric hospital. He was only there a day before he bit off his tongue and took his own life. The attendees had to restrain him for his own safety, but somehow, even with a straight jacket on, he managed to hang himself without anyone noticing or hearing anything." Jason started to open another tab but seemed to think better of it and minimized the screen instead. "It was hard to find any information on him, but the hospital documented everything, and I happened upon it by accident after searching his name. One of the doctors said he screamed about a clown torturing him."

"A clown," Kristina couldn't help but repeat the words. Silently, she wondered if it was the same clown who was torturing her.

"Yeah. Things weren't much better for Klauss either."

Kristina wasn't sure she wanted to know, but Jason kept talking.

"I'm not sure if the two deaths were related, other than Brooks saying they were, but Klauss drowned in a water car being pulled by a train. Apparently, there was a malfunction, and he went to check it out. He climbed into the car from a top hatch, and the thing latched behind him. He fell into the water and couldn't get a grip on the ladder to pull himself out and drowned in there. They found his body when the train made the next stop."

Kristina shivered. She fully believed his death wasn't an accident. "What about the two men who caused the circus train to stall?"

"I haven't found anything on Maurice Stevenson except that one thing from his grandson. I can't even prove he was telling the truth or not. I couldn't find his friend's name either, the one who got fired with him." Jason pulled the photos back from the bottom of the screen and left them open on the desktop.

"Do you think the clown who caused Sargent to kill himself is the same one I've been seeing?" Kristina held her breath, fully prepared for Jason to tell her he didn't think that because ghosts weren't real, and even if they were, why would this one be interested in her?

Instead of rejection, he put his hand on her shoulder and smiled. "I don't know, but I'm going to help you find out."

CHAPTER THIRTEEN

October 15th, 1918

Alonzo Sargent woke up in a cold sweat in his one-story home, nestled in the suburbs of Grand Rapids, Michigan. He'd had nightmares ever since the accident but couldn't recall them once he'd woken up. Apparently, he'd been sleepwalking as well. The night before last, he'd woken right as he was about to step off his roof in pajamas in the middle of the night. At least he was in his own bed tonight.

"Goddamn it all." Alonzo twisted his overweight body to the side, rising, and planting his feet on the cold floor. "What's a man gotta do to get a good night's sleep?"

The ticking clock on the bedside table was just to the far side of midnight. He'd only been asleep for three hours before the terror overtook him. Scratching the side of his head, he struggled to recall what it'd been about.

Pushing against the mattress with closed fists, he hefted his weight upright and stretched. "Might as well pour myself a bourbon. That'll help me drift off for sure." No one was around to hear him. Even the cat ran away the first chance the little beast got when Alonzo returned home from his detainment. He no sooner opened the door that the cat made for the space between his legs and bolted into the night. The train conductor hadn't cared to chase after him. One less mouth to feed.

The bourbon sat on the counter in the small galley kitchen. There wasn't much of anything else to be plainly obvious. The empty space in the cabinets reflected the inordinate amount of time he spent on the tracks. More often than not, he found his dinner in random diners located near railway stations in the towns he stopped in. Some of the mangy looking women who waitressed in the low-class establishments even knew him by name. Hell, he'd gone home with some of them for lack of anything better to do. It wasn't like he'd ever had a wife or kids waiting for his return. Even if he did, it wouldn't have mattered to him.

Alonzo was a heavy-set man, with one great roll hanging over the waist of his pants. He was forever tucking the shirt around his girth, only to have it come loose mere seconds later. The railway company was too cheap to buy him a uniform that fit. They just expected him to run laps or something of that nature. But with all the overtime he worked, who had time for that?

The bottle clinked against the glass as he poured the drink. With an upwards gesture, he lifted the glass high in a salute. "To all those poor fools who burned in the crash. May God have mercy on your souls for all the trouble you put me through."

Bringing the glass to his lips, he allowed the amber colored liquid to fill his mouth. The burn it caused was exquisite, and he recalled once more the sound of the passengers screaming in pain. Swallowing, he stared at the glass, feeling the alcohol scorch his throat.

He poured a second glass for good measure.

Something moved in his peripheral vision. Alonzo turned, the bourbon bottle slipping from his grasp. It didn't break but was full enough to spill the contents across the floor. Muttering a curse, Alonzo bent to retrieve the bottle, grunting as his fat got in the way.

"Goddamn cat must have snuck back in. I knew it was only a matter of time before the animal got hungry. I must have left a window open somewhere." He licked the bourbon off the side of the bottle before setting it back on the counter. "Here, kitty, kitty." He clicked his tongue and patted his thigh. No meow came back to him.

Frowning, Alonzo tilted his head to see into the hallway where the movement first caught his attention. He hadn't bothered to turn on any lights on his way out of the bedroom, and now he kicked himself for it. Remembering the glass he'd poured, he looked back at the counter, located it, and downed it in one swift motion. It burned his tongue just as well as the first had.

"Mittens? Is that you?" He searched the shadows for a burst of black fur. The heart so deeply buried in his chest from years of physical neglect hammered at his ribs as if he'd been running. The dark hallway looked ominous, much blacker than it was when he walked down it before. The floor seemed to stretch out endlessly. The doors were all so far away and closed. When did he shut the doors? Being the only resident in the house, he never had a need for closed doors, so they all sat perpetually open, even when he relieved himself in the bathroom. But now, every one of them was firmly latched in their frames. Alonzo imagined they would be locked if he tried them, but he wasn't sure where the thought came from.

Another shadow crossed his path, and he sucked in a breath. "Mittens! Stop messing around! Come out, and I'll fill your bowl."

The knob on his bedroom door creaked ever so slightly. The noise sounded like a single nail down a chalkboard as the old metal pins turned under an unseen hand.

Alonzo froze in mid-step. Cats couldn't turn doorknobs. Someone was in his house.

"Who's there?" Pressing himself to the wall, Alonzo projected his voice, trying to sound as big and mean as he could muster. It was very possible a squatter took up residence while he'd been held in the God forsaken jail cell. "I'll warn you! I have a gun, and I'm not afraid to use it!"

In reality, the man had never even held a gun, let alone used one.

Low garbled laughter reached Alonzo's ears from his hiding spot against the floral wallpaper. Whispering voices came from behind him, back in the living room and kitchen, but he couldn't make out what they said. Fear trickled down his spine like a lover's caress, light fingertips touching him, prodding him, turning his flesh to stone each place they pressed.

The bedroom door inched open—the dark from the room blacker and yet more alive than that of the hallway. It was almost as if the shadow inside possessed a consciousness. It twisted and writhed across the floor, turning in on itself and winding free. The barely audible chuckles seemed to come from the inky tendrils rolling across the floor.

Alonzo slid across the wall, his sausage like fingers finding purchase amongst the rose print. An icy wall slammed into his back, allowing him to go no further. A dozen or more disembodied voices held him in place, allowing the seething, evil thing on the floor to come closer. It was growing, folding over, and doubling in size every time it did so.

"What are you?" Alonzo screamed at the mass that was nearly the size of a man. "What do you want from me?"

Hands gripped his body from all sides—the icy blast replaced by burning fingers digging into his arms and legs. Each place they touched him blistered and peeled, his flesh turning black and falling away from him like pieces of roasted pork on a spit. Alonzo screamed in agony as he cooked from the invisible flames.

The shadow before him changed, gaining features, arms and legs. The body was much wider than Alonzo had ever been. Eyes formed in the shadowy face, eyes that pierced like knives, seeing into his soul. The grin came next, too wide for the face it graced.

"Dear God, what are you?" Alonzo screamed through his teeth, unable to shake the fiery hands holding him in place.

The whispers ceased, falling away to silence so deep, he could hear his frantic heartbeat in his ears.

The thing before him manifested into the visage of a clown. The frilled color around his neck sat perfectly in place, scorch marks marring the pristine white color. The red frock he wore was similarly damaged and singed. The paint slathered on his face dripped, and the happy blue around his mouth had melted away to look jagged and cruel. Looking closer, Alonzo could discern the puss-filled boiled skin beneath the white exterior as if the man had held his face above a crackling fire.

The fingers dug into Alonzo's flesh harder, reminding him of their presence.

The clown's lips parted, and a red tongue lapped at his parched lips. "Fine night for a train wreck, wouldn't you agree, Mr. Sargent?"

Placing hands covered in white gloves on each shoulder of the terrified man, the clown brought his face to his. The smell of cooked flesh and burnt hair assaulted Alonzo's nose. Trying to turn his face away, one of the burning hands gripped his chin and held him firmly in place. The clown's eyes were mesmerizing, a flame flickering inside each black pupil. Alonzo couldn't help but stare at embers inside, like a moth to the flame, knowing it would end him to get too close.

"Please!" he begged. "Let me go!"

A chuckle rumbled from the clown's bulbous chest. The red fabric of his costume rippled over his girth and a button popped free. The gloved hands felt like coals placed on bare skin. The familiar surroundings of his home melted away around him until a new location flooded in. As Alonzo watched enraptured, he found himself inside a train car. The clown still gripped him tightly, but the other hands vanished. Around him, people slept on beds stacked three high on each side, their trunks and meager possessions pushed beneath the first level of cots.

"Bear witness," the clown whispered, the stench of his breath invading Alonzo's nose. "Experience the pain you caused."

"I didn't cause anything!" Alonzo screamed. "I was acquitted! Or didn't you hear? It was just an accident. Nothing more! It was no one's fault!"

The clown's grin broadened to an impossible length. "Bear witness and pay for all you did. Pay for every life you cut short."

Alonzo whimpered, pulling against the steel like grip on his body. The hands holding him were unmovable like those of a statue. Twisting him to the side, Alonzo was afforded a view through the back of the train and out the caboose. Lights in the distance closed the gap. The train riding the tracks beyond didn't slow, didn't hesitate, didn't acknowledge the warning flares Alonzo could clearly see from where he stood.

"Oh, God!" As he was held in place, pandemonium broke out around him. The second engine perforated the sleeping car, slicing the wood planks in two. The steel undercarriage groaned and snapped, twisting into unrecognizable shapes. The people on board scarcely had time to know what happened to them before the oil lanterns fell from where they hung and ignited everything. Alonzo watched the men, women, and children catch flame. He saw their bodies thrown around like rag dolls as the train was ripped to shreds. The flames licked at his skin, sending waves of pain cascading over him.

The screams of the dying and injured hit him harder than the flying debris. This was far different than his experience in the engine car had been. While in the other train, he'd barely felt more than a shudder as the two trains collided. When he'd been at the wheel and awoke as he'd driven into the rear cars of the circus train, he'd thrown his arms over his face. Now he was forced to see it all.

A man beside him was pinned beneath a bunk, his arm severing at the shoulder as he tried to free himself. The fire crept up the man's legs until it engulfed him completely. He wailed in agony until his body could withstand no more.

Alonzo pulled against the clown, trying in vain to free himself. "Please! I can't watch this anymore! I'm sorry!"

"Bear witness." The clown's grin didn't falter.

At the front of the inferno of wood and oil, Alonzo spotted an eerie likeness of the clown holding him. The twin shielded a woman and child from the flames, putting his round body over them. His efforts were in vain. The wood around them collapsed, pinning the family under a smoldering beam. The child screamed in pain and then fell silent, the roar of the fire drowning out his final breaths.

Alonzo looked at the clown holding him. "That was you!" The conductor smiled despite the immense pain burning through his limbs. "You sorry son of a bitch! You came back from the grave to punish me for killing your family, huh? Well, good riddance! No one will miss a family of nomads, a family of fools! I did the world a favor when I rammed my engine up your train's ass!"

The clown bellowed from deep in his throat. His hands moved to Alonzo's face, pressing his thumbs into the man's eyes. They felt like red hot fireplace pokers as Alonzo felt the malleable surface of his eyeball's compress, pop, and ooze down his cheeks.

"Ahhh!" The man screamed, flailing his arms against his invisible shackles. He kicked out his legs, anything to get free. The smoke choked his lungs as he howled in agony, sucked in a breath, and continued his striations.

He fell, his body tumbling through space. The fire engulfed him, thoroughly charring what used to be his body. Everything was black—his vision ripped from him by the clown's hands.

New hands gripped his arms and legs, restraining him.

"No! No! No!" Alonzo fought his tormentors with all he had. Gnashing his teeth, trying to catch a limb in his mouth, baring his hands like claws, he couldn't fight them off.

"Hold him steady men, don't let him hurt himself any worse than he already has." The voice was alien to his ears. It wasn't the clown or any of the hoard in flames. "Pin his arms down and get the restraints on, quickly!"

Alonzo tried to open his eyes, but there was nothing there. His blindness prevented him from discerning what was happening to him.

"What the fuck did this guy do to himself?" Another voice reeled from closer to his feet.

"Looks like he had a nervous breakdown and clawed out his eyes," the first voice said. "He's damned lucky his neighbor heard him screaming, or he probably would have bled out. We need to get him to the hospital quickly!"

Alonzo felt the cuffs tightened around each wrist and ankle, and a needle slide into his forearm.

"That should calm him down some." A third voice from his side chuckled.

Sweet oblivion began to slide over Alonzo like a warm blanket on a downy soft bed. Before he slipped away completely, he heard the first man chortle. "Hey, I recognize this guy. He's the one in the papers for killing all those circus folks when he fell asleep at the throttle of his train."

CHAPTER FOURTEEN

May 6th, 2018

Getting through the photos for the ceremony was a chore Kristina couldn't commit to. Having no other choice, she mostly supervised, walking Jason through what needed to be done but not actually touching them herself. Every time she saw a happy, grinning, makeup-clad face, her stomach dropped. The strange photo she'd seen the night before was mysteriously absent as if whoever placed it there for her to find, removed it after she'd found it. It didn't help her feel any saner after telling Jason about it.

When they were done, there were fifty photos she felt confident enough to hand to her boss. None of them were the quality she would've normally demonstrated, but they were as good as they were going to get. Attaching all the photos to an email, she sent them to her boss and to the Caster's, as she'd promised to do. She hoped they made them happier than they made her.

"That's it. The Showmen's Rest shoot is all wrapped up. How about we go to Home Depot and get a replacement door before your property owner ventures this way and sees the damage?" Jason shut down the computer and flexed his fingers out before him.

Kristina had forgotten about the broken door completely.

"How much do you think this is going to run me?" she asked, grabbing her purse off the floor from where it slouched against the desk.

"Don't worry about it," he replied. "I broke it. I'll replace it."

"I can't let you do that." Kristina lowered her arms to her waist. "It was my fault you broke it in the first place."

Jason waved her off. "I happen to know for a fact that if I put the door on my family credit card, my dad won't notice. Plus, I know the paper doesn't pay all that great. Let me take care of this."

Kristina's eyes flashed in warning. "I don't need your dad's money to fix my door or anything else, Jason. I'm perfectly capable of taking care of my own problems. I've never had a man take care of me, and I'll be damned if I'm going to start now."

Throwing his hands up in surrender, Jason grinned, squinting his lavender eyes at her. "I didn't mean it like that. I would never insinuate you couldn't take care of yourself. I just wanted to make things easier for you. I'm sorry."

Kristina melted under the sincerity of his expression. "A door isn't going to fit in that little car of yours."

"We can have them deliver it here."

Jason edged her towards the door. She didn't want to admit it, but she didn't want to leave the apartment. She didn't want him to leave her there alone either. It didn't feel safe where they were, but the outside world seemed so much scarier. "Thank you." Kristina paused, thinking of how much harder this would all be if he wasn't there with her. She didn't need a man to pay her way, but it felt damned good to have some company through this madness.

"Come on. Let's get this fixed, get some food, and figure out what we're going to do next." He didn't acknowledge her apology, but she was glad he wasn't going to make a joke about it like he would have done in the past.

Before she got into the car, Kristina couldn't help but check the back seat to make sure nothing would surprise her on the way to the home improvement store. The interior was meticulous, without so much as a straw wrapper on the floorboard. Heaving a sigh of relief, she settled herself into the passenger seat and locked the door.

"You know it does that automatically?" Jason stuck the key in the ignition. "You don't have to lock the door."

"It just felt good to do it myself."

Nodding his head, Jason pulled out onto the street. "Fair enough."

They sat in silence most of the way. Kristina kept her eyes straight ahead, afraid there would be a clown's face looking back at her from the mirrors. At this point, she didn't trust the apparition not to reach out of the glass and attack her. Jason glanced in her direction every few seconds, and Kristina wondered if he was waiting for her to lose it completely.

"You know," Jason turned on his left blinker to merge into traffic. "I found that guy's address while I was sniffy around on the web."

Kristina tilted her face up at him. "What guy?"

"Collin Stevenson."

Kristina bit down hard on the side of her tongue and felt blood rush into her mouth. "So?" She tried to sound as nonchalant as she could, but her words slurred from the bite.

"So," he started. "I was thinking we could stop and see the guy on our way back. Maybe he knows more than what was in the article."

"Why in the world would we do that?" Kristina put her fingers on the bridge of her nose, trying to stabilize her breathing. "That guy doesn't know us, and we don't know him. What if he made the whole thing up to have a good story to tell?"

Jason came to a stop at a red light, the car idling gently. On the curb, a bum held out a styrofoam cup begging for change. His clothes looked dingy with holes and his hair was long and unkempt. He shook the cup next to Kristina's window, imploring her with his eyes. She tried not to make eye contact with him.

"What would it hurt even if he was lying?" Jason looked past Kristina giving the bum the *'get the fuck away from my car'* look. "Worst case scenario, we waste a little time. But the best case is, we learn something new and find out why you're seeing the clown."

The bum slammed his hand on the glass, his face close enough to the glass that fog formed in front of his mouth. He snarled, showing yellowing teeth. "Spare any chance for a down and out ringmaster?" The man trailed his fingers down the glass, leaving smudges in his wake. "I'll show you a trick for a dollar."

Jason hit the gas, leaving the bum standing with his hand still outstretched behind them. "What the hell was that all about? What a creepy dude."

"Did you hear what he said?" Kristina whispered with her hand against her chest.

"Yeah, he asked you for money."

Kristina's breath caught in her throat. Her heart was a runaway train, hammering at a frantic pace, making her dizzy. "He said he was a down and out ringmaster. You think that was a coincidence?"

The car shifted gears and shot forward with a throaty roar. "The asshole was really close to the car. He probably heard me mention the clown and was trying to play on it. Don't worry. Those guys will do anything to get money for their next beer or hit off whatever drug they're addicted to." He smiled at her weakly.

The parking lot was almost deserted when they pulled in and parked close to the front. Kristina thanked her lucky stars that this trip wouldn't be drawn out. She allowed Jason to take her by the hand and lead her through the glass doors that opened automatically as they came close. A whoosh of cold air blew her hair back as they crossed the threshold.

A clerk stood inside the doors holding a stack of flyers in her dainty hands. "Would you like a copy of the sales?" she asked with a smile.

"No thanks. Can you point us in the direction of the millwork department?" Jason implored.

"Aisle thirteen, back row." The girl grinned again mechanically.

"Thanks." Taking her hand again, Jason looked at the ceiling for the aisle numbers and headed towards the one the girl indicated.

When they arrived, Kristina was immediately overwhelmed by the number of doors there were in stock. There were doors with glass inlays, doors with special designs, metal doors, wooden doors, fiberglass doors. The combinations and price tags were endless. "How the hell are we supposed to choose one?"

Jason chuckled. "Don't even look at these. Unless you own your own house, don't bother with the fancy, expensive stuff. Plus, we don't want the landlord to know we damaged the other one, so it's best if we pick one that looks the same as the old one." Leading her down the adjacent aisle, Jason held his hand out in a flourish to the rows of plain white, nondescript doors on the shelves. "Voila. Apartment specials."

"Can I help you folks find something?" A man in an orange vest and a name tag reading 'Jerry' approached them. The balding, middle-aged man didn't look too enthusiastic about his job.

"We need a door delivered to the Park Ridge apartments." Jason took the lead, and Kristina was grateful. She didn't have any idea what they needed. "Do you guys do any installing?"

"We do, but it's an extra hundred bucks." Jerry picked at his teeth with his tongue, squinting his beady eyes at them as if he fully expected them to change their mind on the install.

"That's fine." Jason met his gaze and held his eyes. "We need this door in a size thirty-eight by eighty. We would like it installed with the old hardware, and we would like it done within the next hour."

Kristina could tell Jason didn't like the man.

"Expedited delivery and installation will cost you extra. Or I can schedule you in for next week."

Kristina swallowed hard. She couldn't go a week with no door. "That's not possible."

Jason took up where she left off. "The old door is damaged and no longer usable. I don't care what the price is. Just make it happen."

His dad spoke like that. During the photoshoot, the man took a phone call and used almost the same words, and Kristina saw why. As soon as Jason put on an air of authority, the man's demeanor changed, and he immediately spoke into his walkie-talkie, asking for an associate to come take the door down. While Jerry and the other man fought with the door, Jason crossed a couple aisles and grabbed a bathroom mirror and adhesive to replace the one she'd smashed. He rejoined her within minutes. After gathering the information on the address of the apartment, color of door jambs in case they were damaged too, and processing the payment on Jason's credit card, they were on their way out again.

Must be good to be rich.

Kristina's head spun. The total of the purchase was almost a thousand dollars with the cheap door and mirror. There was no way she could've afforded that even if she'd drained her savings. She didn't know how she would repay him, but she vowed she would. Feeling indebted to someone wasn't high on her list of things she wanted to experience.

"Food?"

Breaking away from her thoughts, Kristina focused on Jason again. "I don't care. But I'm paying."

"I'll let you pay under one condition."

Here it comes, the I spent money on you, so now I own you, speech. Cringing, Kristina waited to hear what her servitude would entail. "What is it?"

"Jeez, you look like I'm going to ask you for a kidney or something." Jason laughed at his own joke. "You can pay for the food if you agree to meet with Collin Stevenson."

Lurching into her seat, trying to become invisible, Kristina weighed her options. She absolutely did not want to go bother a man who could be a serial killer for all she knew, and she didn't want to let Jason pay for lunch either. He'd already spent so much money on her. Which idea did she hate more?

"Fine." She crossed her arms over her chest in defiance. "But you should know I'm not happy with either of these outcomes, and I'm going to be mad at you the rest of the day."

When she looked back at Jason, pursing her bottom lip, eyes lowered in anger, she was shocked to see the heat in his eyes. Warmth rolled off his body in a delicious wave. She swallowed and averted her eyes to keep from giving in.

"I bet I know how to make you forgive me." Pulling into the drive-thru line for a fast-food restaurant, Jason turned his body until he faced her. "I seem to remember doing something with my tongue that made you pretty happy."

A blush made Kristina's cheeks hot. "Just get me a cheeseburger, please." She changed the subject as he came to the speaker.

Jason ordered for them both, and she placed her debit card in his outstretched hand to pay at the window. While they waited for their order, Kristina looked through the glass wall to their left and saw a child's birthday party in full swing amongst the booths. There were streamers hanging from the seats and a big cake in front of a boy who looked to be maybe five years old. Kristina felt a longing to be that young again. What she wouldn't have given to be that free of worry.

"Kris, look out the other window." Jason's voice took a hard tone, and against her better judgement, she looked closer at the party. Off to the side, a clown twisted balloons together to make hats for the children. His eyes were on Kristina. The long cylindrical tubes in his hands were jerked roughly, squeezed, and manipulated into shapes. His grin broadened when he saw her watching. Placing the balloon hat on the head of a passing child, he raised his gloved hand and waved at them through the window.

Jason thrust the bag of food into Kristina's lap and sped away.

"I'm sorry, Kris. I should have chosen a different restaurant." Jason lifted the cup from the cup holder and gulped it greedily. "I wouldn't have pulled in there if I'd known there was a clown."

"It's not your fault." Her voice sounded like a squeak in her ears. She handed him a sandwich and placed her own in her lap, looking at the sad, grease laden wrapper in disgust. She pulled back the edge, and worms fell out into her hands. Sucking in a breath, she wadded the paper up around the burger and tossed it back in the bag.

"Not hungry?"

The worms in her lap disappeared, having never been there to begin with. "My stomach is too tied in knots to eat right now. Maybe later."

Jason took a bite of his food and eyed her curiously. "Stevenson lives about ten miles from here. I promise if he's a nutcase or just an attention seeker, we'll leave quick, fast, and in a hurry. But I'm really hoping he'll know what's going on and why."

Kristina wasn't holding her breath.

CHAPTER FIFTEEN

October 16th, 1918

When Alonzo Sergeant woke next, he was leaning against a padded wall. The room was tepid, neither too hot nor too cold. Drool trickled down the side of his mouth, and when he tried to wipe it away, he found his arms restrained in long sleeves attached firmly behind him. Panic settled in. He tried to force his eyes open, but no matter how far he pushed his lids, his vision remained black.

His stomach dropped to the floor. He didn't have eyes anymore. The clown popped them.

"Hello?" His voice came out barely above a whisper, harsh and thick on his tongue. It didn't sound like he recalled.

A heavy silence answered his call. Alonzo could hear the blood pulsing between his ears. Each breath he took sounded like an echo chamber.

"Hello!" He projected the word as loud as he could, coughing once it passed his lips. He desperately wanted a glass of water and wondered how long he'd gone without. As if in answer, his stomach grumbled. A sharp pang of hunger doubled him over. Squeezing his eyelids together tightly, he was appalled when they overlapped with nothing beneath them.

"Someone fucking answer me!"

There was a noise directly ahead of him. Alonzo wasn't a great judge of distance, but it seemed to be only about five feet or so. It was a hinge bending, a door swinging open, scraping against the padding on the floor. Soft footsteps came near him, and he flinched, expecting the monster once again. But it was a woman.

"Sir, if you'll just stay calm. The doctor will be with you in an hour."

Anger replaced his desperation. "What the fuck is going on here? Why do you have me all wrapped up in whatever the hell this thing is?" He turned his body around in a full circle, trying to figure out how to escape the jacket. "I'm hungry, I'm thirsty, and you have no right to keep me here against my wishes. Take this stupid thing off so I can go home."

When her voice came again, it was softer with a touch of sadness. "Mr. Sargent, we have to keep you here until you're well. When you came in, you were covered in blood. You'd gouged your eyes out, and you screamed a bunch of nonsense about a clown and burning. You haven't been evaluated yet. After the doctor sees you, we'll be able to treat you and get you somewhere more comfortable."

"No!" Alonzo screamed at the woman. "You're going to untie this goddamned thing and get me a glass of water. What am I, some kind of prisoner?"

"No sir, you're a patient."

"I didn't do anything to my eyes, just so we're clear. It was the fucking clown that did it." Sargent ripped at the fabric, trying to use brute strength to force the sleeves apart, but the weak flabby man couldn't manage it.

"Let me get someone to help you, Mr. Sargent." Her footfalls were soft as she left him. A moment later the door closed, and he was alone once again.

His nose picked up the hint of smoke. Inhaling deeply, he tried to ascertain where the smell originated from, but without his eyes, he couldn't be sure. Pushing his back against the wall again, he slid around the room, finding his previous assumption of the door being five feet in front of him to be correct. The room didn't have corners. It was perfectly circular, and if his arms had been free, it was likely he could've touched both sides with his fingertips, it was so small.

The burning smell lingered, growing stronger the more he dwelled on it.

"This place is on fire! Open the door!" Sargent screamed towards where he believed the door was. Doing his circle, he felt no difference in the padding with the side of his face in any spot, so he couldn't be certain he was correct on the location at all.

He smelled burning flesh, melting hair, and kerosene oil.

"No!" Sargent slumped to the floor, burying his face in his crossed arms to protect his face. "Not you! Not again! Haven't you done enough?"

Someone else was in the room. The presence felt like it stood very close by. Sargent could feel the eyes on him even though he couldn't see the person himself. There was no discernible breath, no movement, but he was there.

"What do you want?"

Low laughter filled the room. It was a clown's chuckle, a gay sound of merriment twisted into something sinister. Alonzo sucked in a breath, trying to pinpoint where the creature watched him from. It was elusive. One second, he seemed to be off to his right, the next, his left, but he never made a sound.

"Answer me, you bastard!"

The voice was right in front of his face. "It's your fault they're dead. My Martha and Reginald, all my friends, burned because of you."

The smell of fire choked Alonzo's throat. He couldn't breathe. It felt like smoke poured down his throat, invading his lungs. It grew hotter by the minute. He could feel his skin blistering under his clothes, feel it flaking from his bones. He imagined his lips pulling back away from his teeth—his tongue shriveled like a slug doused in salt.

"Nurse! Nurse!" Alonzo screamed at the top of his lungs, throwing his body on the floor and rolling to put out the flames. It was difficult to get momentum with his arms pinned the way they were, but he scissors his legs to make himself flop. The room was an inferno, an invisible crematorium reducing each limb, each tendon to ash. Any minute now, he would draw his last breath. All the while, the clown laughed.

The noisy hinges turned, and people rushed into the room.

"Can you see him?" Alonzo struggled to keep rolling. He had to save himself at all costs. "Can you see the clown? He's in the room! He did this to me! He took my eyes, and he set the fire!"

"Mr. Sargent, you're not on fire." It was a man's voice, not the lovely girlish lilt of the woman who'd come before. But she said she was getting him help, didn't she? "If you'll just hold still, we're going to give you something that'll make you feel much better."

"No! I need to get out of here! I don't need any—" Alonzo's plea fell off as the needle penetrated his neck, and he floated once more.

THE BIG TENT ROSE BEFORE HIM LIKE A MONOLITH AGAINST A PITCH-BLACK sky. The red and white stripes were lit from within, casting an eerie glow on the surrounding trees. Muffled calliope music drifted on the wind, coaxing him to the flaps held back by thick golden cords of rope.

Alonzo felt his curiosity pique, felt the yearning in his belly to see what spectacles lay within. His eyes were whole, intact, and his vision fine-tuned to the sights and smells overwhelming him. He took a step forward and swung his arms, finding the cumbersome jacket replaced with his conductor uniform. He lifted the cap on his head and repositioned it in a more comfortable position. A train whistled somewhere behind him, almost as an afterthought of his vision.

"Step right up! Ladies and gentlemen, boys and girls!" The ringmaster's engaging words rung clearly through the night air, eliciting fanciful imaginings and dreams come true from the fat old engineer. "You there!" The gloriously dressed showman pointed at Alonzo, his painted face stretching into a grin.

Alonzo looked in either direction, but he was the only person visible.

"What is a man like you still doing outside?" The ringmaster gestured for him to come forward with both hands. "Come! Enjoy the show! See our acrobats and strongman! The Flying Wards are in attendance this evening, and your life simply won't be complete if you don't see them soaring through the air on the trapeze."

Alonzo felt his feet moving beneath him, creeping closer to the man's outstretched arms.

Holding the canvas wide so Alonzo could pass, the ringmaster gave him a toothy grin. "It's the greatest show on earth, Mr. Sargent. You'll never see anything quite like it again."

"How do you know my name?"

Lights of all colors greeted the men as they stepped inside. "We all know you here. You could say we're connected."

Alonzo removed his cap and scratched at the halo of hair around the edges of his scalp. "I'm not sure what that means."

"Well, you killed us, after all."

The music stopped.

The seats were empty. Sargent was the only spectator. The canvas tent flaps were replaced with a heavy metal door, the ringmaster pushed, closed, and locked behind him. The performers on stage stopped tumbling, the trapeze lowered to the ground, and a lively woman in a sequined, turquoise leotard stepped off the bar and glared towards him.

Feeling something in his hand, Alonzo looked down and found the train throttle gripped tightly in his fingers. The metal felt warm against his palm, familiar. The clowns climbed the bleachers on either side of him, happy and sad faces, all trained on him. One clown brought up the center.

"Mr. Sargent." The ringmaster's voice was right by his ear. When had he left the door? "I trust Baldy the clown needs no introduction?"

The clown in question stepped forward, raising his eyes to meet Alonzo's. "Your turn, conductor. Your turn to see hell, to feel the flames. But your suffering won't end with death. Oh no, your damnation will last for all eternity. When I've finished with you, I'm going to introduce myself to Mr. Klauss."

The clown held a length of rope in his gloved hands. He tossed one end over Alonzo's shoulder to the waiting ringmaster.

"After you both have met your end, I'm going to send your

descendants to keep you company so you can watch your blood writhe in agony just as we all did."

Stepping forward, Baldy wrapped his end of the rope around Alonzo's throat, tying it off in a tight knot. He whistled through his teeth and the ringmaster tossed his piece into the air where the second half of the Wards caught it in his sturdy hands.

Alonzo felt himself lifted off the floor, strangling while flying as part of the trapeze act. All the seats were full now. The gleeful onlookers got to their feet, clapping and cheering, screaming for more.

Spots formed in his vision; his mouth gaped for air it couldn't take in. The last thing Alonzo saw was Baldy, waving to him from the ground.

"OH GOD!" THE WOMAN SCREAMED AND DROPPED THE TRAY OF medications she carried. Turning on her heel, she dashed from the room, returning with a pair of bulky orderlies to confirm her discovery.

With a sheet wrapped tightly around his throat, Alonzo Sargent hung from the side of his bed, attached to the iron headboard. His bulbous body was draped across the floor, his face purple. The empty eye sockets were wide and gaping, and his tongue lay on the floor before him, where he'd bitten clean through it as he died.

"How did he manage that?" One of the orderlies asked.

The woman shook her head and made the sign of the cross on her chest. "He's still wearing the straight jacket. He couldn't have done this himself."

CHAPTER SIXTEEN

May 6th, 2018

Kristina really didn't want to do this. The drive wasn't long, Collin Stevenson was just outside of Gary, and she didn't mind being in the car. But her stomach was in her throat. What if he told them something that made everything worse?

"What are you thinking about so hard over there?" Jason offered her a gentle smile from the driver's seat, his hands sliding gracefully across the steering wheel as he made a right turn. "You look so serious."

Biting her lower lip, Kristina tried to put what was bothering her into words. "I'm scared. I feel like I'm being targeted by this ghost, or whatever the clown is. What if we find out I'm destined to die a horrible, painful death or something?"

"He's not a fortune teller, Kris. If you want your cards read, we can go downtown and get some wannabe psychic to tell us we're cursed." Jason never missed a beat to tease her, and now wasn't any exception. "He's just an old man who's related to someone involved in this whole thing. Don't you want to know why this is happening to you? Because

I'm damned curious. You don't have any jugglers in your family I'm not aware of, do you?"

Kristina looked appalled.

"Relax. I was joking."

"You met my parents when they came to the office last month. Do they look like the circus type?" Kristina's brother knew some card tricks, but that was as far as it went in her family. Her father was a postman and had been since opting not to go to college. In contrast, her mother was a real estate agent and a damned good one. Thanks to her, they'd always gone on family vacations when she was growing up. But her mother also shared her fear of clowns. The one and only time she'd seen the circus, her mother refused to go.

"No, but you were adopted, right?"

Turning her eyes to him slowly, Kristina looked at Jason in disbelief. "I never told you that. I never told anyone I work with about that. How did you know?"

Jason swallowed hard. "I may or may not have had an interesting conversation with your mom when she was in. I told her I saw where you got your good looks from, and she laughed at me. I believe her exact words were to stop sucking up and that she knew all about me. Then she told me how they adopted you when you were only a few weeks old but couldn't love you more even if you were biologically theirs."

Kristina warmed at his words. While she didn't understand why her mom told Jason about her past, she glowed, feeling her parents' love surrounding her like a cocoon. "The police found me in an abandoned building screaming my head off. I was malnourished and dehydrated, but other than that, I was fine. The state tried to find my family, make sure I wasn't kidnapped, and when no one came forward, I was adopted."

"How did they choose your new family?"

A smile spread across her face. "The officer who found me, his name was Alex Pallone, he was my mom's brother. He knew my mom and dad had been trying to get pregnant for a while, and they weren't having any luck. So, when I was cleared to get a new home, they asked them first. I don't remember anything before being with them."

Jason nodded approvingly. "I'm glad things worked out for you the way they did. Some kids get stuck in the system all their lives. It's a damned shame. What about your brother?"

"What about him?"

His lavender eyes skimmed my face before turning back to the road. "Was he adopted too?"

Kristina remembered when her parents brought home her brother and introduced her to the golden-haired little boy. He was about five years old, only a year older than she was, and his skin was covered in yellowing bruises. She didn't understand then what that meant. She only recalled thinking he looked like an alien.

"Seth was adopted too. His story was a bit more disturbing than mine." She didn't want to elaborate further. It wasn't her story to tell.

Jason didn't press.

The house the GPS led them to looked straight out of a horror movie. Once coated in white paint, the walls were gray and peeling. The shutters hung crookedly and nonexistent on some of the windows, of which one was covered entirely with plywood. The property was surrounded by a leaning wrought iron fence with sharp points on top. The grass beyond it was as tall as the broken monstrosity, and insects sang from the hidden depths.

"You sure this is the right place?" Kristina felt even worse about this trip seeing the place. "Maybe we can just email him and ask to meet someplace public?"

Pursing his lips, Jason shook his head. "He's a recluse. He doesn't leave the house anymore."

Looking at Jason furtively, Kristina waited for him to say more, but his lips were clamped shut. "Jason, does he know we're coming?"

The muscle in Jason's jaw contracted beneath the skin. He didn't make eye contact. "I spoke to him."

The Mustang bounced across the broken pavement of the driveway, coming to a stop in front of the house's garage door. It sagged from the middle showing several inches of darkness from within. Kristina imagined red glowing eyes peeking over the aged wood, staring at her, warning her not to go inside. She shrunk down in her seat.

"And?" Her voice came out in a whisper.

"And what?"

Kristina sighed. "Is he even willing to speak to us?"

Jason shrugged, pulled the keys from the ignition, and lifted his butt off the seat to push them into the front pocket of his jeans. "About as willing as you are to talk to him. But I doubt he'll say no if we're standing on his porch."

"Jason…" Kristina gave him a disappointed look. "This man doesn't want to be bothered. Why are we forcing ourselves on him?"

"Because we need to know what he knows."

"How do you know he knows anything?" Unbuckling her seatbelt, Kristina wondered again if the old mad had just made everything up for attention. Even if he was, being here was probably better than being alone in her apartment with whatever was lurking there.

"Just trust me on this. Please?"

Before they could make it to the rickety old porch, an old man stepped out the front door. He leaned heavily on a cane and scowled in the direction of the trespassers. "I know you saw the sign on the gate. I don't want to buy whatever you're selling, I'm an atheist and proud of it, and I'm not going to register to vote. I don't give a shit which clown gets elected to office next."

"Mr. Stevenson?" Jason extended his hand while walking towards the man. "My name is Jason Asher. We spoke on the phone?"

The old man's scowl deepened. "You're the one I told to go to hell?"

"The very same."

The old man huffed. "What part of me saying I've said all I'm going to say on this matter was in any way unclear to you? I said my piece on that damned article, and I paid the price for it. Hell, I'm still paying the damned price for it. So, get back in the shiny little car and get out of here. Nothing good comes from knowing anything about the accident."

Kristina shut her car door loudly, hanging on Collin's words. "What do you mean, you've paid the price for it? Are you seeing him too?"

Collin narrowed his steely eyes at her. His chin jutted out as he regarded her carefully. The firm set of his shoulders relaxed, and he dropped his head, looking at his shaking legs. Meeting her eyes once again, he signed. "You both best come inside, I suppose. Looks like it's going to rain."

Jason gave Kristina a thumbs up and locked the car. The beep startled her, causing her to rush to keep up with the two men.

The inside of the house was no better than the outside. Outdated, olive green carpet spanned the small living room and dining room, peeling at the edges, revealing a crispy yellow pad beneath. Old fashioned wallpaper depicting alternating pears and apples covered the walls.

"Come into the lounge. I'll start some coffee." The old man hobbled away, his cane shaking beneath his knurled hand.

The lounge, which was just the living room, smelled foul like years of sweat and hidden mold. Kristina breathed out of her mouth to keep from sneezing. The couch coughed a plume of dust when they sat, and Kristina looked at Jason with frown lines creasing the sides of her mouth.

"Something doesn't feel right here. We shouldn't have come."

Jason shushed her gently. "He's coming back."

With a tarnished silver tray clenched in his hands, Collins returned with a thermos and three cups. His cane was hooked on his elbow, swaying with each step. Kristina noted his tongue protruding from the corner of his mouth as he focused on walking and balancing the coffee.

He settled his burden on the oval coffee table and collapsed into the chair across from them. His hooded eyes narrowed. "Well, what do you want to know?"

Kristina leaned forward on her knees. "Who's the clown, Mr. Stevenson?"

"Baldy." He nodded as he spoke, leaned back in the seat, and crossed one leg over the other, ankle to knee. "If you're seeing a clown, it's Baldy."

"But why?" Kristina asked, recognizing the whine in her voice.

The old man stuck his lower lips out as he met her eyes. "After I wrote that damned article in 1968, he came after my grandfather. For about two weeks, he acted like a madman. He was having nightmares at first, then it started to bleed over into real life. He was old then, seventy-six or so. He'd never told a single soul what he did besides his partner, Robert, who was there when it happened."

"What exactly did he do?" Jason hung on the man's words, breathing heavily, his eyebrows furrowed in concentration.

Collin turned his head and his neck popped with the effort. Wincing, he took his cup off the table and brought it to his lips slowly. After swallowing the brown sludge he thought was proper coffee, he paused with the china still close to his mouth. "He mixed saltwater and vinegar and put it on the circus train's hotbox. They wouldn't have gotten far like that. The mixture rusted it straight through within minutes. My grandfather caused the train to stall on the track. If it weren't for him, that other fellow wouldn't have crashed into them. He was more to blame for the whole thing than anyone else."

Kristina blinked several times, absorbing the new information. "How do I know you're telling me the truth?"

"Missy, I don't rightly care if you believe me or not. I don't have anything to lose, nor do I care. The facts remain that I'm a marked man, and had you come a week from now, you would've been the ones to discover my body. And who knows what kind of state you would've found it in. Lord knows he doesn't leave any of us intact."

Feeling her blood go cold inside her veins, Kristina rubbed her arms. She'd seen the specter of the ghost for three days. Did that mean her life counted down to her own finale? It chilled her to think what might be in store for her. "What happened to your grandfather?"

"You don't want to know the gory details. It's not suitable for the ears of a lady. Trust me. He's dead, Baldy did it, and that's all you need to know."

Jason put his hand on Kristina's thigh as she sucked a breath to speak, instantly silencing her.

"With all due respect, sir. We need to know the details." Offering Kristina a quick, reassuring smile, he told her secret. "My friend here has been seeing Baldy for the past few days herself. We need to find a way to get rid of him."

Collin burst into laughter. The loud, echoing sound grated on Kristina's ears. It ended in a hacking cough, and the man smacked himself on the chest several times to stifle it. "Young man, it's admirable what you're doing to save her. But it's best if you wash your hands of it and leave her be. If Baldy's marked her, she's going to die. He doesn't stop until we're dead. I used to resent the fact that I'd never married or had children, but it was a blessing because once my grandpappy told me the story and I wrote it all down and shared it with the world, anyone I sired would've been added to that list."

Jason opened his mouth and snapped it closed when Kristina spoke.

"I don't understand why I'm part of all this. I'm just a photographer. I was hired to cover the centennial anniversary of the crash, and I did that. Why did he choose me?"

The old man narrowed his eyes and licked his cracked lips. "Did you have relatives on the train, or were you related to either of the men on the second train?"

"Kristina was adopted," Jason blurted to her dismay.

"Well, you're at a bit of a disadvantage, aren't you?" Collin poured more coffee into his cup. The other two hadn't touched theirs. "How do you plan to fight him if you don't even know which bloodline you came from? Was it a closed adoption?"

"I was abandoned."

Collin shook his head sadly. "Even worse. I'm sorry to hear that."

"Mr. Stevenson, please tell me what happened to your grandfather." Kristina implored him, holding his gaze with steady eyes. "If this thing's coming for me, I need to know what to prepare for."

"It won't be much help. Everyone dies a different way. I heard that Sargent man hanged. Gustav Klauss drowned. Maurice Stevenson, my grandfather, set himself on fire. His partner, Robert Sarno well, he took the sharpest blade he could find, and sliced his skin off. He started with his face, then his legs. He was working on his left arm when he bled out and died. I believe he would have kept going if it weren't for that." Collins lifted his cup but seemed to think better of it and placed it back on the table. "So far, he's tried to kill me by car crash, when that failed, I stopped driving altogether. I think I've survived the longest of everyone. No one else has lasted more than two weeks."

"So, it's possible to avoid him?" Kristina asked.

"Yes and no. Yes, you can find ways to keep yourself alive, but the bastard never stops. It's going to come down to how long you want to play cat and mouse and how strong you are to know what's real and what's not." Collins grunted as he uncrossed his legs. "It's not always easy to tell when you're awake and when you're dreaming. You need to remember, when Baldy's involved, your dreams can kill you."

"Like to see the fucker come after me." Jason huffed, puffing his chest out.

"Be careful what you wish for, son. Baldy doesn't react to challenges well."

Kristina began to cry, wiping away the tears as fast as they came. She held her chin high and tried to stay brave even though she felt like she was crumbling inside. "What does he want? Why does everyone have to die?"

Collin grew thoughtful. His face fell, and he looked almost sympathetic to her emotional plea. "He wants revenge. Plain and simple. His wife and boy were killed. Now everyone who was involved will suffer the same loss until there's no one left."

Jason pulled Kristina under his arm, crushing her against his ribs. "But all the main players are dead. None of them even knew the people he's killing now except for maybe your grandfather. What good is it to keep killing?"

Collin shrugged and scratched at his dandruff infused hair. "He's dead. Maybe time's different for him. In any event, we're doomed. I'm getting too old to fight back. It won't be long now for me."

"There has to be a way to stop all this." Jason's eyes burned with a fire from within.

"If there is, I hope you find it. Now take your woman home. Love on her, make her last few days perfect because what's coming will be bad enough to haunt her into her next life."

They all stood. Jason kept Kristina close to his side, her own personal shield against the evil to come. The old man followed them to the door.

"I really wish I had some better news for you. But you came here looking for answers, not for me to blow smoke up your asses." He didn't go past the porch as the other two made their way to each side of the car.

"Thank you for being honest with us," Kristina said as the old man stepped back inside with a wave. The screen door smacked the frame behind him.

They sat in silence, taking in what they'd learned. "We shouldn't have even come. All we learned is that it's hopeless, and I'm going to die. I'm not sure I'm any better off than I was before you talked me into this."

"I'm—"

The sound of a gunshot shook the car. Looking at each other, Jason and Kristina opened their doors simultaneously and rushed towards the house. Jason called for emergency service while Kristina fumbled with the door, managing to open it with shaking hands.

"Mr. Stevenson!" she screamed into the darkness. When he didn't respond, she felt for the light switch as Jason pushed past her. Yellow light flooded the parlor with a sickly glow. A pair of feet protruded from the floor in front of the couch. Varicose veins marred the ankles attached to the black velcro shoes. Jason got there first and pressed his hand to his mouth.

"Don't come over here, Kristina. Just stay where you are."

Never one to take orders, she went around the couch on the opposite side as Jason turned his back to the mess, his complexion going green as he struggled not to throw up. Collin Stevenson no longer had a face or much of a head for that matter. The ruined hamburger remaining left the man unidentifiable. A gun in his right hand smoked from recent use.

Kristina gasped and fell to her knees, barely missing the widening pool of crimson blood spreading across the floor. Sirens wailed in the distance with no one to save. "We were just talking to him. He was just alive. Why did he do this?"

Jason didn't turn to her. "He said he was getting too old to fight back."

"Is this all I have to look forward to?"

CHAPTER SEVENTEEN

November 15th, 1918

The train whistle blew, announcing it would be moving soon. Gustav Klauss wiped the sweat from his brow, baring his teeth in the heat. After the trial, he couldn't find a rail company who would take him on as a fireman or an engineer, the two jobs he'd previously held. The best he was able to do was a position as a brakeman. It cut his pay nearly in half, but at least he was still working on trains. They'd always been his first love, followed closely by beautiful women and liquor.

"Klauss!" The second brakeman yelled from below, cupping his hands over his mouth to make his voice carry.

Klauss rolled his amber colored eyes and brushed his bushy black hair out of his face. The asshole treated him like he didn't know what he was doing when he had far more experience than the kid.

"What the hell do you want, Tony?"

The younger man cupped his hands again. "You got that last pin in? Surry wants to get a move on. We're supposed to be in New Mexico by five in the evening on Friday. We can't afford to waste any time!"

"It's only Monday," Klauss protested. They were in Missouri, and no other stops were scheduled save for food and fuel. There were two engineers on board with a sleeping car, so they'd be sleeping on board. The drought in the lower states had become critical, and they were bringing tankers full of drinking water, thirty thousand gallons in each car, fifty cars long. Enough water to save a state dying of thirst. Klauss didn't give a rat's ass about saving anyone, but the extra paycheck for a straight through job was a real nice bonus.

"Just passing the word around, Klauss." The boy headed back the way he came. The kid was a suck-up and kept himself plastered to the big guns up front leaving all the hard work to Klauss.

Adjusting the straps on his faded overalls, Klauss huffed at the receding form of the younger man and muttered a few choice words under his breath. This was the last trip he was going to make with this company. Come hell or high water; he pledged to find something better. There had to be a line out there who hadn't heard about all the trouble in Indiana. Besides, he was acquitted, absolved of all responsibility. So why did everyone continue to turn their noses down to him?

After the final pin was struck in place and he'd done the final walk through to make sure the hatches on all fifty cars were secure, Klauss retired to the sleeping car with a bottle of vodka tucked beneath his arm. At least the liquor still tasted good, even if the rest of his life had fallen to shit.

The other men in the sleeping car ignored him. He'd heard whispers from a few of them saying he was a murderer, and he should have hanged. It wasn't even him who'd hit that circus train; it was his partner, Alonzo. If anyone was to blame, it was him. As far as Klauss was concerned, he shouldn't have even been charged. The other man hadn't come to him asking to be relieved, so how the hell was he supposed to know he was drowsy? None of it was his fault. Because of this whole mess, his wife left him, announcing on the way out that his son had been sired by the local butcher while he was out on a train—the traitorous whore.

It wasn't like anyone worthwhile had died anyway. It was all carnies, and everyone knew those kinds of people were to be avoided.

The whole lot of them were rapists and thieves. Secretly, he wished the first half of the train had stayed with the rear so they could've taken out more of the scum. Smiling at the thought, he gulped at the bottle, feeling the familiar fire coat his tongue and throat.

Klauss grabbed a hold of the railing to the top bunk at the end of the row and hoisted himself up with a grunt, depositing the vodka beneath his thin mattress and the side of the train. The springs beneath him bent with his weight. He propped his head up on his extra pair of boots and let the sway of the train carry him away.

A dream overtook him at once.

The smell of sweaty men enclosed in a small space melted away. The rumble of steel wheels on an iron track no longer existed. He went back to a time before his name had been destroyed before he'd met Alonzo Sargent and was brought on as his fireman and second in command. He was just starting out, working a job he loved somewhere in Ohio.

Back then, he'd been engaged, and in his dream, he still was. The haggard face of his ex-wife replaced by the girlish features of her youth. Lying flat on his back, just as he'd been doing in his bunk, he felt the girl's long chocolate locks dusting his face as she rode him. The sheath surrounding his cock contracted like a fist, pulsing with her orgasm. Klauss could see the girl throw her head back in ecstasy and could feel her tender nipples rolling between his thumbs and forefingers.

"Gustav, I love you!" Her voice was breathless, sated.

"And I, you, Violet." Klauss smiled, reliving the happiest time of his life. Running his hands across her rib cage, he watched her, waiting for her to look him in the eyes once more. But her head remained tossed back, and her breathing quickened once more.

When she began to move against him again, Klauss squirmed. The sensitivity was too much. He ground his teeth together, trying to withstand the second round.

"I want you, Gustav." Her voice dropped an octave.

"Honey, please! I'm not ready to go again. Give me a few minutes to recover." Gustav pleaded with the girl, trying to hold her hips still with his seed spilling out and running down his balls into the crack of his ass. "I only need a moment or so and I'll fuck you proper, I promise."

She was too strong. He couldn't get a grip on her slippery flesh. The muscles inside of her flinched again, painfully squeezing his member. "You like that, train conductor?" It wasn't her voice any longer, but a man's Gustav didn't recognize. He fought to pull himself out from beneath her, but her thighs held him in place like a vise.

"Who are you?" Gustav recognized the change in his own voice. This wasn't the sound of his youth as the dream had begun. This was him now, in the present day. When had that happened?

Violet's head rolled forward on her thin neck until her hair obstructed her face. Gustav squinted to see what lay hidden beneath the tresses. She parted it down the middle and pulled it to the side revealing silver irises. Violet's eyes had always been brown; this wasn't her. Struggling anew to escape his captor, the girl mounting him put her hands around his throat and began to squeeze.

"You don't like me so much when I look like this, do you, train conductor?"

As he watched, her beautiful youthful skin turned pasty white. Red paint came to the surface surrounding her toothy grin, and her silvery eyes became encased in blue. She'd transformed into a clown as he watched. They were no longer naked, his cock was safe back inside his trousers, but the hands around his windpipe grew to the size of a man's. She changed into a very large, very round man, dressed as a clown would dress.

Gustav tried to speak but couldn't utter a word under the force of the hands crushing him.

"What's wrong conductor? Do you fear death?" The clown held fast while Gustav struggled to breathe. "You who killed so many, you with so little remorse, are you afraid of what lies on the other side for you?"

Gustav felt lightheaded. He knew he would pass out any moment.

"I'll let you in on a little secret, conductor."

The clown leaned in close to Gustav's ear. He could feel a freezing cold breath against his cheek.

"Everything you've imagined about hell is true. The fires are real.

The demons truly await sinners to punish them for all of eternity. I've seen them cut the flesh from bones, and the person did not die, didn't even lose consciousness. They remain awake to experience everything done to them. I watched them scream in agony, watching pieces of themselves fall away until there was nothing left to cut. And you know what the beauty of it was? When the demons ran out of flesh, the person was restored, and they started over again. Imagine eternal suffering, never-ending pain, ceaseless agony. You did that to me when you killed Martha and Reginald. I'm in this hell, not because I was bad in life, but because you damned me for all time."

Sparks flew behind Gustav's eyelids. He knew he was going to die. He wondered if the other men in the train car could see what was happening to him and if they could, did they care? Did they pretend not to notice? His life force ebbed. Giving survival one last shot, he bucked his hips, pushed out with his arms, and was ecstatic when the hands vanished, and the clown faded away into nothing.

His movement caused him to flop over the edge of the bunk. He slammed into the floor face and chest first, knocking the wind out of himself anew. Blood poured from his nostrils, and he could taste it in the back of his throat.

"Hey guys, look at this!" The younger brakeman sat on his lower bunk, putting his bare feet on the floor. "Clown killer Klauss had a nightmare, and it scared him right out of his bed!"

The other men in the car laughed, pointing fingers at him. Klauss's vision was blurry, an after effect of being choked, but he met each man's eyes, and as he did, they quieted down. They were afraid of him. Raising himself onto his hands and knees, he squeezed his eyes closed, willing his head to stop spinning, then got to his feet shakily.

"What were you dreaming about, Klauss? We all heard you moaning like you were getting a ripe piece of ass. Oh, look!" The man pointed at Klauss's breaches. "The clown killer made a mess in his pants! Bet it was the bearded lady you were banging!"

Klauss lunged for him, catching the younger man around the waist and knocking him off the bunk. Hitting him in the face over and over, Klauss watched the blood dripping from his nose mix with the blood from the man's face until it was indistinguishable what belonged to who. Two other men had to pull him off.

"Come on now, Klauss!" one of the men cajoled. "He was just poking some fun at you. "You don't want to kill the lad for being a dumbass. I heard the trial was a messy business. You don't really want to do that again, do you?"

Klauss allowed himself to be pulled away before turning and striking the man who'd mentioned the trial just for good measure. Climbing back on his own bunk, he turned his back to the other men and pressed his sleeve to his nose to stop the flow of blood. What the hell just happened to him? It felt so real, almost like the clown was actually here, choking him. Klauss knew if that ghost was the real deal, he was truly out to kill him. He wondered if Alonzo was getting the same visitations.

Taking the vodka into his palm, he finished the bottle allowing himself to be good and drunk. If something were going to kill him in his sleep, at least if he was wasted, he wouldn't feel it.

"Come on clown," he whispered. "I'm ready. Take your best shot."

He closed his eyes and felt the blackness overcome him. The dream didn't return that night.

CHAPTER EIGHTEEN

May 6th, 2018

"He killed himself." Kristina hugged her knees against her chest. Somehow, they'd made it back to her apartment without her having a nervous breakdown. When the police arrived on the scene, they didn't keep them long. Apparently, they'd been to the house several times, and the state threatened to lock old Collin Stevenson away for psychiatric reasons quite a few times. It didn't surprise anyone when they found he'd shot himself. No one even bothered to ask Jason and Kristina what they were doing there or why. No one cared.

"Kris," Jason squatted on the floor in front of her trying to pull her legs down so he could see her face. "He was going to do it whether we came there or not. This wasn't your fault. If anything, our visit may have prolonged his life by the hour or so we spoke to him. He must have already had the gun loaded and ready to go to have done it so quickly."

"That doesn't make me feel any better." Kristina relented and lowered her legs. "I'm next, Jason. Baldy's going to kill me. I'm not strong enough to fight him off for years like Collin did. Hell, I already feel like I'm losing my mind."

"You're not. You're a fighter, and no clown will be able to get to you. Except me, of course." Jason grinned at her, tilting his head the way he did when he tried to make her smile.

Kristina looked past him to the newly replaced front door. It still smelled like fresh paint in her apartment, and they'd opened the windows to help it dissipate. She hadn't been brave enough to check out the new mirror in the bathroom, afraid she'd see the same face in this one the last one had held.

"That's easy for you to say." Kristina huffed. "You don't see him every time you close your eyes."

Jason put a hand on each of her knees, lowering himself down onto his backside. "I see him every time I look into your eyes, and that's enough to know I hate him."

"How can I protect myself from something that comes after me while I'm asleep? I mean, it's bad enough I see him when I'm awake, but in a nightmare, anything can go. I'm completely powerless." Kristina twisted her fingers in her lap absently.

"You act like this guy's Freddy Krueger or something." Jason chuckled. "He's just an angry clown." He got to his feet and took the seat next to her, pulled her hand into his lap, and intertwined his fingers with hers.

"What's the difference? They can both kill you while you're asleep."

"Yeah, but Freddy was born bad. He was a true psychopath. This guy wasn't evil while he was alive. Something tragic happened to make him that way. So, they aren't the same at all." Kissing her knuckles one by one, Jason's lips felt like velvet against her skin. "Does he talk to you? Like a conversation? I know he's said things to you, but does he allow you to respond?"

Kristina thought about each encounter she'd had with the clown. "No. He's said things to me, but he doesn't respond to anything I've said to him."

Jason rubbed his chin. He hadn't shaved, and black stubble covered his cheeks. "Okay, so the chances of you having a sit-down type of conversation and explaining you had nothing to do with the accident and you don't even know your real family is pretty much zilch."

"I don't think so."

The phone lying on the sofa cushion beside Kristina vibrated. Her body tensed as if a gun had been fired at her. Three rings later, and she hadn't reached for it.

"You going to get that?" Jason asked, looking at her puzzled. "I doubt Baldy the clown's calling your phone."

When Kristina didn't make a move for it, Jason reached over her and lifted the device to his ear, accepting the call. "Kristina's phone," he said cheerfully. His face fell when the voice on the other end responded. "Oh, hey boss, yeah, we're together. Why?"

Kristina rolled her eyes. That was just what she needed when a psychotic clown was out to murder her. Work. "Tell him I'm sick," she whispered dramatically.

Jason held up a finger, effectively silencing her. "That's not possible, sir. We went over each photo and made sure everything was perfect before we sent them over."

Feeling her heart drop to her stomach, Kristina couldn't fathom what could've been wrong with their work. She knew she wasn't operating at one hundred percent, but they still weren't bad. After completing editing, she'd gone through each frame personally to ensure none of the rejected stills made it through to the final batch, and nothing out of the ordinary caught her eye. The picture she'd seen that didn't belong had disappeared, and no other surprises popped up in its place.

"I understand, sir." Jason's eyebrows scrunched together. "We'll be right there." Jason ended the call and tossed the phone back to the far side of the couch, where it landed with a little half-hearted bounce.

"Well?" Kristina asked when Jason didn't speak right away.

"I'm not sure." He shrugged. "Sullivan said there's a problem with all of the photos, and the clients are pissed. He was so mad he wasn't spitting out coherent sentences. I thought the pictures were pretty decent."

"I sent the email from my computer. Let's go look at them." Kristina pushed off Jason's thigh to stand and looked back to make sure he followed her. "We should be able to see whatever he's upset about."

The computer booted up with a hum, and Kristina typed in her password. Her screensaver was set to a floral display of lavender she'd taken herself on another job. It was her favorite assignment to date. The fields of flowers seemed to stretch forever in waves of purple swaying in the breeze. It was so relaxing, and the smell was heavenly.

Clicking on the file labeled '*Showmen's*', Kristina waited while a hundred thumbnails loaded one by one. They were thoroughly destroyed. Ripples of color smeared the frames, like an action shot taken by a bad photographer. The colors were washed out, and some of them were just black with nothing to be seen at all. Only one photo remained pristine.

"I didn't take that picture." Jason pointed at the screen.

"I know." Kristina recognized it as the photo that appeared as if by magic denoting her weary frame from behind and Jason in the foreground, the Nikon dangling from his fingertips. In front of him, the clown leaned over to stare at her. "This is the picture I saw the first time I went through them. It's the one I told you about but then it was gone, and I couldn't show you."

"Who the fuck took it?"

"He did." Kristina pointed at the screen. The clown's eyes seemed to be staring straight through her. Her heart made angry palpitations in her chest, threatening to vacate a place that was no longer safe.

Jason leaned over her shoulder. "That doesn't look like the clown I spoke to at the event."

"What do you mean?"

"The guy I talked to had purple hair. This clown has red hair. My guy had music notes on his cheeks; that one doesn't. And the clown in the picture is way fatter too. It's not even the same costume." Placing his hands on his hips, Jason nodded as if agreeing with himself. "I'm telling you, Kris. That's not the same guy at all. I don't know who he is. I don't recall seeing anyone dressed like him there."

Swallowing the rock forming in her throat, Kristina turned to her friend. "That's Baldy. He's the one who's after me. I don't know how he got the picture in there, but he did. And he ruined the rest. He's going to destroy me before he murders me."

"How are we going to explain this to Sullivan?" Jason nudged the computer bag with his toe. "We can't tell him a ghost from the accident sabotaged us. He would never believe it."

Kristina sighed. "We're just going to have to tell him the truth."

"Which is? Because I thought the truth was the ghost clown story."

The computer fell silent after Kristina clicked the shutdown key. She stared at the screen for a long moment before licking her lips and turning to Jason. "Defective memory card in the camera. The pictures all looked fine when we shot them, so we didn't feel they needed any editing. We got lazy and didn't go through them before we sent them. We apologize a lot, and you offer to pay back the client for the money they paid us because, let's face it, I don't have several grand lying around for emergencies."

"You're a really expensive person to hang around; you know that?"

"I'll make you the beneficiary on my will so you can sell all my stuff once he kills me. That's about the only way I'll ever be able to pay you back." They both laughed at the joke, albeit nervously.

"That's a pretty grim statement." Jason nudged her with his elbow.

"Well, we need to make light of this situation I suppose, or it'll drive us insane. Smoothing the tendrils of hair breaking free from her ponytail, Kristina stood and followed Jason back to the living room.

"I meant that you think your junk would be sufficient to pay your debt."

Kristina punched his shoulder. "I happen to like my junk."

"Hey, Kris. Someone stuck a note under your door."

A white slip of paper protruded from the gap between the door and the floor. Kristina's fingertips tingled and her mouth turned into a desert, suddenly dry and hot. She didn't want to touch the note. She didn't have any desire to see the words written on it.

Jason snagged it from the floor, and she held her breath, waiting for his hand to catch on fire or fall off. When none of that happened, she carefully took it from his outstretched hand. It was folded into three sections and wasn't sealed. The handwriting on the inside flowed with an outdated script. Kristina dropped the paper, and it fluttered to the carpet gracefully.

"Kris?"

"It says, *'You're the last performance and the final curtain is closing.'* How can a ghost shove a letter under a door?"

"I don't know, and I don't want to think about it right now. Let's get the hell out of here." Jason grabbed her hand and pulled her towards the door, snagging his keys off the counter in the process. "Let's get this thing over with the boss so we can get back to trying to figure out how to save your life."

"I don't know why we're even bothering. I don't need a job if I'm dead." Allowing him to lead her down the stairs, Kristina felt a wave of emotion roll through her. What if the train wreck project was the last job she'd ever do? What if she never took another photo? She felt like everything she'd worked for her entire life was slipping through her fingers like sand in an hourglass, and when it was all gone, she would be too.

"Stop talking like that. Dammit Kris, it's like you've already given up." The door to the apartment building slammed open under his touch, and he caught it before it could smack her. "We're going to figure this out, I swear to you."

"Don't make promises you can't keep."

He held the passenger door of the Mustang open for her, and she slid inside. When Jason got in on the other side, she probed him. "You think Sullivan will fire me?"

"You're the best photographer he has. He won't fire you. Me? Maybe. But not you."

The intimidating brick building was only three blocks away on the busier side of town. The first-floor offices had large windows on the street side with azalea bushes planted beneath each one. The second floor was all business with the printing press for the paper that was so loud, you needed to wear earplugs to be in the same room with it. The company couldn't afford to upgrade to the quieter laser printing yet, even with Jason's sizable donation to secure a job.

Sullivan's office was on the third floor, and when Jason and Kristina arrived, they went straight to the elevator at the far end of the building. Kristina felt like everyone watched her and knew how badly she'd screwed up. She wanted to hide her face and wallow in her shame privately. But it would have to wait until after Sullivan ripped her a new one.

"You okay?" Jason whispered.

"Everyone is staring at us."

Jason chuckled. "Probably because you have a death grip on my hand, love."

"Oh!" Kristina released him immediately, wiping her sweaty palm on her jeans. The elevator dinged, and they both stepped inside away from the accusatory stares. Sullivan waited on the other side of the door when it opened again.

"Before either of you say a goddamned word to me, tell me how you're going to fix this?"

Apprehension rolled through Kristina's gut. Everything she'd been prepared to say fluttered from her brain like a butterfly away from a flower and left her speechless. Her mouth opened and closed repeatedly, grasping for the words that wouldn't come.

Jason cleared his throat. "It was my fault, sir. Kristina got sick after we went to the cemetery. She threw up in my car, and it still smells in there."

Sullivan didn't look amused.

"Anyways," he continued. "I told her I would take care of all the pictures while she slept it off, and I guess I screwed it all up. I sent the files over thinking they were good before she ever got to see them. She isn't responsible for any of it."

Sullivan narrowed his eyes and shifted his gaze to Kristina. She blanched under his scrutiny and took a step back. "Why didn't you tell me you were sick? I would've gotten another photographer to go with him. Now we have some really pissed off clients and no way to fix this for them."

Jason interjected on her behalf valiantly. "Actually sir, I'm prepared to offer the Caster's double the money they paid you for the services and I'm willing to donate to their charity. It was my fault, and I should be the one to fix the problem. I'll apologize to them personally and make sure they know that no fault lay with the paper."

Some of the heat left Sullivan's eyes. "I'd appreciate that, Jason. We can't let them leave unsatisfied. A hit like this would destroy this paper."

"Leave here?" Kristina squeaked.

"Yeah. Norman and Beatrice Caster are in the conference room. They've been waiting to speak to you both since I called you."

Kristina thought of their kind faces and it made her heart hurt. They'd wanted the celebration to be perfect, and instead it was a total wreck. How was she supposed to face them now? "I guess we better go and speak with them then."

Sullivan didn't join them, instead taking a seat behind his massive L-shaped desk and flashing them a thumbs up before they entered the room. Kristina prepared herself to offer them her firstborn child if it would put them at ease about the pictures. Not that she'd ever get the chance to have kids. Jason held the door open for her and the elderly couple stood as they came in.

"Norman, Beatrice, it's such a pleasure to see you both again. I'm sorry it had to be under these circumstances." Taking the hand offered to her, Kristina thought the Caster's were being far too polite to her. "You both remember Jason Asher?"

"We do, yes," Norman said. "Ms. Perdue, could you please tell us what happened to our photos? Your boss was a bit vague and I'm afraid we didn't really understand.

"Are you okay, honey?" Beatrice asked, looking at Kristina with motherly concern. "You look like you've seen a ghost."

It was the word that did it. Kristina burst into tears, disregarding the whole speech Jason was preparing to deliver about money and fault. There was something about these two people compelling her to tell the truth.

"You have, haven't you?" Beatrice inquired.

"Now Bea, don't go putting words in the girl's mouth. Let's hear it from her." Norman chastised his wife gently. "Come and sit with us, young lady. The photographs can wait. Tell us what's going on."

Jason leaned against the door with his arms crossed over his chest. As Kristina crossed the room, she got the distinct impression he was listening for Sullivan to make sure he didn't walk in while she spoke about the clown. She was grateful for his insight.

Beatrice wrapped her arms around Kristina and patted her on the back. "Calm yourself, child. We'll never understand a word if you keep crying like that."

"Ever since I said yes to the train wreck job a clown has been stalking me. He's in my dreams, he's in my apartment, he came out of my bathroom mirror. I feel like I'm losing my mind."

The Caster's looked at each other as if they knew what the other thought. "What did he look like?" Norman asked.

Kristina wiped her tears on a handkerchief Mrs. Caster held out to her and sniffled. "He's very round, tall, he wears a red costume, and his face is painted like a clown. I don't know how to explain it, but he ruined the pictures. They were perfectly fine when we sent them over. I swear to you."

"I'll give you back double the money you paid for the shoot, and I'll match whatever donations you got last year for your charity to make it up to you," Jason added from the other side of the room. "Kristina wouldn't have messed this up on purpose. She's a phenomenal photographer and she takes pride in delivering the best possible photos to her clients and the paper."

"That's very generous of you, young man." Norman smiled at him. "Let's talk about money later, shall we? I'm more concerned about Ms. Perdue's visions now. I'm sure you can understand that."

"Yes, sir." The side of Jason's mouth tilted up in a grin.

"Tell us everything, honey," Bea encouraged.

"When we left for the cemetery, I saw him in the window of my apartment; then he was behind the car as we drove away. I thought I was seeing things because I'd always been afraid of clowns. My mother's deathly afraid of them as well. Then the random photo appeared with him looking at me and it wasn't a picture either of us took. It was mixed in on our memory card, though."

Bea was nodding. "We saw the picture you're referring to."

"That night, the night I found the picture, I found a clown nose on my floor in the middle of my kitchen. I thought it was Jason pulling a prank on me and I got mad, but he didn't do it. When Jason drove back to the apartment, I saw the clown slithering out from under my couch. He tried to grab me!" Kristina took a deep breath and held it, trying to stop her tears. "Then he came out of the mirror and licked me."

Bea made a disgusted face. "He made physical contact with you when you were awake?"

"Yes, but I had a nightmare about him that night too. He's everywhere."

"That would be Baldy then," Norman said matter of fact. "Honey, I didn't know you were related to anyone involved in the accident. Had I known, I would've insisted someone else take the photos."

"You know about this then? You know it was Baldy, and you know I'm related to someone who caused the accident. Why hasn't anyone stopped him?"

Bea removed her arms from Kristina and looked down in shame. "Honestly, we thought they were all dead. We didn't know there were any more relations out there. Once, we tried to protect them, but nothing anyone did made a difference. He got them all."

"I wasn't the only one left this morning." Kristina scoffed.

"What do you mean?"

"Collin Stevenson committed suicide this morning. He blew his own face off. He said he couldn't hold out against the clown anymore. Apparently, he'd been after him for years." Jason filled in the gaps.

Norman scratched his scalp and looked at his wife. A puzzled expression played across his wrinkled face. "I'm sorry, I'm not entirely sure who that is? Was he a relation to Alonzo Sargent or Gustav Klauss?"

Kristina shook her head. "No, he was the grandson of Maurice Stevenson, the man who caused the circus train to stall on the tracks."

Bea gasped.

"You'll have to excuse our reactions. This is all new news to us. We've never heard someone was responsible for the breakdown. It had always been assumed that part of the story was nothing more than a tragic accident." Norman flexed his crooked fingers on the shiny surface of the table. "Lord knows how many more people died because of his folly."

"He had a partner named Robert who helped him. Apparently, he's dead too. The clown got him." Jason crossed to the table and took a seat, forgetting all about their employer. "We don't know his last name though."

"So, there could be more people out there related to both of them and we won't even know." Bea sniffled.

"I'm the last one," Kristina said. "Baldy told me so today. This ends with me."

"Lord have mercy on you, child." Norman patted Kristina's hand sympathetically.

"Tell us everything you know about him," Jason said. "Maybe we can figure out what needs to be done to stop him before he gets to Kris."

"We can try," Bea said. "Our minds aren't at all what they used to be."

"I'm sure you can both understand, I just found my way to the woman I'm meant to spend my life with. I won't settle for the time we've had so far. That's unacceptable to me. I love the woman sitting across from me, and I'll go to hell myself to find a way to protect her."

Kristina's eyes welled with fresh tears looking at the man who just admitted to loving her.

CHAPTER NINETEEN

November 19th, 1918

Gustav woke early, surveying the sleeper car while the rest of the men slumbered. It reminded him of that damned circus train, and he thought to himself, this must have been how the other train looked inside before they ran into them. He remembered sitting on the ground while the charcoal lumps that used to be people were pulled from the rumble and how hard his heart beat with a rush of adrenalin.

A cold fall wind overcame them during the night and the morning was significantly cooler than the day before. Gustav put his spare pair of long johns on under his overalls to fight the chill. He didn't like how bulky it felt, but at least he wouldn't be shivering with frozen balls while he climbed across the train cars. There was also less of a chance of the clothing being stolen if it was on his body. He didn't trust any of the other men. Especially since the outburst the previous evening. There was nothing like beating the tar out of someone to make a few enemies.

Exiting the sleeping car by the rear hatch, Gustav inspected the pinion to the next car and found all was well. He would need to check all fifty before noon. He checked his pockets, making sure he carried all the necessary tools to fix any problem he came across and a rag to wipe his greasy hands on, then began the arduous task of a fifteen-point inspection on the tankers.

He preferred starting before anyone else was awake. Everyone had their own job, and he was left alone for the most part, but he was more than happy to go without the sneers and jokes made at his expense.

The wind whipped up again and almost knocked him from the narrow walkway between the cars. He placed a dirty palm on top of his hat to prevent it from being caught in the gust.

"Goddamned wind. Gonna make this whole day shit if I'm battling it the whole day." As if in response, another burst of air whistled through the space, making it hard to take a breath.

A metal ladder stood at the front of each car extending to the catwalk on top and then resumed the form of a ladder down the far side. In the center of the walkway lay a hatch into the bladder of the tanker. The water level was less than a foot below the opening, and the liquid was frigid. Part of Gustav's job was to inspect each hatch daily to ensure none had come loose with the train's vibration and resecure them if they did. After he checked each pin, he would climb the ladder, inspect the hatch and descend on the other side. Then the pattern would repeat for the rest of the cars.

Already this morning, he'd inspected twelve cars in with no issues to speak of.

On the thirteenth car, he found the latch on the porthole open, and the seal broken. The side of the tanker was wet where the water sloshed out, running down the iron sides, turning the black paint a darker shade than the rest surrounding it. Gustav swore under his breath.

"I checked this fucking car yesterday, and it was fine. Hatches don't just unlatch themselves. I bet this was those idiots who started trouble with me yesterday. They're just trying to give me a hard time."

Gustav Klauss got down on his knees and pulled his lambskin gloves over his hand to keep the metal from biting into his calloused skin. The handle wouldn't turn no matter how much pressure he applied.

"Come on, you bitch!" He gritted his teeth as he tried to find a grip allowing him the leverage necessary. Something must've been in the way below. Gripping both palms around the wheel, he pulled hard, flipping the hatch open the rest of the way. He leaned over the opening and peered inside, shielding his eyes from the sunlight above. He ran his hands around the opening and felt nothing hindering the normal operation.

"Help!" A small voice pleaded from within. "Please! Someone, help me! I'm going to drown down here!"

Gustav froze, unable to see anything in the murky depths of the dark tanker. There wasn't so much as a ripple. "Who's down there?" he yelled, tilting his head to the side to hear the reply clearly.

"Please! I only wanted a little drink and I fell in!" Someone inside splashed the water around.

"Stay where you are! I'll go fetch a rope!" Gustav started for the ladder.

"No! Don't leave me! I can't swim much longer." The voice stopped him. "If you come down, you can lift me up."

Gustav scoffed. "What are you, daffy? If I go in there, I'll drown too."

"No!" The voice insisted. "You're strong! You can push me out and pull yourself out. I'm not strong enough to do that, and I'll die if you leave me for a moment!"

The darkness below him was absolute. It was a black hole with no end, and he couldn't see where the shadows stopped, and the water began. A strange sensation in his belly warned him to run and not look back, but Gustav was no coward. He swallowed back the feeling of dread and steeled himself for what needed to be done.

"Please, mister. I'm cold!"

The turmoil in the person's voice gave him pause. It was a high enough pitch that it could be a woman or a child—he wasn't sure which. It wasn't in his nature to go around saving anyone, no matter who they were. But it wouldn't look good on him if they found a body in the tanker, and he was the one supposed to make sure the hatch stayed closed. He planned on quitting anyway, but it would be another dark mark on his record he didn't need.

Hell, maybe if he climbed in and rescued whoever was in there, he could get a promotion or an offer for a better job. He could pretend to be a hero for one day to further himself.

"Please!" The voice sounded as if it went under water on the last gasp. The sound of flailing and bubbles emanated from inside.

Gustav flopped onto his backside and looped one foot under the rail that ran the length of the car for safety and began unlacing the boot on the other. He stuck the set securely under the bar so they wouldn't fall while the train barreled on and added his socks and jacket to the pile. His breath was a fog before his mouth and nose, and he knew the water would be freezing. Stripping out of his overalls and the first pair of long johns, he lowered himself into the tanker until his toes touched the black water within.

"Fuck, that's cold!" Second thoughts fought their way to the forefront of his brain, and he started to pull himself back up. "To hell with you. You're on your own!"

Something curled out of the water and latched itself around his legs. The skin on the creature felt like a dead fish, cold and slimy. Gustav kicked his legs, trying to free himself from the fingers digging into his thighs, fingers with talons like that of a bird of prey.

That was no child or woman. That was a devil, there to drag him to the pits of hell.

"Please, train conductor! It's so cold down here!"

When did the voice start calling him that? That was what the clown called him during the nightmare. He imagined the hands around his throat squeezing, remembered what it felt like when his life drained away. With renewed force, he kicked against the phantom, feeling the claws dig into his flesh harder.

"Let me go, devil. I'm not interested in going to hell just yet!"

"Devil?" The voice rolled with laughter. "I'm not a devil, conductor. I'm a clown! I live to make people happy. Oh, but that's right, I don't live anymore at all!"

Gustav looked down into the hole and saw the silver-white eyes looking back at him. The face contorted into a sinister grin with rows of yellowing teeth showing behind the red ring framing the mouth. The hands gripping onto his skin were sheathed in white gloves with razor sharp claws protruding through the fabric. As he watched, his skin began to tear away, peeling away in strips where the clown pulled at him.

Letting out a pitiful cry, Gustav groped for the safety rail to heave himself out of the tanker. No matter how he stretched and turned, it was just out of reach. Warm liquid flowed down his legs, and he knew without a doubt it was his own blood he felt.

"Come on down, conductor! The show is just getting started! You wouldn't want to miss the first act, would you?"

His fingers steadily lost their grip, the blood loss making him woozy. Gustav wouldn't be able to hold his body weight up much longer. "Please! I don't want to die here!"

The clown threw his head back and let loose a string of chuckles, but his hands didn't release him. "Oh, Mr. Conductor, no one ever wants to die, especially not tragically. I don't believe a single soul wakes from their nice warm bunk and says, I would really enjoy dying a horrible fiery death in a train crash today, for instance."

"It was an accident!" Gustav screamed.

"Yes, an awful accident, but you didn't feel bad, did you? Not one shred of remorse flickered through your mind. I believe the words you used to describe my family and friends were they're nothing but rapists and thieves, and the world's better off without them?" The clown pulled one hand off his thigh and moved it higher, latching onto Gustav's hip.

Gustav's sweaty palms searched the rim of the hatch for anything to save him, but the iron was smooth under his fingertips. Each time the clown jerked on his legs, his hands slid closer and closer to the ledge. Closer to the oblivion below.

The clown pulled on him a final time, and he couldn't hold out any longer. Gustav plunged into the icy water, feeling the cold envelope his body. His lungs paralyzed with the cold; his vocal cords rendered useless. Pumping his arms and legs to try to stay afloat, Gustav looked above him in terror and watched the hatch lift and close and he heard the wheel locked tightly. Even if he could get himself to the exit, he couldn't escape. The clown laughed a sinister chorus of chortles somewhere nearby.

"You're a regular Houdini in the water, conductor. Do you have a trick up your sleeve?" The clown lay across the ceiling, illuminated in a space where there was no light. He had his legs crossed, his enormous shoes sticking straight out. His arms were casually folded under his head with big red sleeves fanned out around him. Gustav reached for him, pleading with his eyes for help, but the clown only laughed. "Let's see you get out of this spot of trouble just like you did at the trial."

Water flooded Gustav's mouth, forcing its way down his throat like an angry snake. He felt his lungs fill, felt the cold freezing the organs, shutting them down. No more air would expand his chest, the cavity was occupied. Gustav opened his mouth wide and gasped, and nothing happened. Sparks shoot off behind his eyes, his vision going blurry as his brain began to misfire.

"Do get on with it, conductor. I'm a very busy clown. I have places to go, people to kill. By the way, your family will join you shortly. I'm going to take the bitch who forced you out from between her legs first, then anyone else with a blood connection." The clown laughed his evil laugh again, pointing a long, gloved finger at Gustav as he did so.

Gustav sank below the surface. His limbs stopped working. His eyes could only pick up shades of color, nothing more. The water got warmer the deeper he went; it was almost pleasant. Then color erupted from below. Oranges and reds swirled around him. The floor burst open with a rumble rattling his eardrums. There were flames below, licking and snaking around the destroyed bottom of the tanker.

Before his heart took its last beat, Gustav felt the sensation of burning, and he knew what it was like for those people on the train to burn alive.

CHAPTER TWENTY

May 6th, 2018

"The night after the tragedy, Baldy visited all the survivors in their dreams and told them he was going to get revenge for what was done to them." Norman looked at his hands in his lap with a semblance of guilt. "I understand the ringmaster's second got a much more personal visitation, to which I can only assume was because the fool happened to pass out on his grave."

"Do they really need to know this part?" Bea questioned from beside him.

"It's time to be honest, my dear." Norman patted her hand affectionately. Clearing his throat, he looked at the younger couple, and Kristina noticed the glimmer of tears. "When he came to our relatives and their friends, he asked each one of them for permission to proceed, and every one of them said yes. It's very embarrassing to admit the living are the reason this all came to be and not the dead. It's not to say that it isn't Baldy who's exacting a pound of flesh for the damage done, but they allowed him to do it. They made him strong. And for a very long time, they searched out the relatives of those who caused the accident, and when Baldy came to them while they slept, they gave him the names."

Kristina felt revulsion building in her stomach. These two old people who'd seemed so sweet were entwined in a conspiracy to eradicate bloodlines because of some injustice done to their ancestors. "But Alonzo Sargent didn't hit the train on purpose. He didn't set out that night to become a weapon of mass destruction. Why does he and the other man deserve this kind of revenge?"

"Because they were careless, and they put themselves above the welfare of others. A bloodline holding that type of personality traits shouldn't continue." Norman met her eyes. The sweet smile Kristina was used to crept back onto his lips. "I suppose, my dear, that you prove the notion of nature over nurture incorrect because I see none of that in you. But if Baldy has decided you need to die, their blood most definitely runs in your veins."

"Honey, we don't condone the decisions they made. It was done long before we were even born." Beatrice spoke when she saw the twin expressions of hate on Jason and Kristina's faces. "Baldy can't move on until he's fulfilled his vow to kill all blood relations of the men responsible for the accident. I wish there were something we could do to help you."

"If your relatives gave him permission, why can't you take it away?" Jason slammed his fist down on the table and bit his lip. "Obviously, he cares about what the chosen few thinks about things, so tell him you've changed your mind."

Bea shook her head sadly. "Baldy hasn't visited anyone from this generation. That stopped with our parents."

Kristina saw Norman squeeze Bea's hand as if in warning.

"You're lying." Kristina looked each of them in the eye.

"What reason would we have to lie?" Norman asked with a wide eyed, innocent expression.

All eyes were on Kristina as she stood and walked to the window. "I know you're lying because when the article was written about the other two men who were involved in the crash, the previous generation was already gone. Baldy couldn't have found out about those two unless you told him."

Norman and Beatrice looked at each other, and Norman slowly grinned.

"Perhaps you should have been a detective instead of a photographer, Ms. Perdue. Alas, as far as either of us knows, Baldy hasn't visited this generation. There are more than just us, though. Maybe it would be worth a visit to see Charlie Kent's granddaughter, Matilda. He was the ringmaster back then. She may know more than we do on the matter."

"Where do we find her?" Jason pulled his phone out of his back pocket and opened his notepad application to take notes. "What's Matilda's last name and an address or phone number where we can reach her?"

"Matilda Russo," Norman said. "She's very easy to find these days. She was committed three years ago to the local mental hospital. She isn't very good on the phone—she doesn't really understand what they are. But if you go there, she's very talkative. If you tell the receptionists Norman Caster sent you, they'll let you right up."

"What's wrong with her?" Kristina spoke in a quiet voice, not sure she wanted to know the answer.

"She sees things that aren't really there." Beatrice swiveled in her chair to face the younger woman.

"Like clowns?" Jason asked.

"Yes, exactly like clowns." Norman clasped his hands before him as if praying and bowed his head. "Now, I believe we've said all we're able to say. If you'll excuse us, Ms. Perdue, Mr. Asher. We have a very busy day ahead of us. I'll let Mr. Sullivan know we're all set before we head out, and the problem has been rectified.

Jason stood as the Casters rose from their seats in a show of manners.

"Here's my card, boy. You may contact me with the number printed there on the bottom so we can work out a payment arrangement for what we discussed." Taking his wife by her petite hand, Norman Caster led her to the door.

Pausing, Bea turned back to Kristina and offered her a smile. "I meant it when I said I wished I could help you. I think you're an exceptional young lady and I'm so very glad we got to meet you before—"

"Come along, Bea. That's more than enough." Norman pulled her through the door and closed it softly behind them.

The silence following their departure was unbearable. Kristina felt it in her bones like an itch she couldn't quite reach. Shadows seemed to rush at her from every corner, closing in like a hunter stalking a prized buck.

Jason broke the spell.

"I guess we're going to the state mental hospital then."

Sullivan was nowhere to be found when they left the conference room. The Casters must have appeased him enough that he was no longer concerned with whatever they did. Kristina was careful not to look at Jason in any way that could be construed as anything but a working relationship between two coworkers as they walked through their place of employment. No one gave them a second glance this time through, and Kristina felt relieved.

Once safely outside, she exhaled. "I'm so tired of this wild goose chase."

"Oh, come on. You don't find this the least bit exciting? Where's your sense of adventure?" Jason held the door of the Mustang open for her to slide inside and shut it carefully behind her. He was in the driver's seat a second later, looking for the address to the state facility.

Kristina rolled her eyes. "My sense of adventure died somewhere around the time I found out I was going to be brutally murdered by a psychopathic clown out for revenge against people he already killed. Something about that just doesn't excite me."

"Party pooper." The volume of the GPS was way too high and the woman's voice coming from the speaker made them both cringe. Jason twisted the knob and brought the sound down to a manageable level. "The place is about an hour away. You need anything? Food? Bathroom?"

Kristina shook her head. "I'm fine. Let's just get this over with."

Jason took the curvy road at rally car speed, gunning the engine on the straights and only slightly braking for the turns. Usually, Kristina would have clutched the edge of the seat in terror, but today, it didn't seem like it mattered. The inertia of the car pushed her two and fro, and she was more than happy to just go with the flow.

"Do you think she's going to know anything more than anyone else has?" Kristina tilted her blue eyes towards Jason, looking for words that would ease her stomach. He only shrugged.

"Everyone we've spoken to has known a bit more than the last person. Don't give up. We'll find the missing puzzle piece, and when we do, this will all be over with." His brows knotted as he executed a particularly tight turn.

"I wish I was as optimistic as you are."

"Look," Jason grinned at her before turning back to the road. "Today's already been better than yesterday. How many clowns have you seen today?"

Kristina smirked. "Besides you?"

Jason clutched his chest as if he'd been shot. "Ouch, Kris. That hurt. My nose isn't that red, is it? I mean it, you haven't seen a single thing that scared you today. Maybe the fat fucker already moved on."

"Jason, don't talk like that."

He looked at her again. "Why? You think he can hear me talking about him? If he can, good. Maybe he'll go after me and leave you alone.

The sun peeked through the clouds and momentarily blinded them both, prompting the visors to go down. Kristina traced a pattern of a warm ray on her leg with her finger, feeling the difference in heat from the lit portion to the part in shadow. She yearned to forget all this, and head east to the ocean and just lay in the sand. When she closed her eyes, she could almost feel the grit of the beach against her skin, hear the gulls calling from the air, smell the salt in each intake of breath.

She wanted to be far away from Indiana and its ghosts.

If she made it out of this alive, maybe she would take a loan and see some of the places on her bucket list. Maybe she would invite Jason. Maybe they could—

"You're awful quiet." The vision of beaches and sand in places it should never be evaporated.

"I'm just thinking," she said.

"About what?"

A wistful grin spread across her mouth. "How nice a vacation would be right now."

Jason reached across the center console and took her hand. He rubbed his thumb across her knuckles and the warmth she'd felt on her leg extended to that part of her. His gentle touch, the way he caressed her, made the beach seem so much closer than it was. The sunlight suddenly dimmed as a large, heavy cloud floated across the sky. Kristina looked out the window and saw a large storm front rolling in from the west.

"Well, it looks like this day is about to get wet and wild." Jason wiggled his eyebrows at her before blowing her an air kiss. "Have you ever fucked on the hood of a car in the rain?"

Kristina snatched her hand back and leaned away from him. "You're never going to change, are you Jason Asher?"

"Not if I can help it, no."

CHAPTER TWENTY-ONE

December 1st, 1968

The first snow of the year fell gracefully, making the world a winter wonderland. Already, several inches coated the ground and there would be a lot more before the storm passed. It began in the early morning hours and now, at noon, it showed no signs of stopping. Maurice Stevenson hated snow and he would tell anyone who'd listen just how far that hate extended. Hate was too nice of a word, a more appropriate one would be loathed. He loathed the snow.

The tavern on this side of town was just far enough away from the little one room hovel he rented that his legs were wet up to the knees when he sauntered in and found an empty seat among the merrymakers. Everyone else was excited, almost gleeful—but not Maurice.

Being alone in the world, this time of year brought him no joy. Families were preparing for Christmas; trees were going up with fancy decorations. He'd had a family once, but when his wife caught wind of all the tarts he had on the side, she'd taken their son and left. That was years ago. His son was an adult now, and he even had a grandchild in his twenties. In Maurice's dank room, nothing mirrored the spirit of the season other than a label on a tin can denoting some holly and a fat man with a red coat.

"Fucking snow," Maurice said, pulling his withered frame onto a stool beside another gentleman wearing the same frown as he.

"What's wrong with the snow?" The stranger looked in his direction for a moment before turning his eyes back on the frothy glass before him.

Maurice signaled to the bartender to bring him a glass then ran his hands through his greasy gray hair, showering the floor in flakes, some his own and some cold and wet. "I can't stand the shit. It makes your feet cold, your hands hurt, and your nose run. There isn't anything good about it."

The stranger shrugged and ignored him after that, set to scowl on his own.

"Well, you're very engaging." Maurice pestered the man.

"I like the snow. I don't like crazy old men trying to talk to me out of nowhere." The man lifted his beer and meandered away to another seat.

Not one to be ignored, Maurice yelled after the man. "It's no wonder you like the damn snow. You're just as cold as it is! I bet your woman has icicles hanging from her nipples." For good measure, he grabbed a handful of peanuts and launched them at the man.

It was his loss of temper that caused him to be thrown out of the bar. A large man, nearly double his size, came out of a rear room Maurice hadn't noticed and approached the bartender. When the man pointed an accusing finger at him, he felt himself blanch. The brute crossed over to him and grabbed the back of his trousers where they were planted on the seat. Suddenly upended, Maurice threw his hands out to prevent his face from slamming into the floor, his old bones aching from the assault.

"Now, now, friend. I was just joshing with the fellow. I didn't mean nothing by it." The door and the frigid outdoor temperatures loomed closer. "Can't we talk about this? You wouldn't throw a man in his seventies out in this mess, would you?" He asked, gesturing towards the water seeping in from under the door.

"You've been warned about your attitude before, Stevenson. We told you last time, if you lost your temper again you wouldn't be allowed back in here." The man opened the door with his right hand and held Maurice clutched in his left. "I don't give a damn what the weather's like out there. You'll figure it out."

"I hate the goddamned snow!" Maurice protested.

The man threw Maurice like a bowling ball, his face sliding across the blanket of white. His body sunk into the accumulation when he finally came to a stop, with his clothes saturated and the hated mess filling his mouth and nose. Maurice got to his feet quickly, brushing himself off, and turned back to the door where the other man was already disappearing.

"You'll be sorry! I know what to do with the likes of you!"

It wouldn't be the first time someone treated him poorly. The last time it happened, a bunch of people died. They should've known better than to mess with him and his partner, Robert. They were a force to be reckoned with—or at least Maurice was. He'd always been the smart one in the duo.

Maurice knew exactly what to do to break that train down. They hadn't expected the other train to take them out, though. That was a serendipitous event. Shortly after the accident, the two men parted ways, thinking it better if they were nowhere near each other in case the law came looking. Maurice couldn't fathom why anyone would come looking for them, though. That all occurred fifty years ago.

There were still several hours before he was supposed to meet with his grandchild. The boy called him the previous evening and asked if they could meet. There was something about a thesis paper for college and him writing about the circus train accident. Maurice told the boy about it once or twice when he'd been growing up, much to his father's dismay. Collin wasn't like his dad though; he was smart, and he needed to know a little bit about everything. He was a lot different from his grandfather too. All Maurice ever accomplished in life was a string of bad debt, a failed marriage, and a never-ending slew of odd jobs encompassing everything from digging graves to a circus clown. Nothing ever stuck.

Maurice pulled his collar closer around his wrinkled neck and shivered. "I'll show him. That asshole will wish he never messed with me."

A car horn blared as he crossed the street, sliding in the slush to avoid hitting him. Maurice flipped him the bird and got another beep as a result.

Collin was coming to his room after he got out of class. Maurice intended to be five sheets to the wind before his arrival, but that wasn't going to happen now. He had something to tell the boy that was important. For the first time in his life, he was going to tell another soul what really happened the night of the train accident. His grandson probably wouldn't want anything to do with him after he heard the story. But he was getting up in years and who knew if he'd ever get another opportunity to clear his conscience.

His little couch was indented from years of sitting in the same spot. It was threadbare and smelled like a church garage sale, but it was his and he liked it. When he got back to his place, he went to it first, sighing when his body fell into the hollow spot he'd created.

His arthritic fingers went to work unlacing the old cloth boots. They were soaked straight through and would have to go next to the radiator to dry overnight if he had any hope of wearing them tomorrow. He draped the socks over the grate, above the boots.

He turned the knob on the little radio on his counter and the velvet voice of Frank Sinatra came through the crackly speaker. The days of the Rat Pack were when the world was doing something right. Lord knew he would never know what the world saw in the Beatles. That garbage wasn't music. In ten years, no one would even remember their names, but Frank Sinatra was forever.

Before long, his eyelids began to feel heavy, and he drifted away.

A loud pounding on his door awoke him from a glorious nap.

"Grandpa? You in there?" Another loud knock, rattling the thin frame. "You're starting to scare me. Are you alive?"

Maurice braced himself on the armrest of the sofa and hefted himself to his feet. "Goddamn it! Stop beating on my door like that. You want the neighbors to call the authorities?" His body felt sore from being handled so roughly and getting across the room was slow going. "I'm coming. Hold your damned horses, Collin."

When Maurice threw the lock and revealed his grandson on the other side, he was shocked to see how tall he was. The last time he'd seen the boy, he scarcely came to the old man's shoulder. But the man before him towered over him like a giant. He had his grandmother's eyes. For just a glimmer of a second, Maurice felt a yearning for the woman, but he locked that down tight inside of his subconscious.

"When did you grow so much?"

Collin smiled and his grin looked just like his father did at that age. "Well, you haven't seen a lot of me over the years, Grandpa. I had to grow up eventually."

Maurice harrumphed and crossed his bony arms. "I would've seen a lot more of you if your grandma hadn't poisoned my own children against me."

"To be fair, if you hadn't cheated on her, she wouldn't have left you."

Maurice dropped his arms. "How do you know about that?"

"Dad told me when I asked why you weren't invited to Christmas dinner." Collin stepped inside and closed the door behind him. He walked the short distance to the couch and opted for the far side Maurice usually occupied. "Just so you know, I advocated for them to still invite you, but they wouldn't go for it."

"I wouldn't have come anyway."

"That's what Dad said." Opening the backpack slung over one of his shoulders, Collin took out a pad of paper and a pencil. "Come talk to me. I really need a good grade on this paper, and I bet no one has a story as interesting as yours."

"That's debatable." Maurice took the seat beside his grandson, feeling his rear sink into the worn-out cushion. "Why didn't you ask your dad about his time in the Navy?"

"Boring."

Maurice chuckled. "Well, all right then."

Closing his eyes, Maurice remembered back to his days in the circus. "We were hitchhiking across the state. We had nothing but a bag on our back with a few changes of clothes and a spare set of boots."

"Who's we, Grandpa?" Collin wrote down every word.

"My good buddy, Robert Sarno. We did everything together. I was already married to your grandmother then, but I had an itch that just couldn't be scratched. I wasn't happy unless I was exploring and along with that came taking every woman who'd go to bed with me. Robert was the same way and I think that's why we were such kindred spirits." Maurice paused, remembering his friend's rough face. Unless Robert shaved twice a day, he would have the beginnings of a beard by nightfall. "The women found Robert to be irresistible, and they would bring their friends to entertain me while they got a crack at him. It was a good arrangement."

Collin's pencil froze on the paper. "So, how did you and Robert end up working as clowns? That's not a very sexy job. I can't imagine you got very many ladies dressed like that."

Maurice chuckled. "Well, we were running low on money. Robert loved to drink, and I loved trying to keep up with him. After a while our pockets were empty, and we had to find a way to keep going. Neither of us wanted to return home to our boring wives and snotty children. Luck would have it that we came across a flyer attached to a storefront for the Hagenbeck-Wallace Circus. The greatest show on earth. They were looking for performers."

Crossing his legs at the ankle to make a tray for the notepad to sit more comfortably, Collin gazed at his grandfather in admiration. "Did you ever get to pet a real tiger, Grandpa?"

"I sure did. His name was Khan, and he was better trained than most dogs I've met."

Collin looked astonished.

"Anyways, the flyer told us where to be to try out and gave us the Ringmaster's name. If I recall correctly, his name was Charlie. Or was it, Chester? My memory isn't what it used to be these days." Years of drinking and not taking particularly good care of himself make him far more feeble than other geezers his age. At least he thought so. "I guess his name isn't important. Call him whatever you want on that paper of yours."

Maurice paused as if trying to remember a series of events more clearly.

"When we showed up, there were only a handful of people there and none of us had any worthwhile talents the circus could use, so they took four of us and made us into clowns. It's important to mention that the ringmaster was a no-nonsense man. He didn't allow any drinking before or during shows and for Robert and me, that was damn near impossible. It was only a matter of time before we tripped up.

Collin uncrossed his legs and bent forward, enraptured with the tale. "How did they catch you?"

A smile grew across Maurice's wrinkled lips. "The same way most drunk men reveal their secrets. We went out with the troupe after a show and ran our mouths. We didn't know the Ringmaster's second in command sat directly behind us, and he could hear all the shit we were spouting."

"Oh, no." Collin put a hand to his mouth, his eyes wide in disbelief.

"Oh yes, and he followed us both outside and single handedly whooped us both."

His grandson began to laugh.

"Oh, yeah sure. Laugh. It wasn't funny then. It made us very angry. The second in command fired us both and demanded us to collect our belongings from the train and never come back."

"But you told me you were involved in the crash?" Collin tilted his head, not realizing how involved his grandfather really was. "If you were fired, you weren't even there."

"You're right. I wasn't there. But I was involved." Maurice rubbed his cheeks, feeling the familiar heat he always felt when he thought about the crash seeping into them. "That night when we went to get our belongings, I concocted a plan. I was going to make them pay for firing us. They needed to be held responsible for spoiling our fun and I knew just how to do it."

"How?" Collin asked.

"I used to listen to this radio program about science and getting reactions by mixing certain things together. I knew that if you mixed saltwater and vinegar together and poured it over something made of iron, it would rust immediately. I knew the worst thing that could happen to the circus was to miss their shows. We kept a bottle of vinegar in our bags to remove the clown makeup. Getting salt and a ladle full of water was an easy feat. I mixed the components together and made Robert stand watch while I doused the hotbox of the first sleeping car with the rusting formula. I watched as the iron went from gray to brown with rot."

Maurice felt ashamed to be disclosing his darkest secret. But he couldn't stop now. He needed to get it off his chest.

"That's terrible," Collin told his grandfather. "All those people."

"Good people too. We had immense respect for the other performers. Even though we didn't know them very well, most everyone was kind to us. It was a stupid, selfish thing to do."

"What happened next?"

Maurice shrugged and massaged his thighs with his fingers, not knowing what to do with his hands. "We took our bags and left. We didn't have money to get home, so we stuck out our thumbs and got picked up that night. A few days later, we heard about the crash over the radio, and we knew it was our fault. They indicted the engineer of the other train on murder charges, his fireman too, and I was so relieved when they were found not guilty. Those men didn't deserve to hang for something we caused."

"How come you didn't turn yourselves in?" Collin asked.

"When the crash happened, Robert decided we should separate so we couldn't be hunted down and questioned as easily. I never saw him again. He abandoned me as soon as the going got tough. Some friend he was. Without him to go in with me, I was always too afraid and ashamed to admit to the crime. What good would it have done anyway? They were all dead already."

CHAPTER TWENTY-TWO

May 6th, 2018

The gates surrounding the facility looked like a prison. Tall and iron with spikes adorning the top the birds wouldn't even land on. The corners were flanked with large rectangular blocks of stylized concrete, which were taller than the fence itself, creating a foreboding, imposing feeling to anyone outside of it. The parking lot was separated by a street and a guard shack with a bleary-eyed older gentleman donning an official looking cap and jacket. When the Mustang pulled beside him and Jason rolled the window down, the guard held his hand out.

"Identification please."

Rummaging in her purse, Kristina produced her license and slid it into Jason's hand on top of his own. He gave them both over and waited patiently for the man to return them.

"Neither of you are on the approved visitor list. You'll have to fill out some forms and mail them to the hospital chief for approval." The man took a folder from somewhere beneath the window and licked his fingers to separate the pages within.

"Sir," Kristina leaned forward to speak over Jason. "Norman Caster sent us to speak to Matilda Russo. He told us to give you his name so we would be let in."

The man settled the papers back where they came from. "Well, why didn't you say so. If Mr. Caster sent you over, I'll get the gate open. First, here's two visitors' badges. Put them around your neck, and don't lose them. Those will be the only thing separating you from the patients and you don't want the nurses thinking your residents. The crazies in there will try to take them from you, so tuck them in your shirts and only take them out if a staff member asks for them. Don't get lazy. There's some really bad people in there."

Jason took the lanyards from the man's fingers along with their identification. "Thanks."

"One more thing. Leave your bags and wallets in the car. I've already checked you out, so you have no need for it in there. Those people are good at turning everyday objects into weapons, and they're insane enough to use them." The man pushed a button beside the window and a loud buzzing noise accompanied the gate swinging open. "Godspeed, you two. I hope you find whatever it is you're looking for."

He slid the glass window closed and settled back into his chair as Jason gave the car enough gas to push forward. "That was odd."

"What kind of place is this if the patients are just running free? This seems dangerous." Kristina rubbed her arms, her eyebrows pinched together in worry. "How are we going to find Matilda if the staff doesn't know patients from visitors?"

"I agree. Something about this doesn't seem right." Jason pulled into the first spot in a long row with visitor's spray-painted on the ground. There were no other cars in the designated area.

Heeding the gate guard's advice, Jason locked his wallet and Kristina's purse in the trunk of the car. Both of them put their lanyards around their necks and tucked the dangling cards into their shirts. The plastic felt cold and alien against Kristina's skin.

"This place gives me the creeps." Jason grabbed her hand as they made for the entrance.

"No kidding. This is almost worse than the cemetery."

Jason eyed her suspiciously. "There were clowns at the cemetery. I haven't seen one here yet."

"Keyword in that sentence is yet." Kristina squeezed his fingers back. "I'm willing to bet we'll see at least one before we leave here."

"At least you're optimistic."

The metal, windowless doors opened with a whoosh as they stepped close to them. Past them was another set with a window situated against the wall in between. A young woman in a white uniform greeted them with a smile. "Hello! May I see your badges please?"

Both Kristina and Jason tugged them out of their shirts and held them up for the girl to see. She scrunched her face as she peered through the glass. Her face resumed the smile when she was satisfied.

"You may put them away." She gestured with her hand and blood red nails caught Kristina's eye. "Who are you here to visit?"

"Matilda Russo." Jason recited the name as if he'd been repeating it to himself so he wouldn't forget it.

The receptionist's smile faded. She pressed a button on the counter that began to blink. Wiping her brown bangs away from her eyes, she settled a stone-cold stare on the couple. "I'm afraid Ms. Russo isn't allowed to see visitors. She's far too mentally unstable for us to allow anyone but trained professionals into her room."

Jason and Kristina looked at each other, then back at the woman. "Norman Caster sent us to speak to her. She knows something that could save someone's life." Jason told her.

"Mr. Caster sent you?" The girl's smile returned. "Everything should be fine then. Let me buzz you in." Hitting a second button on the desk, a buzzer did indeed sound while the second set of metal doors slid open.

"Where do we find her?" Kristina asked.

"Second floor, room number two-oh-one. Make sure you knock three times and don't stand close to the door. Ms. Russo will only let you in if you do that." The girl closed the window and went back to whatever she'd been doing before.

The door closed securely as they passed through and the sound of an air lock sliding into place echoed through the hall. An intercom system adorned the wall on the inside with a screen to scan their badges on the way out. The hall itself was empty. The gate guard made it sound like there would be people wandering the corridors unsupervised, but that wasn't the case. A sign pointing straight ahead showed them where to go for the elevator.

"This place is depressing." Jason walked beside her, glancing at each door they passed. There was a little window in each one, but it wasn't big enough to see the occupants unless you pressed your face to it. Each one on this floor had a scanner on the wall outside, presumably for the doctors to let themselves in.

"It's way too quiet." The absence of sound was unnerving. There weren't any of those little speakers in the ceiling offering background noise or beeping from equipment. There was just nothing. "Where is everyone?"

The elevator doors opened with a loud ding as they approached, welcoming them inside its gaping mouth with cheery lighting and music. It was so out of place among the eerily quiet halls that Kristina was reluctant to step inside, looking around for a stairwell that may be a better choice. When she didn't see one, she heaved a sigh and followed Jason inside. Surgical steel coated the walls of the box, reflecting a blurry image of the people it captured. Kristina stayed close to Jason's side, not trusting the sudden tranquility.

Jason hit the illuminated button for the second floor, and the elevator gave another signaling ding and the doors slid closed. "You ready?"

"Nope. But what choice do I have?"

There was a significant uptick in movement in the hall when the doors opened once more. Patients lined the floor against the pastel blue walls, their white gowns tied at their backs. They howled and cried, beat their hands on the floors, and drooled, all while the nurses rushed from person to person attending to their needs. Kristina was appalled to see one man in particular masturbating beside another woman who seemed to be sound asleep. As she watched, unable to look away, a nurse rushed over and took him by the arm, pulling him from the floor, and stopping his frantic jerking.

The man looked her in the eyes as the nurse led him by and smiled. Kristina felt the need to vomit.

When they were finally noticed by the staff, Kristina was already prepared to get back in the elevator and leave. Jason had his arm locked firmly around her waist, holding her in place as if he knew what she was about to do.

"I'm sorry! I didn't notice you two standing there. It must be a full moon or something because they're really acting out today!" She gestured to the people on the floor simultaneously wiping the sweat of exertion from her brow. "There's far too many of them and not enough of us."

A woman screamed at the top of her lungs and the nurse grimaced.

"We're here to see Matilda Russo. Can you please point us in the direction of her room?"

Kristina was grateful that Jason spoke. Her tongue felt like it was five sizes too big for her mouth, hitting the inside of her teeth like a wrecking ball.

The nurse dropped her arms down to her sides and stared at them with her jaw hinged open. "They're allowing her to have visitors? That's very odd."

She didn't ask any more questions, just gestured for them to follow her. They had to step over legs and arms on the venture down the hall. The patients sought to make the trip difficult, moving into their path and swinging out at the last moment to make them trip. The ecstatic laughter each time they succeeded put Kristina's nerves even more on edge. The throng dispersed the further they got down the hall.

"They like to group together down there. It makes it easier for us to keep track of them, though. Most of them don't go down to the far end of the hallway. It's the strangest thing. The rooms on either side of Matilda's are vacant as well. We can't get anyone to settle near her. Every time someone's placed in those rooms, they scream and pound on the doors all night until we move them." The nurse pulled a ring of keys out of her pocket and sorted through them until she took one in her palm. "Matilda's very particular about who comes into her room. Only certain nurses can get in without trouble."

"The lady downstairs said something about knocking twice and standing back?" Jason recalled out loud.

"Three times," the nurse corrected. "If you deviate from that, she'll attack you and she's clever. When we secure her, she finds a way to get free. We have a camera in her room and even with that, we can't figure out how she's getting loose. It's like she's possessed."

Kristina squeezed Jason's arm.

"When we get to the door, stand back about four feet so she can see your faces when she looks through the window. She'll decide if she wants you in there or not." According to the numbers on the doors. They were nearly there. "Do you want me to come in with you?"

Kristina wanted to say yes but knew what they needed to talk about would make them look just as crazy as the woman inside. "No thank you. The questions we need to ask her are confidential. The fewer people who know, the better."

"You guys work with the police or something?"

"Or something," Jason said.

"Here we are. I'll be just out in the hall if you need me. If you scream, I'll come running."

Jason followed the directions given, and knocked exactly three times, pulling Kristina back against him roughly four feet away. In seconds, a face filled the space in the glass and stared at each of them. The heavy bags under her eyes looked purple against the too white skin. Then the door opened.

"Do we just go in?" Jason whispered to the nurse.

"That's her invitation. Go on in." She ushered them forward with her hands. "Good luck guys. I hope you get what you came for."

The room was plain, painted white with white trim and pale blue tiles squares on the floor. The bed was similarly colored with sheets and pillows the exact color of snow. The only other shade in the room was the dark brown desk against one wall. There weren't any windows. Kristina saw restraints attached to the bed at the top and bottom for wrists and ankles and had a desire to rub her own where she knew the leather straps would lie against her skin. They didn't see Matilda at first.

"Welcome to my room." The door slammed closed behind them

and Kristina jumped. Matilda materialized behind them from where she'd been leaning against the wall. She was short and had brown hair down to her waist. Her face was lined with her age, but Kristina didn't think she could be any older than forty. "I've been waiting for you. He told me you would come."

"Mr. Caster?" Kristina asked, her voice cracking, betraying her fear.

"No, stupid. Baldy." The woman tossed her hair as if annoyed. "He told me you would come soon and here you are. You're a surprise, though." She eyed Jason hungrily.

Kristina felt his body tense against her.

"What else did he tell you?" Jason asked.

Matilda smiled, and Kristina saw the yellow color of her teeth. "Oh, he tells me lots of things. He tells me when people are going to die mostly. And he tells me all about each one. For instance," she pointed at Kristina. "I know you don't know who your family is."

Kristina gasped, placing a hand to her mouth in disbelief.

"Do you know who they are?" Jason quizzed the woman.

"Of course, I do! Do you think I'm stupid? I listen when they talk to me. That's why they all still come. No one else wants to listen. They've forgotten what he's done for us. They're all stupid." Matilda crossed her arms over her chest and her hair obstructed her round face. "I know you've seen him. Isn't he glorious?" She was looking at Kristina again.

"If you say so," Kristina whispered. Jason elbowed her in the side. "Oh, yes, so glorious," she corrected.

"Do you want to know who your real family is?" Matilda taunted.

Kristina's mouth went dry. Did she want to know? She'd made it this far in life without the knowledge. Did she need it now? "Will it help save my life?"

Matilda laughed. It was a huffing painful noise that sounded unnatural in Kristina's ears. "No, silly. Nothing's going to save your life. Baldy's going to have you and he has something fun planned. But if you want to know who they are, I'll tell you. He didn't tell me I couldn't."

"Has he told you anything you're not allowed to tell us?" Jason asked.

"Yes," she told him.

Fidgeting nervously, Kristina wondered what she could know and if the knowledge would help her in any way. "Do you want to talk to us about those things?"

The woman laughed again. "I'm crazy, not dumb. Don't try to manipulate me. It won't end well for you. Do you want to know about your family or not, Kristina?"

"How did you know my name?"

She flicked her hair again. "Baldy told me." Matilda crossed the room and took a seat on her twin-sized bed, spreading her legs suggestively and looking Jason in his eyes. She licked her lips and grinned, patting the bed beside her. "I can tell you like this. You wanna know what it's like to fuck on the hood of a car in the rain?"

Jason's mouth dropped open.

Those were the words he'd said to Kristina on the way to the hospital. Kristina shook herself, clearing the fog that settled over her brain. If she knew what they'd said in conversation by themselves, then Baldy was in that car with them. Was he here now?

"Yes, I want to know about my parents."

Matilda's eyes darted to Kristina and she crossed her legs, pulling the long shift down over her exposed thighs. "They abandoned you so no one would know who you were. They knew Baldy would kill you if he found you. You're the granddaughter of Maurice Stevenson and a performer named Adelaide Thompson who survived the crash. You're half the enemy and half the victim. Before Maurice was fired, he raped her in her tent. She never told anyone, but several weeks later, she realized she carried your mother."

Kristina felt like she was going to pass out. She was far more entwined in the Hagenbeck-Wallace circus than she ever thought was possible. "What happened to my grandmother?"

"Nothing. She was a survivor, not an enemy. She wasn't one of the men who caused the deaths. She lived a long time and died happily. But your mother—she was half enemy and Baldy took care of her. It was your grandmother's fault. When your mother turned eighteen, she told her the truth about who her father was. Speaking the words out loud made it known to Baldy. She already had you and a fellow who wanted to marry her when Baldy began to stalk her. She'd grown up with the stories of his vengeance all her life and she knew what was going to happen to her, so she abandoned you. She thought if no one knew who you were or where you came from, you'd be safe."

"Safe, left to rot in an empty building with no one to take care of me?" Kristina questioned.

"She called told the police where you were." Matilda played with her hands in her lap, picking at her nails absently. "They knew where to find you, just not where you came from. You were always safe."

"How did Baldy find out who Kristina was in the first place?" Jason asked.

Matilda tilted her head to the side and closed her eyes as if someone else spoke to her from inside her head. "Adelaide recognized her blood when you came to the cemetery the first time. The time before you brought him." She leveled a thin finger at Jason. "Her body is there. When she remarked to her friends how lovely her granddaughter had grown to be, Baldy heard her. She pleaded with him to leave you be, but he took an oath with the devil to eliminate the bloodlines, and that's what he'll do."

Jason caught Kristina as her legs went out from under her. "The man who shot himself, Collin. I was related to him. My grandmother was on the train when the accident happened. My mother was a product of rape. This is too much."

"Can you go now? I'm tired and Baldy says I said too much." Matilda laid back on the sterile bed.

"He's here?" Kristina asked.

"He's everywhere." Matilda laughed putting her arm over her face. "I'm going to be punished. I told you something you weren't supposed to know."

"What?" Jason asked.

Matilda shot up from the bed. "Get out! Get out now! Don't come back!"

Jason and Kristina rushed to the door that opened on its own in front of them. Once they were through it closed again, rattling the frame. The nurse looked at them bewildered as Matilda started to scream from within.

"I'm sorry! I didn't mean to say all that! It slipped out! It's been so long since someone wanted to talk to me! I'm—" A loud crash and a moan came from inside. The nurse fumbled with the keys to get the door opened. When she did, they saw Matilda Russo splayed across the floor. She's ripped her own throat out with her fingernails and lay in a pool of her own blood. She blinked twice, took a breath, and then she was gone.

The nurse screamed.

CHAPTER TWENTY-THREE

January 1st, 1968

Collin called his grandfather a month later to tell him not only did he get a perfect grade on the story he wrote, but it was being published in article form for the local newspaper. He was so excited to be featured that he never considered how the other man might feel about it. Maurice was infuriated.

"I told you all that for your school paper. I didn't want the whole goddamn world to know what happened. I thought your professor would see it and that would be it. When you came here, you never told me there was any chance of it being published." Maurice wrung his hands, balancing the bulky phone on his shoulder, careful not to get too far away from the base and have the cord yank the receiver away.

"What are you so mad about? It happened years ago. It's not like they're going to charge you with anything now." Collin protested.

"You don't know that." Maurice opened the avocado green fridge and searched for a can of beer. The inside was emptier than his bank account and that was depressing. He could really use a drink. "What about Robert?"

"What about him?"

"Did you at least change his name?" Maurice asked. "You don't have his permission to publish his name."

Collin laughed. "Grandpa, what are the chances he'll ever see it? It's the local newspaper. It's not the Times. Does he even still live in the area?"

"I don't fucking know. I haven't seen him since the crash. He could be anywhere."

"Then I'm probably safe using his name then." Collin sounded like he was getting irritated.

"You should have asked first."

Collin huffed. "Just like you asked Grandma to let you sleep with those other women? You know she let me go through your old trunk that you left behind when she kicked your sorry ass to the curb. I saw all the photos in there. There had to be at least fifty different girls. Do I have any half aunts and uncles out there?"

"What does that have to do with your shit article?" Maurice was more than mad. He was seething.

"Everything. You can't act all indignant when all you've done in your life is stomp on other people. You can't be all righteous and be a sinner too. You have to pick a side and stay there." Someone spoke in the background and Collin put his hand over the receiver to muffle the voices. "Listen, I have to go. I thought you'd be happy for me but you're obviously not. I'm going out to celebrate with people who are proud of my accomplishment."

"That's your father I hear, isn't it? Well, you tell him to kiss my ass."

"No Grandpa. You've told him that through your actions all your life. I wanted to give you a chance. I really did. But you'll never change."

The line went dead.

Maurice slammed the salmon-colored phone back into the cradle. How dare he take the story public like that. What of the local authorities tried to talk to him about it? Maurice decided then and there that if the police did show up on his doorstep, he would pretend to be a feeble old man. He was certainly old enough to play the part. If he seemed non-threatening, maybe they would just leave him to die alone in his rented room. He couldn't afford to disappear so that would have to work. He sunk into the weathered old couch and massaged his temples.

Someone knocked on the door. "Damn that was quick," Maurice mumbled in a hushed tone. "Who's there?" He tried his best to make his voice quake like that of an invalid.

No one responded but the knock came again.

"Goddamn it." Pushing himself out of the chair, he grabbed the cane he only occasionally used lying against the side of the couch and bent over it, thrusting his backbone out and turning his feet in the wrong direction. He squinted one eye closed and let his mouth droop at one side. "I'll be right there."

He took his time, not wanting to seem too spry. The knock came again.

"Hold your damn horses. Don't you know I'm old?"

The person knocked again, more persistent this time. Maurice slid the chain lock free and twisted the deadbolt. On the other side of the threshold stood a fat clown with a wide grin. In his hands was a small box wrapped in glittering red paper. He pushed his hands forward, offering the parcel to Maurice. "For you, Maurice."

"If you're some sort of special delivery person, shouldn't the package come with a song or a dance, and who's it from?"

The clown set the box on the floor and kicked his feet up in the air. He finished with a flourish with both arms extended out dramatically. He retrieved the package and held it out again.

"Would've been better with a song." Maurice snatched the box away and tore at the red foil paper anxiously. The package inside was made of ordinary looking cardboard. Sliding a finger under the lip, Maurice peeled back the top to reveal the contents. On a small velvet pillow lay a straight razor, not that much different than the one occupying space on his bathroom sink. The edge was honed a razor sharp, and it gleamed in the meager light from the standing lamp beside his couch.

"This is especially for you, Maurice." The clown took a step into his living room uninvited.

"Who the fuck said you can come in my house, clown. And what the fuck is this? Who would send me a razor?" Maurice tossed the box onto the floor and made to push the clown out the door, but he was a brick wall. His hands sunk into the bulbous stomach like a sponge, but the clown didn't move an inch.

"Your time has come, Maurice Stevenson. I'm here to exact justice for the crimes you committed. For every soul whose flesh melted off their bones, I will take a pound of flesh from you." The clown reached down and took the straight razor into his gloved hand, balancing it, admiring the weight. The light reflected off the sharp surface in a line across the jester's face.

Maurice moved backward without the use of the cane, back straight and feet set in the proper angles. "Get out of my house! You're not welcome here! This is my home!" He bellowed, feeling behind himself for anything that might hinder his escape.

The clown advanced, his large flopping shoes smacking the faded rug with each step. His eyes glowed an unearthly silver and his mouth stretched wide showing the rows of teeth previously concealed. "Eighty-six souls, eighty-six pounds of flesh to cut away. Do you have enough on that saggy body of yours?"

"I don't know what you're talking about," Maurice stuttered, hitting the edge of the couch and collapsing into the hollow space. "I haven't killed anyone. I'm just an old man, I have a family, you have me confused with someone else, clown."

A red tongue snaked out of the grinning mouth, running down the length of the blade. It bit into his flesh and blood oozed to the surface, coating the surface of the razor. "You were one of us. You learned the circus ways and people liked you. You bedded our woman, you drank with our men, you put your blood and sweat into our shows, then you killed us in our sleep like we were no better than dogs."

Maurice blanched as recognition washed over him. "Baldy?"

The clown cackled, slicing the weapon through the air. "Now you recognize me! Am I that forgettable?"

"Baldy, you were always such a good man. Why are you here? You're dead! You died with all the others." Maurice started to stand but eased back into his seat when Baldy leaned in close to him. "Are you a reaper? Is it my time to go?"

Baldy chuckled the gay circus clown giggle Maurice heard a million times before. "It is in fact your time to go. But I'm no reaper. I'm here to deliver you to hell for your sins. It's your final show, Maurice. You'll pay in flesh, and when that runs out, you'll pay with your soul."

"I never meant to kill any of you," Maurice sobbed. "It was a stupid mistake, nothing more."

Baldy dropped to his knees before the quivering man. His frilled collar tilted down in front where his chin lowered menacingly. "I watched my Martha burn to death. I saw her skin melt off her bones. I listened to my boy scream in agony as the oil from the lantern ignited him like a human torch, but you never paid. None of you did. No one took any responsibility for what they did. Now you will."

Maurice's hands felt glued to the couch. He couldn't move away, couldn't escape. "What are you going to do?"

Baldy chuckled again. "I'm going to skin you like a deer. I'm going to start with the leather on your face and we'll see if you last. If you do, then we'll keep having fun. The show must go on, you know."

"Please don't hurt me!" Maurice cried in earnest now, squeezing his lids closed and turning his face away from the encroaching blade.

The white gloved hand took his chin in his hand and turned his face forward. "Now you hold still. This might hurt a little."

Starting with his eyelids, Baldy sliced away the flesh. Maurice's eyes darted frantically, blood flowing over the irises. The cheeks were next, exposing the white bone beneath. He cut the lips away, making Maurice look like a gruesome Halloween prop with all his teeth showing all the way to his molars. He continued to scream.

"That's right," Baldy crooned. "Show me your pain." He dropped the strips of skin and blood in a pile on the floor.

The skeletal teeth chattered making unintelligible sounds.

"There. Aren't you beautiful? What shall we do next? How about your legs!" Ripping the trousers down the seams, Baldy exposed the man fully. He started at the ankle and removed skin and muscle alike until nothing remained but the two bones of the lower leg. "Such nice bones for an old man! You should be proud!"

Maurice was fading fast. Baldy got halfway through the left arm when the man's heart stopped its frantic pace and stilled in his chest. Placing the straight razor in the man's right-hand Baldy chuckled. "Such a pity he committed suicide. The guilt must have finally gotten to him."

Baldy's expression turned sour as he stepped away from the corpse. "See you in hell, old man. May the rest of your eternity be filled with flames."

The clown's form slowly faded until only the eyes were visible, then blinked out completely.

CHAPTER TWENTY-FOUR

May 7th, 2018

Kristina woke covered in sweat and panting. Her surroundings were unfamiliar to her and she panicked for the split second it took her to remember they were at Jason's apartment, not hers. The previous evening, after listening to Matilda die either by the phantom clown's hand or her own, the last thing she wanted was to go back to her place. The silk sheets twisted around her torso felt like ropes in the darkness, squeezing her in a vice grip. The back of her throat felt like sandpaper and each breath she sucked in hurt. Jason slept soundly with his back to her, snoring gently.

The room was bathed in darkness with a patch of light shining from beneath the en suite bathroom door. Kristina insisted on leaving it on as a night light. Something stirred in the corner, drawing her eyes to it like a moth to a flame.

She saw the red pants first, then the matching top with the ballooning sleeves, and the frilled collar. As the clown took a single step into the light, his face paint became clear, face white as a corpse, mouth red as a whore's, and blue circles around the silvery pupils of his eyes.

Kristina was rooted to the bed, unable to scream, unable to reach for Jason. The only thing that seemed to move was the frantic pounding of her heart and the rise and fall of her chest with her marathon like breathing.

"Did you think I couldn't find you here, Kristina?" Just like the first dream she'd had of him, his mouth didn't move, but she heard his words loud and clear inside her head. "I can find you no matter where you go. We're bonded by my oath. The blood in your veins calls out to me like a ringmaster to his troupe."

"Why did you kill Matilda?" Kristina heard herself speak, but she knew her lips were still. It was projected through thought and not sound. "She was on the winning team; she didn't have to die."

"She betrayed us."

"Us?" Kristina tilted her head to the side trying to understand.

"The dead, the survivors, and I." Baldy took another step forward, his monstrous red shoes flapped against the thickly carpeted floor. "She almost told you everything."

"If you're going to kill me anyway, why can't I know everything?"

Jason stirred, rolling over onto his back. One arm draped over his face and he moaned. Kristina willed him to wake up and to protect her, but he continued to snore.

"There will be no secrets once you're dead."

Moving of their own volition, Kristina's legs kicked out from under the blanket and swung off the side of the bed. She rose to a seated position and she fought an internal battle with her body to stop responding to the silent commands of the ghost before her and lost.

Baldy put a gloved hand out and beckoned her with a finger. "Come to me. Let's end this tonight so I may finally be at rest."

"No!" Kristina screamed, audibly this time, finding her voice through the paralysis. Jason twisted around onto his hands and knees, ripped from sleep by the intrusion of sound. Kristina reached for him as her legs began to propel her forward. Lunging like a cat, Jason tackled her to the floor, pinning her appendages beneath him like a linebacker. "Hold on to me! I can't control it!"

The clown howled in anger, pulling at his wisps of red hair at his temples, his mouth falling open to a cavernous black hole.

Jason flinched against the onslaught of power projected by the scream, putting his hands over his ears with his elbows still caging in Kristina. "I see him! Oh, God, I see him."

Flailing against Jason, Kristina struggled to get free and get to the clown. Her body bucked and squirmed and she cried out against the force controlling her. The louder Baldy screeched the harder her limbs fought. Her brain swam with visions of fire and death, implanted by the same being controlling her body. Kristina ground her teeth together trying to force him out.

A blinding white light filled the room. Jason put a hand over his eyes and Kristina shoved her face into his chest. The clown's murderous scream turned to one of pain as he covered his own eyes. His flesh began to smoke, filling the room with the smell of rot. Kristina gagged, trying desperately to breathe through her mouth.

All at once, there was nothing. The light vanished, taking the clown and the noxious odor with it. Jason hesitated to remove his weight from Kristina, looking at her first for reassurance that she was no longer under the thing's control. When she relaxed against the floor, breathing heavily, he got up on his knees.

"What in the fuck just happened?" Looking into the corner from where the being had assaulted them, Jason tried to discern what occurred.

"I—I don't know," Kristina stuttered, trying to catch her breath.

"I think it's gone." Jason got to his feet and hit the light switch on the wall revealing an empty corner where the clown had been. Nothing was out of place. There weren't even lines in the carpet where he'd stood. Crossing the space and standing exactly where he'd seen the phantom, Jason waved his hands in the air and then shrugged his shoulders. "It's like it was never here at all, but I saw it with my own fucking eyes."

"Now you believe me?" Kristina asked from the floor.

"I always believed you, but goddamn!"

Tears ran down the sides of her cheeks and she put her arms over her face to hide it. Her body shook with the sobs she couldn't hold back. "I'm not crazy. I'm not seeing things like Matilda. This thing really is out to get me. And now you've seen it too."

Jason went back to the broken woman on the floor, pulling her into his lap and cradling her against him.

"I understand why Collin killed himself," she wailed. "I can't live like this, Jason. I'm not as strong as he was."

Kristina had a raging headache when she woke the second time. Jason volunteered to stay awake the rest of the night to keep watch so they wouldn't be taken by surprise again. By the time the sun rose, and Kristina's eyes shot open, his were bloodshot from lack of rest. The stubble on his chin was past the five o'clock shadow mark and Kristina had never seen him look so scruffy. Knowing he'd let his appearance go to make sure she was okay made her heart burn with appreciation.

"Take a nap, I'll make breakfast," she told him as she made for the kitchen.

"What if he comes back while I'm sleeping?" he asked. "I can't leave you alone."

Kristina smiled and pulled out a skillet. "He never comes back that quickly. I think you're safe for an hour. I'll have eggs and bacon ready when you get up."

Jason crossed to the stove where she stood. He wrapped his arms tightly around her waist and buried his face in her hair. "God, I think I love you."

"That's the second time you've said that." She grinned.

"Must be true then."

"How do you like your eggs?" Kristina pulled out of his embrace and moved to the refrigerator, pulling the cartoon off the top shelf in the door.

"Scrambled, please." She heard his voice trail off as he made his way to the couch and soft snores started almost immediately after.

Busying herself in the kitchen, Kristina distracted herself with the menial task. She took her time cracking each shell, measured out the perfect amount of milk, salt and pepper, and a dash of shredded cheddar cheese. For good measure, she added diced jalapenos, but not too much, just enough for some extra flavor just like her mother always had for her.

Her mother.

The face of the woman who raised her popped into her mind. So many secrets revolved around her birth and her abandonment, or of her being hidden as she supposed she should think of it now. It was a curious thought to wonder if maybe her adoptive mother and father might know more than they had let on. It wasn't normal protocol for a cop to decide where a baby who was found abandoned would go. Usually, the state would step in and the child would go to an approved foster home until a blood relation could be located or an eventual adoption occurred. But that didn't happen to her. The day they found her, she went home with the Perdue's and that was where she stayed.

Kristina wondered if they'd ever looked for her real family at all. She'd always believed them when they said they did. But now? She wasn't sure.

There was a package of thick cut bacon in the fridge drawer, and she cut the plastic wrap open carefully, separating the pieces and laying them aside until the skillet heated up. The bowl of eggs sat to the side waiting their turn.

On a whim, she pulled out her cell phone and located her mother's phone number. After staring at the screen trying to make up her mind and build up her courage, Kristina hit the call button and listened to the ring on the other end.

The chipper woman answered on the second ring. "Kristina! This is a pleasant surprise."

"Mom. Can we talk please?"

"Sure, honey. What's up?" Whispering to someone else in the room, her mother suddenly giggled. "Sorry sweetheart, your father is in a ripe mood this morning."

Kristina rolled her eyes. "Mom, I need to know how you adopted me." Killing the fire under the burner, Kristina scooted the bacon away from the edge of the counter and turned to lean against the cleared space. "I know that's not how a normal adoption works, but I never questioned it because I was happy."

Her mother sighed. "Honey, you've heard the story about how we came to adopt you so many times. It was just a lucky series of events. We were in the right place at the right time. Bringing you into our family was meant to be." Pausing, Kristina could almost hear the other woman gather her thoughts. "Why's this coming up now? Are you not happy anymore?"

The choice to sugarcoat what needed to be said or to come right out with it was a hard one. Unsure whether her mother would be truthful either way made it a bit easier to pick between the two options. "Baldy the clown has found me and he's going to kill me. I need to know what you know to try to save my life."

Silence. A minute passed, then two. Her mother didn't utter a sound.

"Mom?" Kristina pressed the phone to her ear harder. "Are you still there?"

"How?" It was all she said, and it belied so much information in one single syllable.

Kristina smiled, not because she was happy, but because she felt like she was getting somewhere. "So, you do know then. Why did you hide it from me?"

"If I'd said it out loud, even to you, he would have found you much sooner. I had to protect you, Kristina. I couldn't let that man—that thing—get to you like all the others. I promised your father—your real father—that I would keep you safe." Her voice choked on a sob; the long-hidden secret finally exposed.

"Who is my real father?"

The other woman hesitated. "Your uncle Alex."

Kristina was stunned into silence. When she reclaimed her voice, the questions spilled out in a torrent. "He was the one who found me in the abandoned house. He knew I was there the whole time, didn't he? I was never actually abandoned at all. No one ever looked for my real family because you all knew who they were. Did the state even get notified about me, or did you just snatch me up before anyone was the wiser?"

Jason was awake and watching her carefully from the couch.

Kristina mentally kicked herself for raising her voice and disturbing him. She mouthed, I'm sorry, to him.

"We had to be very careful with the paperwork. You couldn't be traced back to your original family in any way or you would still be in danger. That's why we had to say Alex found you in the building. You were never actually there at all. Grace handed you over to your father as soon as she knew her life was in jeopardy, hoping Baldy wouldn't already be aware she had a daughter." Her mother was in tears now as she described the sequence of events that occurred before Kristina was old enough to know what happened to her. "Alex had a friend in the social work department, and he begged her to let you stay with us. He told her how we'd been trying for years to have a baby and had no luck and told her how much better it would be for you not to go through the system. And somehow, she agreed. It was done through a closed adoption with your origins unknown and the state made you a new birth certificate."

"What about Dad?" Kristina asked. "Does he know about all this?"

"Which father are we speaking about now? Alex or—"

Kristina clenched a fist at her side. "I don't care if Alex aided in my procreation. He's my uncle, not my father. I'm talking about Dad."

"He doesn't know anything. He only knows the story we told him. He's been more than happy with it all these years and I don't think he should know now. He'd be devastated if he knew Alex was your real father."

"Guess no one cared how devastated I might be if I found out the truth." Kristina sulked.

"Would you rather we let you be hunted down and killed by an angry ghost clown?"

Kristina scowled even though the woman couldn't see her. "What difference did it make. He's going to kill me now anyway."

"How did he find you?" The woman asked for a second time.

"I went to Showmen's Rest on a job for the paper. According to a mental patient at the state asylum, my grandmother's spirit recognized me and when she did, Baldy was alerted to my existence." Kristina remembered the feeling of warmth that overtook her while standing in the place that seemed so out of place with the irrational fear she'd felt the rest of the time.

"Adelaide."

"Yeah, I guess you knew who she was too then, huh?" Kristina was becoming more and more annoyed.

"I was told she was a very kind woman. It's a shame what happened to her."

"If it hadn't happened, I wouldn't be being hunted now." Kristina whispered, feeling resentment towards her biological grandfather for raping the woman. It was the first moment she'd agreed with anything Baldy had done and hoped Maurice's death was especially gruesome.

"You also never would have been born."

"Oh, well." Turning the fire back on under the burner, Kristina decided this call was over. She didn't care about anything else her mother had to say. "Listen Mom, I've got a lot going on, so I'll call you back later."

Jason entered the room and took her place at the stove, placing strips of delicious, fatty meat into the pan. The smell wafting from the stove was hickory and pig and Kristina suddenly felt famished.

"Please be safe sweetheart. God, I hate clowns."

Kristina smiled despite her mood remembering how her mother expressly forbade the kids from going to the circus when they were younger because of her fear of clowns and how her father took them anyway. He'd lied and told the woman they went to the zoo and the kids followed his lead. Now she understood why she didn't want them there.

"Okay, Mom. Bye."

Tossing the cell carefully on the counter, Kristina pulled her hair into a ponytail behind her head and secured it with a band on her wrist. She watched Jason expertly flip the meat as she composed herself. "I was supposed to be cooking for you."

He shrugged. "You were busy."

"Things just keep getting more and more convoluted."

Jason grinned, pulling the meat from the pan and placing them on a plate covered in paper towels to soak up the grease. "I take it you found some more puzzle pieces."

"You could say that." Kristina blew the stray hairs out of her face. "I found out my uncle Alex is my real father, and my mother knew who my biological family was the entire time and hid it from me. She knew about Baldy and what he was doing to my relatives and hid my origins from the state so I could stay with them."

"That's beyond fucked up." Jason turned and met her eyes. "So, I guess we need to speak to your uncle dad then huh?"

CHAPTER TWENTY-FIVE

January 15th, 1968

Robert Sarno was a hard man to find. He never used the same name twice and this week he went by the name Frank. It wasn't a good name or a bad name, just something random that came to mind when someone asked him who he was. Last week he was Jerry, and the week before that he was Michael. But new town, new identity. That's how it worked.

Life was never something Robert, or Frank as he was today, was good at. He started his existence of disappointment in a troubled home with alcoholic parents who beat him every time the booze ran out. Back then, things were simpler and so much harder at the same time. No telephones, no televisions, no distractions. But there was also no way to get help when you were a child trapped at home and no one cared about you anyway.

When he was ten, the state finally stepped in after an extended bout of truancy to his school. A home visit revealed a malnourished kid with yellow skin from healing bruises and a mother who swore he was just the clumsiest thing you ever did see. The caseworker didn't believe her and took him away that very day.

Life should have gotten better at that point.

Instead, he went to his first of fifteen foster homes. He was beaten worse than he ever was at home. He was put into a room with ten other boys who were already numb to the system, and in one home, he was sexually abused. Life was never meant to be good for Robert Sarno.

When he turned eighteen, he walked out of his last group home and never looked back. He survived by stealing, petty robberies, and purse snatches. He got odd jobs here and there, but nothing ever lasted long.

In his twenties, he befriended a man named Maurice and hitchhiked across the country until they ran out of money. That ended in a stint in the circus as a good for nothing clown. There was nothing Robert hated more than dressing up in frilly clothes and putting makeup on his face like a damn woman. Luckily, that didn't last either.

After Maurice vandalized the circus train and it caused a wreck, they went their separate ways. The last thing he needed was to go to jail for something that nitwit did. He hadn't seen the guy since.

That was years ago.

Robert honed his thieving skills to deadly precision in that time. But now he was a wrinkled shell of who he once was. He lived in a halfway house full of alcoholics and drug addicts and he wondered how he'd ended up exactly like his parents whom he hated so much even seventy years after being removed from their home. He didn't know what happened to them and he never cared to try to find out. As far as he knew, they'd never looked for him either.

"Frank?" The teenager with all the metal in his face sat on the big couch in the common area with his legs spread out across the cushions. "You got a couple dollars to spare?"

"Get a job, you bum."

The boy sat up, indignant at the slight. "You stole whatever you have anyway. You've never had a real job in your life. At least I have a chance to fix myself. You're just going to shrivel up and we'll find you dead in your bed someday. And when we do, we'll take everything you've stolen from others and you won't be able to say shit about it."

Robert didn't give a rat's ass what the kid said. He twitched as he spat his venom, a sure sign that whatever high he had was wearing off and he would need another soon. "When I'm dead I don't care what you do."

Hobbling out of the room, Robert made for the street. He didn't have any money to give the boy even if he'd wanted to. The halfway house only provided dinner and that was seven hours away. He'd have to acquire food another way. It was easy enough now that he was getting up in age. His tactics changed, but the rewards were the same.

Dressed in tweed pants and a button-down shirt with suspenders, Robert looked the part of any grandfatherly gentleman. But his eyes always watched for someone he could be take advantage of. And he was good at weeding them out.

It was cold outside, and he didn't own a jacket. His breath puffed from his open mouth like an angry dragon as he made his way down the street to a little diner he'd been having some good luck at. He waited outside until a younger couple approached the door and began to pat his pockets.

"He robbed me!" he proclaimed. "That punk stole my wallet!"

The younger couple stopped, obligated to make sure an elderly man was okay while the commotion interrupted their lunch break. "Sir? Is there anything we can help you with?"

"I just got off the bus and a young man was trying to chat me up before we reached my stop. I haven't eaten since yesterday and I really wanted a cup of joe and some breakfast. Now I can't eat, and I've got no money to get back home. I don't know what to do." He willed tears into his eyes, sealing the deal.

The girl looked at her man, begging him to do something. With a heavy sigh, the man pulled out his wallet and handed Robert a twenty. "This should be enough for a meal and to get home. I hope he didn't get anything other than some cash from you."

"I keep all my important things at home." Robert smiled at the two and thanked them graciously. "You're both angels, true angels. Thank you so very much."

"It's our pleasure." The man smiled at his girl and she beamed at him for his good deed. "Get yourself something to eat, huh?"

"Oh, I will. Thank you again."

Robert didn't go inside the diner. There was a convenience station right across the street and that was his real goal. Crossing the street as quickly as his old legs would manage, he opened the door with the little bells on it and the cashier greeted him by his fabricated name.

"Hey, Frank! How's it going?"

"Same as always I suppose." Robert headed for the beer fridge in the back of the store. He grabbed a twelve pack of the cheap stuff and a pre-made sandwich on the way to the register. Those idiots didn't even question what he wanted money for. They just handed it over without a second thought. This was almost too easy.

"You staying warm out there, Frank?"

Robert huffed. "Yeah, this invisible winter coat keeps me toasty."

The cashier laughed as he scanned the items on the counter. "You know, instead of buying beer every day, you could go down to the Goodwill and pick up a second-hand coat for pretty cheap. You're going to end up catching pneumonia dressed like that."

Robert took the beer, and the weight made his shoulder droop. "It's not going to be cold much longer. Besides, I prefer the cold over the heat."

"Whatever you say, Frank."

The short walk to the halfway house was made more difficult with the heavy burden in his hand and the ice on the pavement. Eating the egg salad sandwich as he went, he almost cracked one of the cans open to wash it down. With any luck, he could sneak back into the room before any of the other loser residents saw his prize.

Some bums on the other side of the street warmed their hands over a fire in a trash barrel. Robert couldn't stand fire. It made him nervous. Ever since his buddy Maurice compromised that circus train and the damn thing went up like the fourth of July when the other train ran into it, fire made his stomach hurt. Maybe it was the thought of all those people burning after the kerosene from the lanterns coated the wooden boards of the train cars and then ignited. Whatever it was, it caused a lifelong phobia he couldn't shake.

The teenager was gone when he threw the door open and walked through the common area. Surprisingly, no one was around. Robert thanked his lucky stars and hustled to his room. Locking the door behind him, he settled on the small cot and cracked the first beer.

Robert guzzled the first half and came up for a breath. He didn't get lightheaded from beer anymore. On the contrary, when he drank now, he felt more aware, more in control. When the second half of the can filled his belly, he felt alive.

Voices from outside his window drew his attention. Robert was nosy and he liked to know everything going on around him so he could best avoid problems. Sitting perfectly still to hear what was said, he was startled to hear his real name.

"I finally found you, Robert Sarno." The man who somehow knew who he really was chuckled. The sound was cheerful and maddening in the same breath. Although there wasn't anything inherently sinister about the sound, it made the alcohol in his belly rear up into his throat, nonetheless. Something about it was familiar. The laugh was something that shouldn't be. "Did you think you could hide what you did forever, Robert? You knew I'd come to find you sooner or later."

Robert stiffened, his hand on a fresh can of beer. "It can't be."

"You know who I am, Robert." The voice came closer to the window. "Come and face me like a man, or like a clown, I suppose I should say." The person chuckled again, and Robert knew exactly who stood outside.

"Baldy," he whispered. "That can't be. You died over fifty years ago."

CHAPTER TWENTY-SIX

May 7th, 2018

"That's awful." Kristina turned up her nose. "Please don't call him my uncle father. This isn't an episode of Jerry Springer."

"Whatever you say, sister, cousin, wife." Jason laughed as he shoved a piece of crispy bacon in his mouth. The crunch that followed made Kristina's stomach grumble.

"You're absolutely awful." Taking the bowl of raw eggs, Kristina bumped Jason out of the way and dumped them into the skillet on top of the bacon grease. They sizzled and popped as they met the hot surface and she whisked quickly to prevent them from sticking or burning. She brought the flame down to a manageable level and within seconds, they began to look like proper scrambled eggs.

Jason snagged another piece of bacon before she could smack his hand away. "I get my winning personality from my dad who's also my cousin."

Kristina rolled her eyes. "This is all you can come up with this morning?"

"I didn't sleep well. Once I'm well rested, I'll have some better jokes for you." He handed her two plates and she put food on each of them. "Maybe. I guess it's debatable if my jokes are ever good."

"Not hardly." Kristina poured two glasses of orange juice and set one in front of him.

"These eggs are great. I could get used to you cooking for me every morning. You wanna move in?"

Kristina choked on her juice.

"Too soon?" he smirked.

"Way too soon."

Jason nodded thoughtfully, making Kristina wonder if that was another joke as she thought or if he was serious. She didn't ask to find out, feeling a bit embarrassed that she'd shot him down so easily.

"So, where is your uncle these days?"

Kristina took a bite of her bacon. After she swallowed, she tried to recall the last time she'd even spoken to the man. It had to have been around the time of her graduation, maybe eight years ago now. She didn't have a clue if he still lived in the same house or even had the same phone number. He'd never married or had any kids that she knew of, other than her. While he'd been present a lot when she was younger, as she'd reached adulthood, their contact drifted away to where it was now. Nonexistent.

"To tell the truth, I'm not really sure. I haven't seen him in a while. I know he's still a cop for Gary, Indiana, but beyond that, your guess is as good as mine."

Jason's plate was already empty. He took the dish and rinsed it in the sink, placing it in the dishwasher for later. "Guess we can go to the police department then. Maybe we can catch him there. If not, someone can point us in the right direction."

"I could just call him." Kristina offered him the rest of her food and he took it happily, devouring the last few bites as she watched. "His numbers in my phone as long as he hasn't changed it."

"Well, you should have said so in the first place," Jason chided, playfully.

"You asked where he is, not how to reach him." Kristina laughed.

Jason nodded. "Touché."

Kristina located the number in her list of contacts and hit dial.

She'd never been nervous to call her uncle Alex before, but this time her heart had a stranglehold on her chest, making her lightheaded listening to each ring on the other side. Just as she was about to hang up, the man answered.

"Hello?"

Kristina forced her mouth to work, and her words came out sounding funny to her ears. "Uncle Alex, it's Kristina. We need to talk."

The sharp intake of breath on the other end told Kristina this was a conversation he'd been dreading for a long time. "About what, sweet cakes?"

The childhood nickname brought back happy memories before she realized he was deflecting. He already knew what this was about. "About the fact that you're my father."

Jason motioned for her to put it on speakerphone so he could listen in and she obliged. It was too late now to worry about the man knowing all her dirty little secrets. He might as well be privy to this conversation as well.

"I knew you would find out someday. I really wished you wouldn't have."

"Because of the clown?" Kristina wasn't going to spare him anything. She needed answers and she needed them yesterday. He wasn't going to be able to get out of this one. "We're already well acquainted."

"What happened? I'm on my way to you." There was a rustling in the background and Kristina knew he was rushing out the door. "Did he hurt you?"

"Not yet, but not for lack of trying."

Jason rocked back in his barstool, putting the piece of furniture on two legs as he gripped the edge of the counter. Kristina almost scolded him for it, then remembered they belonged to him so if he broke them, it wouldn't affect her.

"How did he find you, Tina?" The panic in her uncle's voice was palpable. "We were all so careful to make sure that never happened."

"Grandmother."

"What?" he asked.

Kristina smiled, feeling the warmth envelope her yet again. It was like her grandmother was always around now that she'd found her. Even though she probably imagined the feeling, it still felt good. "Grandma Adelaide recognized me at the cemetery. She could feel the blood in my veins and knew it was the same blood coursing through her own when she was alive. When she noticed me, Baldy did too."

"Adelaide's dead. Are you talking about Showmen's Rest? What in God's name were you doing there?" The door slammed closed on the other end of the line.

"Baldy's dead too, but that's not stopping him, is it?" Kristina countered. "Yes, I was at Showmen's Rest. I'm a photographer and I had a job shooting the centennial anniversary ceremony for the train wreck there. Uncle Alex, I'm not home. I'm at a… friend's house. You'll have to meet us here. He can give you the address."

Jason cleared his throat and said the address.

"That's quite the neighborhood." Alex sounded impressed. "To live somewhere like that, you must have some impressive family members, young man. What's your name?"

"Jason Asher, sir."

Alex sounded like he choked. "Of *the* Asher's? Jesus Christ. Good job, Tina."

"Okay, Uncle Alex, we'll see you in a few minutes then. Bye." She hung up the phone before he could fanboy over Jason any harder.

"Awe, your uncle dad likes me!"

Kristina rolled her eyes as hard as she could manage. "Please don't say that in front of him."

Jason put his hand to his heart. "I would never."

Cleaning up from breakfast took hardly any time at all with both of them working. Everything was in the dishwasher and the counters wiped down before the buzz from the gate came over a speaker in the kitchen. Jason looked at the screen over the intercom built into the wall and hit a button allowing the car idling outside to come through. Although it was technically apartments, the opulence in each one was equal to a lavish home, easily five times the size of the apartment Kristina rented.

Her uncle parked in the visitor's space and Jason had to buzz him in again to enter the building. Three floors later by elevator and he knocked on the door.

"I'll let him in," Kristina said.

The man standing on the other side of the door had aged significantly since the last time she'd seen him. Salt and pepper hair flanked the sides of her uncle's head and wrinkles extended from the corners of his eyes and mouth. He tried to pull Kristina into a hug, but it ended up being clumsy and awkward and they both pulled away quickly.

"Come inside." She held the door open, and his eyes wandered the living space as he entered.

"Damn this place is nice." He whistled when he saw the seventy-inch TV on the living room wall and the twelve-foot ceilings above it. "I bet the football games look great on that thing."

Jason took a breath to brag, but Kristina shot him a look and his mouth closed instantly. "You're not here to talk about the Indians season, Uncle Alex. We need to know exactly what you know so I can try to stay alive."

His head hung in embarrassment. "You're right. I'm sorry." He raised his eyes and tried to smile. "I was never able to say it before, but you look so much like your mother."

Kristina blushed and she wasn't sure why. "Uncle Alex, please?"

"I don't know what I can tell you that would help, Tina. We didn't know if there was any way to stop him. That's why we hid you the way we did. I think it's too late to try that again. It was agony knowing what I knew all these years and having to pretend I didn't know it. Watching you call them mom and dad knowing they weren't. Or maybe they were. They did raise you, and they did a fantastic job. But I would've given anything for you to have called me dad. I would've cut my own arm off to have married your mom and had a family with you. Baldy ruined that for all of us." Tears filled his eyes and he blinked them away quickly. "I've always thought of you as my little girl."

"What did he do to my mother?"

Alex squirmed. "You don't really need to know that, do you?"

"I need to know everything if I'm going to fight him." Kristina felt

Jason's hand slide into hers and it gave her the confidence boost she needed to keep going. "No information's useless knowledge as far as Baldy's concerned."

"He pinned her to the wall like one of those circus wheels and threw knives at her. Only in the circus, the knife thrower always barely misses. Baldy didn't miss." He didn't stop the tears this time. He left them where they fell on his cheeks, running across his lips. "I found her after it happened and had to pretend I didn't know who she was. I almost quit the force after that."

"All the other deaths he caused that I could find have been ruled as a suicide. They couldn't have possibly thought she did that to herself." Kristina surmised.

"Nope. It was ruled as a suspicious death. It wasn't a homicide because the door was bolted from the inside. The windows were all locked too. There weren't any fingerprints in the home except for hers and mine and mine were justified because I was the lead investigator. We didn't have forensics past that back then. With nothing to go on, no evidence, and no entry point, they couldn't rule it as a homicide even though I knew exactly who did it. Didn't do any good though. It wasn't like I could go arrest the killer."

Jason squeezed her fingers.

"Did you ever see him?" she asked.

"The clown?" her uncle questioned. "No. As far as I'm aware, no one's seen him except the ones he's killing and the family members of the survivors."

"I've seen him," Jason said. "Last night he came for Kris and I woke up. I saw him in my bedroom."

Alex looked bewildered. "That's a new development. Are you related to anyone from the circus?"

"Not that I'm aware of. I guess it's not outside the realm of possibility since Kris had no idea she was related to them either." Jason moved behind Kristina and put his hands on her shoulders, massaging lightly. "But that was the only time I saw him, and I've had multiple opportunities."

"If you are, you may be the best way to keep her safe, because you can see what's coming too," Alex said.

"Or it might have just been a fluke." Kristina didn't want to get her hopes up.

"That could be as well," Alex agreed. "What have you discovered so far?"

Kristina shrugged, knocking Jason's hand loose from her. "Not a whole lot. Only that Baldy systematically murdered every person related to the original four men who caused the crash. The Casters told us he came to each of the survivors and asked them for permission to seek revenge. Apparently, they were all so hurt and angry that they granted it."

"Why can't the descendants just revoke permission then?" Alex asked, scratching his thinning hair. "If he needed their permission to kill, then it seems reasonable to assume if he doesn't have their permission, he can't do it anymore."

This was a possibility Kristina and Jason hadn't thought of. How many descendants of the survivors were there? Could they feasibly contact all of them and convince them to demand the clown to back down? Would he just kill them for standing against them like he did when Matilda gave her too much information? The woman said she was the only one he still spoke to because she was the only one who listened. Did that mean he no longer cared what the descendants had to say about anything? Might be worth a shot to speak to the Casters again.

"That's a brilliant suggestion, Uncle Alex. We're going to need to make some phone calls to see if it could work. I'm in touch with a few people who could help with that."

Alex stood and eyed the watch on his wrist. "Will you please keep me informed? I'll help however I can, but I have a shift starting in an hour."

Kristina nodded. "I will. Thank you for telling me about my mother. I wish I could've met her."

"You should know, Tina. Your mother loved you more than anything in the world. There wasn't anything she wouldn't have done for you. When she had to give you up, it tore her apart. She didn't fight when Baldy came for her. She didn't try to save her life like you're trying to do. She just welcomed death. I think she believed it would all end with her and he would go back to wherever he came from. I wish she was right about that."

Alex headed for the door, turning away when the emotions threatened to take him over again. Kristina wished she could hug him and give him some solace, but things were just too strained between them right now. Maybe someday, though. Perhaps when this was all over, they could get to know each other again with no secrets holding them back.

"I love you, Uncle Alex," she said as he reached for the knob.

He nodded but didn't respond. Jason stood and walked to the intercom box to buzz him out when he reached the downstairs door. When they were alone again, Kristina folded herself in against his chest, breathed in his scent, and tried to work through her emotions.

Jason hit the button and let the man out. He wouldn't need him for the gate.

"Do you think the Casters will want to talk again?" he asked.

"I don't know, but we need to try." Accepting there was more between them than there was before, Kristina raised her face and met Jason halfway in a kiss that was both sweet and terrifying. Admitting to herself that she loved this man as much as he seemed to love her was a revelation she wasn't prepared for. To say she valued his strength and understanding was an understatement. The need to say it out loud overwhelmed her and she searched his eyes for the courage to give voice to the truth. "Remember when you said you loved me?"

"Twice as I recall." Jason smiled and went for a second kiss. She placed a hand to his mouth to stop him.

"I need to tell you something."

Jason's eyes fell. "If you're going to say you're not ready for that, I totally get it."

"I love you too, Jason."

CHAPTER TWENTY-SEVEN

January 15th, 1968

The chuckling continued. Robert fled from his room, leaving the beer he'd worked so hard for behind. The halfway house was empty. The usually bright space was dim and alien. Fluorescent lights blinked overhead, the bulbs humming in his ears. The TV that was perpetually turned on, was smashed in, sitting lifeless in the corner. Windows that would be thrown open in the spring to let in fresh breezes had slabs of wood nailed over them and light didn't creep in from between the slats.

"You can't hide from me, Robert." The voice was closer, inside the house somehow. "Are you trying to play hide and seek?'

Looking down at his feet, Robert saw the linoleum tiles he'd hated since moving in. They were in a checkerboard pattern of alternating black and white squares. Except now the squares were faded and dusty, the white almost the same shade as the black. Robert scuffed his shoe across the surface trying to see the original freshness, but the filth didn't budge. What the hell happened to this place? It was normal moments ago when he'd arrived. This dilapidation couldn't have occurred this quickly. Someone had to be messing with him.

Robert slowed his pace and looked around more carefully. Where were the damn drug addicts? This had to be their work. They were trying to scare him to death so they could take his beer. The kid said earlier that he would die in his room and they would take all his shit. A slow smile spread across Robert's face as the realization dawned on him.

"All right, you got me." He slapped his thigh and laughed. "You can all come out now. I have enough beer for everyone."

He thought if he offered to share, the gig would be up, and things would turn back to normal. But no one jumped out from behind the old couch. No one came out of the shadows to take responsibility for the gag. Sweat broke out across the old man's forehead which he wiped away quickly, noticing how cold and clammy his skin felt beneath his fingers.

"Where you at, Jasper? Helena? Murphy? I know you all did this." He all but begged the other lowlifes to appear. "Come on out so we can get drunk."

"No one's here to save you, Robert." The voice was just behind him now. "Just like no one was there to save them."

Robert turned around quickly, swinging at the vacant air where he'd heard the man speaking. He was still alone. No one was in the room with him. The doors in the hallway all slammed shut at once, the one to the kitchen followed suit, trapping him in the living space with nowhere to go. His body began to shake. This wasn't a prank. Those assholes couldn't have put something together this good. They would have given up halfway through to get high then forgot what they'd been doing altogether.

"Do you know what it smells like when a human body burns?" Behind him again, the voice taunted, just out of reach.

Robert quickly turned around, trying to catch the culprit in the act, but as before, no one was there. "Why are you doing this? I'm just an old man. I mean no harm to anyone."

The voice was in his ear. "It smells different than anything else you've ever smelled. It's a pungent odor, sickening. Nothing like beef or pork. Add to that the rancid smell of hair catching flame, curling up on itself, then melting away completely. It's something your nose could never forget." It moved to his other ear. "You wouldn't know. You and the other dealt the death sentence then went on your way. You didn't stick around to see the fruits of your labor. You were too worthless to go down with the ship you crippled."

"We didn't mean to kill anyone," Robert exclaimed. "We just wanted to inconvenience them a little. "It was the second in command's fault, truth be told. Yeah! Gregory, that was his name. If you want someone to blame, you should blame him. If he hadn't treated us so badly, he hadn't embarrassed us in front of everyone, we wouldn't have done anything at all. But we had to teach him a lesson. You should understand that. That's what you're doing after all, right? Teaching me a lesson?"

The voice was back in his right ear. "Lessons are learned where lessons are due. You broke the rules, and you were dealt with appropriately. Gregory broke no rules. There were no lessons to be learned except to trust one's gut when it came to men like you."

"Men like me?"

The clown chuckled again from behind him. "Murderers."

"I'm not a murderer."

More chuckles and the meager light in the room lowered until Robert couldn't see his own hand in front of his face. The furniture disappeared. The room became an echo chamber of darkness. Robert's breathing hitch and he caught himself panting. He opened his eyes as wide as he could trying to find a single fractal of light to make out his surroundings, but there was none to be had.

"You killed eighty-six people." The clown moved in front of him without him noticing. "You wounded nearly double that."

Robert shook his head. "I didn't kill anyone, Baldy. Maurice came up with the plan to stall the train. He knew how to mix things together to make the parts rust. I didn't know any of that stuff. I wasn't smart, I was just a thief. He poured it onto the train, not me. I'm not responsible."

The maniacal chuckles grew louder. "Everyone says they aren't responsible. Not one of you had any remorse for what you did. Even when you die for your sins, you'll still believe you're treated unfairly. When you're burning in hell, you make sure to tell whatever demon is assigned to you how unfairly you've been treated and see how that goes for you."

"What are you going to do to me, Baldy?" Robert asked. "You were always so good to me before. You helped me do my makeup and taught me how to be a clown. You were patient and took your time."

"I'm still patient. Do you know how long it's taken me to find all four of you?" The lights raised enough for Robert to make out the white face. "And it'll take me even longer to hunt down every person you and the other men have sired and commit them to the flames with you."

"I don't have any children." Robert spat the words out like he was taking away some of the clown's fun.

"You don't, but the others do."

"Leave me be and go get them." Robert tried to bargain with the ghost. "They probably deserve it more."

The clown threw his head back and laughed. "So sure of yourself."

"I'm an old man, I can't do any more damage. You should go after the young ones, the ones who still have the time and strength to commit crimes. Your efforts would be better suited to killing them before they commit new crimes than to kill an old man past his prime."

The lights grew brighter yet in the room and a single table stood in the center. Robert saw the light came from the lantern sitting on top. The orange glow grew as the wick soaked up more oil from the reservoir. It was the same type of lantern used on the Hagenbeck-Wallace circus train back when he'd been employed with them. The same type that exploded in the crash and burned all the performers alive who didn't die when the engine of the second train tore their sleeping car apart.

"No..." Robert whispered, taking a step back to get far away from the table.

"What's wrong, Robert," the clown asked, bracing his white gloved hand behind the man's back to prevent him from moving away. "Not afraid of a little flame, are you?"

Robert whimpered, pressing hard against the hand of the clown.

The flame of the lantern reflected in his pupils, dancing even though the air was stagnant in the boarded-up room. Pressing him forward, the clown corralled him closer to the table. Robert's feet scuffed across the floor, trying to prevent himself from moving, but the clown was inhumanly strong, his hand like a steel bar, cold and unwavering.

Before long, the wood pressed into Robert's thighs and he braced his hands on the surface to keep from falling forward. The lantern was only inches from his face, and he could feel the heat from the flame on his nose.

"I want you to imagine what those people felt when the oil coated their skin. Think about what went through their minds when it ignited, and they could smell themselves burning. What was it like when they heard the screams of their friends as they died?"

As if on cue, screams arose around them, pained pitiful sounds of the dying and injured. Robert lifted his hands and slammed them over his ears to block the sound. Baldy used that moment to nudge him from behind, knocking him face first onto the table. The lantern wobbled as if it would fall, and Robert held his breath before it righted itself.

"Are you ready to face your demons, Robert Sarno?" Baldy pressed his hand to the side of Robert's head, holding him against the warm wood.

"No! I don't want to die! I don't deserve to die like this!"

Baldy chuckled and the sound made the beer in Robert's stomach bubble to the surface, coating the table in front of his face with bile laced with alcohol.

"Splendid," Baldy said. "The alcohol will help the flame burn hotter."

Taking the lantern in his other hand, Baldy tilted it on its side, spilling the kerosene down Robert's face and neck. It rolled down his back and onto his legs, soaking his clothes. It seemed to never empty, forming puddles around his feet. When Baldy set it down again, it was just as full as it had been before, and the flame was just as alive.

"How do you like the feel of it on your skin? Is it refreshing?"

"No! No! No!" Robert screeched, trying to break free.

The flame on the lantern came to life, shooting towards the ceiling, wild and out of control. Baldy chuckled and Robert's pupils grew large, his breathing came in bursts, and his heart was on the verge of exploding.

"Now where did I put my marshmallows?" Baldy asked, patting his pockets theatrically before grinning at his own joke.

Taking the lantern into his free hand, Baldy admired the flame. When he was sure Robert watched, he dropped it on the floor. The reservoir shattered and the puddles of kerosene caught fire. It quickly spread up Robert's legs and Baldy released him to try to extinguish himself.

"Whoopsie. I'm so clumsy!" Baldy held his hands up just like he would do during a show when he would pretend to be inelegant to make the kids laugh. No one laughed now. But Robert screamed.

The man threw his body around the room, rolling against the walls, and screeching with everything he had. His body was fully engulfed, and the clown did a little happy dance, kicking his feet in the air and grinning ear to ear. When Robert fell to the floor and the noises stopped, Baldy approached him, looked at the melted, blackened body, and tilted his head to the side watching the flames extinguish themselves.

"Well, that was very entertaining, Robert. You put on one hell of a final show, but as they say, the show must go on."

THE FIRE DEPARTMENT DEPLOYED THEIR BIGGEST TRUCK TO TRY TO PUT OUT the flames that erupted at the halfway house for criminals and drug addicts on the bad side of town. It was a three-alarm blaze and most of the building was already destroyed. Worries were that it would spread to other buildings in close vicinity and so they worked tirelessly to get it under control.

The occupants of the home stood on the opposite side of the street watching their sanctuary disappear little by little. An officer took statements from each person.

"Do you know how the fire started?" he asked the teenager with facial piercings and dark eyes.

"Yeah. It was the old guy, Frank." The teenager met the officer's eyes with a soulless gaze. "I told that fucker to give me one of his beers. He said he'd rather burn alive than give any of us anything. I laughed at him and told him he was just an old fucker, and I didn't want his shit anyway."

"What happened then?" the officer prodded.

"He went out to the tool shed and came back with a gas container they use for the snow blower. I asked him what he was doing but he told me to shut the hell up. He dumped it all over himself then lit a match. I ain't never seen a fire burn so fast. I got the hell outta there and everyone else came out behind me. I didn't think the old man had the balls to do something like that."

The officer nodded. He'd seen things like this before. An elderly person with no prospects, tired of having nothing, takes their own life in a way that draws attention to themselves. It was like a final fuck you to a world who didn't give a shit about them. The officer thought it was sad that anyone thought they had to do something like this, that their lives were worth so little. When he finished with the statements, he called a bus to take the residents to another state-run house where they could stay until other lodgings were found for them. He would have to wait until the corpse was located in the shambles of the burned building to make a positive identification to inform his family of his passing.

CHAPTER TWENTY-EIGHT

May 7th, 2018

"Mr. Caster gave you his business card, right?" Kristina asked Jason. The kitchen fell dead silent after she confessed she was in love with him, and she needed to change the subject to feel less awkward. She expected Jason to be happy, or say something, but he didn't and now she just felt stupid. Maybe she misread him and shouldn't have said anything at all.

Jason shook his head as if clearing his thoughts. "Yeah, it's in my wallet."

"Can I have it?" Kristina held out her hand, a little pushier than she meant to be. Her feelings were hurt, and she was having a hard time hiding it.

"Kris, I—"

Kristina put her hand up. "Don't. I'm not interested in whatever excuse you come up with for why you think it's okay to tell me you love me, then when I start to feel secure with you, when I start to feel like you could be safe, you suddenly don't feel the same way anymore. But please, if you're just going to play games with me, stop.

I told you before, I refuse to be another name on your list of conquests."

"That's not it at all. I—"

"That's exactly what it is. I open myself to you and tell you I love you and you clam up so fast it makes my head spin." Kristina snatched the card out of his outstretched hand and took a deep breath to calm herself before she made the call. "I'll go back to my apartment tomorrow. I don't need you to look after me just so you can try to get lucky."

Jason grabbed her arm and spun her around. Whatever she was about to say died on her lips when he claimed her mouth. He wasn't gentle and he wasn't savoring the moment. He thrust his tongue inside her mouth like she was the last glass of water on earth, and he was parched. Running his hands down her back, pressing into her skin hard, he splayed his fingers at her waist and gripped her ass in his fists.

Kristina moaned into his mouth, feeling the moisture pooling between her legs.

Jason broke the kiss. "Close your damn mouth and listen to me for two seconds. I never expected you to fall in love with me. I don't deserve you. I've been nothing but a whore and you're so perfect. I didn't respond when you said you loved me because my brain was processing what you said, it was trying to convince me I heard you correctly. If you believe I could lie and say I love you when I don't, you don't know me very well. I've never once told another woman I loved them. Not. One. Time. There's only ever been you."

Grabbing the card away from her, Jason dared her to say something, but her tongue was tied.

"Let me take care of this for you. Sit down, relax, get ready for what's coming because tonight, I'm going to show you how much I love you."

Kristina's legs felt like rubber under her. Hobbling to the couch, she did as she was told and took a seat. Jason grabbed a blanket over the back of the couch and draped it over her lap, placed a pillow beside her, and kissed her on the forehead. The roughness was gone, and Kristina wanted it back. But things needed to be done. Squeezing her thighs together, she willed the heat to a simmer and watched him dial the number on the card.

"Hello Mr. Caster, this is Jason Asher," he paused. "Yes, of course, Norman."

There were a few moments of silence while Jason listened to whatever the man said, and Kristina wished he'd had the presence of mind to put the call on speaker.

"Yes sir, that seems like a very appropriate amount for the check." Jason saw her looking and figured out what she wanted, switching the phone over so she could listen in.

"I'm so very glad you called us today. The wife and I were just talking about you."

"Oh? That's funny because Kristina and I were just talking about you as well. We actually have a few things we would like to discuss with the two of you if you don't mind."

He paced as he spoke, glancing at her every few seconds and giving her a smile.

"That sounds delightful. We're headed to the cemetery to put flowers on Henry Caster's grave. Today's his birthday. You're both welcome to join us if you'd like. I understand if Ms. Perdue would rather stay as far away from there as possible, but he's still my family, and I must go." Norman Caster's voice sounded pleasant. He didn't seem to harbor any negative feelings about the loss of the photos. Kristina was happy Jason was able to resolve that for them.

Looking at her with a questioning expression, Kristina realized Jason waited for her to say yes or no to respond to Mr. Caster's invitation. He was right, she would rather not go back to the cemetery since that was the reason this all started in the first place, but she needed to tell them about what her uncle suggested. She gave Jason the thumbs up and hoped she wouldn't live to regret it.

"We can do that, Mr. Caster. What time would you like us there?"

"We'll be arriving around noon. If you hurry, you could get there around the same time." Bea's voice could be heard in the background, but Kristina couldn't make out what she was saying. "Beatrice says she'll pack enough sandwiches for the both of you. We're having a picnic lunch there."

"That would be delightful. We'll see you soon." Jason ended the call and clutched the phone in his closed hands. "You sure about this?"

Kristina nodded. "We can't waste any time."

"Yeah, but I feel like we're walking into the lion's den. What if this is exactly what Baldy wanted so he can kill you there?" Jason laid the phone down and joined her on the couch. Kristina lifted the edge of the blanket and he slid under it with her, caressing her thigh through her silky pajama pants.

"Then so be it. I have to face him eventually. Might as well be there."

"I don't like this." Jason didn't budge when she moved her side of the blanket and got to her feet. "I think we should wait until we know more before we get reckless."

Kristina smiled and exhaled sharply through her nose. "We're never going to know enough to be fully prepared against him. There are always going to be variables we don't know. We just have to hope for the best and try our damndest. I'm going to get dressed. You should probably take a shower. You need to shave that beard you're trying to grow."

"You don't like it?" Jason tugged on the short hairs.

"Not even a little bit."

Jason tossed his head back in mock disappointment. "Fine." He exaggerated the word so it sounded like a complaint, but it was made lightheartedly.

KRISTINA FELT A SICKENING FEELING IN HER STOMACH THE CLOSER THEY got to Showmen's Rest. The bravery she'd shown back at Jason's apartment had worn off and now she felt apprehensive and afraid. Another three blocks and they'd be passing through those iron gates. The stone elephants would greet them just inside and she'd be at the mercy of a homicidal ghost clown. She wasn't ready to forfeit her life— not when she'd just found love. Internally, she knew she'd fight like hell if it came down to it.

"You doing okay over there?" Jason's questions pulled her out of her own thoughts.

"I'm fine. Just a little scared." She saw the fence in the distance and her heart beat a bit faster.

"I'd tell you not to worry, but I guess you'd know I was full of shit, huh?" He grinned at her.

"Yeah, just a little bit."

"We don't have to do this, Kris," Jason said. "Say the word and I'll turn this car around and we'll go back home. I'll take you to Paris, or Italy, or anywhere else you'd like to go. We'll just keep moving and Baldy the psychopathic clown won't be able to keep up."

Kristina laughed. "He's a ghost, Jason. It's not like he needs to buy airline tickets. I'm pretty sure he can materialize anywhere he wants to be, and that would include anywhere we run away to. This needs to end. I want to have a life where I'm not running scared. I don't want to end up like Collin."

Jason cringed. "I don't want that either."

"I want to have kids and not worry about how Baldy's going to kill them." She looked at him wistfully. "I'd love to see which one of us our kids would look like."

Swallowing hard, Jason pulled on his collar. "Kids?"

"Someday, maybe." Kristina looked out the window as he pulled into the parking area. "Not while I'm waiting to die, though."

The Casters got out of their Lincoln Continental when they saw Jason and Kristina pull in. They were dressed casually in jeans and tennis shoes, looking like ordinary people compared to the previous times they'd met. The first time being when they were dressed in period clothes from 1918 and the second at the paper when they wore business apparel, looking like a million dollars. They slowly sauntered over to where the younger couple stood, Norman leaning heavily on a cane while Beatrice gripped his arm tightly.

"Ms. Perdue, it's so nice to see you again and know you're still well. We've been worrying about you greatly. Mr. Asher, we're pleased to see you're taking such good care of the young lady. It was very nice for you to join us here today. We have a basket in the car with the food and a bouquet of flowers if you'd be so kind as to fetch them for us?"

"No problem." Jason rushed over to the car and pulled open the rear door, collecting the items in his arms.

"How are you holding up, Ms. Perdue?" Beatrice asked with a genuine smile.

"We took your advice and visited Matilda." Kristina wasn't sure if they knew she was gone or not, so she treaded water carefully.

"I do hope she was helpful," Bea said. "The hospital called and told us what befell her. They believe she did those awful things to herself, but I suppose we know better than that, don't we?"

Kristina frowned. "It was Baldy. He was angry she told us things he didn't want her to say. She told me who my real family is, and it turns out my biological father is still in my life after all."

The ground was soft and uneven. When Beatrice stumbled and almost took her husband down with her, Kristina took her opposite arm and the old woman looked at her appreciatively. "My balance just isn't what it used to be. Getting old's a burden." She looked at Kristina as if she regretted her words, but she pretended not to notice the slight.

"What is it you wished to speak to us about, dear?" Norman asked. "Hopefully something happy and not about that dreadful clown business."

Kristina bit her tongue. Was there anything else to talk about? "I'm sorry, but it is about the clown. Although, depending on how you look at it, it's happy too. We have an idea about how to get him to stop trying to kill me." The elephants towered over them on either side, their trunks faithfully down, mourning those no longer alive. Kristina envied their ability to stand strong after so many years. They were untouched by the elements, as clean and solid as the day they were molded, and they would remain that way for hundreds of years to come.

The stone markers were at their feet. There were so many marked unknown. Kristina was struck again by how unfair it was that these people didn't even have a proper headstone proclaiming who they were. They died the way they lived, shielded behind a mask of ambiguity, their identities hidden from the outside world. Did it bother them that no one knew who they were? Were they sad their families didn't know where their bodies lay and never visited them? Kristina guessed there was no way to truly know.

"Dear, I know you're desperate for a solution to this mess, but people have been trying to outwit Baldy for a hundred years now. He always wins in the end." Norman pulled the party to a halt when Henry's grave lay at their feet. "Hello, Grandfather, happy birthday."

Out of respect for the dead man, Kristina lowered her eyes. She clasped her hands together before her and said a short prayer for the man beneath their feet. Jason handed the flowers to Mrs. Caster and she placed them gingerly below the headstone. It was a large collection of flowers with daisies and a purple flower Kristina didn't recognize. Baby's breath was mixed in between making a breathtaking arrangement.

Norman closed his eyes and knelt, placing his palm on the headstone. "Sometimes, I feel like I can hear him talking to me when we're here."

Beatrice turned to Kristina. "While my husband communes with the dead, tell me about your idea. I also have something to tell you that we should have told you before."

Jason sat the basket down and came to Kristina's side.

"My uncle—"

"Who's really her father." Jason completed the sentence eliciting a look from Kristina.

"He asked why, if Baldy came to all the survivors to ask for permission to take revenge against the responsible parties, why can't you all revoke it now? It makes sense if he cares about how you all feel about what he's doing, he might care if you tell him to stop."

Norman got to his feet. "Baldy cared about what the survivors thought. We aren't the survivors. They're all dead now. You saw what he did to Matilda for giving you information. What do you think he would do to us if we stood against him? I can't put my wife at risk like that. Especially when there's only one person left in the bloodlines he's targeting. I'm sorry, I think you're a very nice girl and I wish I could help, but I have to put my family first."

Bea made a noise and her husband looked at her quizzically.

"Norman, can we at least talk about the possibility?" she asked.

"It's a very logical question and we're old. We've lived our lives and we've had a great time doing it. Look at these two kids. They're just starting out and they have so much ahead of them. Would you really let them die so we could have maybe ten years more?"

Jason looked back and forth between the two. "How many of you are left?"

"Survivor's children and grandchildren?" Norman asked. There are three now that Matilda has left us."

"Who is the third?" Kristina asked. "If we have any hope of doing this, we should have all of you here."

Beatrice gave her husband a loving look, imploring him to be gentle. "Him." She pointed at Jason.

"Me?" Jason pointed at himself. "I think you're a bit confused. "I have a very large family. I can't be a descendant, if I was, all my family would be too."

Kristina looked at Jason. She was thoroughly confused.

CHAPTER TWENTY-NINE

July 17th, 1985

Scott Brooks paced back and forth in the hospital corridor. His hands trembled and every noise he heard made him jumpy. His wife, Cora, had been in labor for over twenty-four hours and things weren't looking good for her or the baby. Every time a doctor rushed through the hall, Scott feared the worse.

The waiting room was too small and claustrophobic for his liking. The chairs, although designed to be comfortable, were too confining. No matter how many times the nurse told him to take a seat and calm down, he couldn't bring himself to do it. Cora needed him to be ready if they called him in.

This was their first child, and they already knew it was a boy. As a couple, they'd spent the last eight months buying baby clothes and painting a nursery. Everything was in hues of baby blue and they'd brought the perfect onesie for him to wear home. It was a navy-blue striped outfit with the words, *daddy's little slugger,* emblazoned on the front. Scott couldn't wait to hold him in his arms.

The doctor pushed through the heavy sterile doors wearing a solemn expression on her pretty face. "Mr. Brooks?"

"I'm here!" Scott rushed back down the hall to where she waited and noted the dark red stains on her scrubs. "Is my wife okay?"

"Mr. Brooks, perhaps we should sit down."

Scott's body went numb. His tongue stuck to the roof of his mouth. He tried to get to the chairs before his body could give out on him. From the set of her mouth and the dull look in her eyes, he already knew what she was going to tell him, and he didn't want her to speak. The longer he could draw it out, the longer he could pretend it wasn't true.

Sitting in the chair right across from him the doctor took a deep breath and Scott recognized the doom in her voice. "She's going to be all right. Right?"

"No, Mr. Brooks." She slowly shook her head from side to side as she voiced the words. "As you know, we took her in for an emergency cesarean section. Your son was breach, and his heart rate was very low. Unfortunately, while we were inside of her getting him out, she hemorrhaged. We didn't notice the blood because it came from the bottom of her uterus and we were focused on the top." She placed a clean hand on his thigh. "I did everything I possibly could to save your wife's life but there was just too much bleeding."

Scott broke down, placing his hands over his face. He howled in agony over the loss. Cora was his everything. They'd been dating since high school and she waited for him while he was in the Navy. When he introduced her to his father, Gregory, the man gave his son the seal of approval, loving her like a daughter instantly. Now his dad was gone, and so was she. How was he supposed to raise a baby without her?

"How's my son?" He wasn't sure how he managed the words. It sounded like they were coming from someone else's mouth. A wave of resentment passed through him. How come the infant got to live but Cora didn't? How dare he take a breath as she took her last.

"He's going to be fine." She gave a small smile. "He's very strong and wants to survive. Do you want to see him?"

Scott hesitated. "Not yet. I'm not ready. Can I just sit here for a little while? Can I see my wife?"

The doctor nodded. "Yes, you can see her. Come with me."

Following the woman through the doors, Scott imagined Cora's cold form on the operating table. He wanted to take her hand, kiss her forehead, and tell her he loved her. He wished with all his heart she was Snow White, just waiting for true love's kiss to rise from her deathbed anew. But fairy tales weren't real. Dead was dead.

She brought him to the last door in the surgical wing and turned to him before she opened the door. "Mr. Brooks, your wife's gone. I want you to go in there knowing this will be your chance to tell her goodbye. I don't know if a spirit lingers after death, but I like to believe they stay with their bodies until they see their loved ones. If you believe that, know that she can hear whatever you say to her and tell her you love her so she can move on."

Scott nodded, stepping closer to the door.

When the doctor opened it, Scott's eyes were drawn to the puddle of blood beneath the gurney. How did no one know she was bleeding out? There was so much blood. The white sheet was pulled over her head, revealing nothing of her except her form. Scott ached to pull the sheet back and see her pretty face. Once again, he imagined her lavender eyes opening and smiling at him, telling him he was a dad now.

No one he'd ever known had that shade of eyes and he told her all the time how special she was. He'd joked with her throughout the pregnancy that their son would inherit that strange shade of eye color and she wouldn't be the only one with them anymore. She'd laughed back and said she didn't mind that at all.

"Mr. Brooks?" The doctor was already poised to pull the sheet back and he was still loitering at the door. "We don't have to do this if you're not ready."

"I'm ready."

The sheet turned down and the face he expected to see wasn't there. The flesh was sallow and gray. Her lips that were always a pale shade of pink, like a blooming rosebud in the spring, were dark purple. Scott sucked in a breath.

"Why does she look like that?"

The doctor clasped her hands in front of her. "Her heart isn't beating anymore. When the blood stops pumping it begins to pool at the lowest point. So, the parts of her you see look pale."

Scott quickly kissed his wife's forehead and took a step back. He didn't like the way her cold skin felt on his lips. It felt like kissed a wax duplicate of his wife, not the real person. He wiped his mouth on the back of his hand expecting there to be a residue. "I love you so much, Cora. I would do anything to trade places with you and let you live."

The door opened and the coroner came in with two other men. "Oh, I'm sorry. I didn't know anyone was in with her. We can wait in the hall." He turned and started to leave.

"No," Scott called out. "We're done here. You can cover her back up, doctor."

Pushing past the waiting men, Scott made it back into the hall. His stomach rolled and before the doctor could rejoin him, he bent over and vomited on the floor. He stayed braced on his knees, staring into the fluid. The doctor put a gentle hand on his back as he straightened.

"Don't worry about that. We'll get someone to clean that up."

Scott licked the bile off his bottom lip. "Can you take me back to the waiting room? I need a few minutes before I can see the baby."

"Absolutely. Right this way."

She walked at a fast clip and Scott made no effort to keep up with her. As long as he could see the white lab coat ahead of him, he wasn't worried. She waited for him when they returned to the maternity waiting area. The little storks holding bundles in their beaks on the walls made him nauseous all over again.

"Let the receptionist know when you're ready and someone will bring your son to you."

Scott looked at the younger girl sitting behind the desk and she smiled at him. "What if I can't take care of the baby? What then?"

The doctor softened. "Mr. Brooks, I know this is going to be a huge adjustment. Especially without your wife. But it's not impossible to be a single father. Your son's going to grow and the older he gets, the easier it'll be. I think you'll be a great father."

Apprehension overwhelmed him. "I'm not sure you're right."

"I have to get back to my other patients. Julia will help you as soon as you're ready."

The receptionist waved and he ignored her. He sunk into one of the plush chairs as the doctor disappeared. Three chairs down, a couple around his same age sat holding each other. He watched them, saw how the man caressed the arm of the woman, how they whispered to each other, and seemed so excited. They looked exactly how he and Cora looked when she went into labor.

Another doctor came through the doors and knelt in front of the couple. "Mr. and Mrs. Asher?" The couple got to their feet and the doctor crossed to them. Scott watched with rapt fascination to see how it should've gone when the doctor came to him. He knew the doctor was going to say the baby arrived, was healthy, and momma was doing fine. He resented that family's happiness when his was gone.

"I'm sorry, but the baby's heart stopped beating midway through delivery."

Mrs. Asher began to cry.

"I'm so terribly sorry." The doctor looked like he didn't know what to say.

Scott got to his feet. "It sure seems like a lot of people are dying in this hospital tonight." He looked at the couple. "They just told me my wife's dead and I'm stuck raising the thing all by myself now."

Mr. Asher looked at Scott with tears in his eyes. "We can't have children. We were adopting a son to raise as our own."

"I'm never going to be a mom," Mrs. Asher wailed.

Scott knew what the resolution was. He didn't even want to see the baby who killed his Cora, let alone raise it. These people wanted a son, and he just so happened to have one.

Taking the seat beside him, he leaned in. "You want mine? It's a boy."

The couple was quick to agree, and the hospital sent someone over to do the appropriate paperwork. Scott and Cora planned to name the infant Gregory after Scott's father, but now he didn't care what he was called. Bentleigh Asher, the baby's new mother, chose the name Jason. Scott didn't even look at the bundle as they placed him in her arms. He wasn't his anymore.

He walked out of the hospital and drove home, numb to everything around him. Back in the house, the first thing he did was walk into the nursery, then he cried. He sobbed until he didn't have any tears left and then began to destroy the room. The crib was reduced to a pile of broken wood, the same with the changing table. He scraped under the edge of the wallpaper and pulled it from the walls. When the room was no longer recognizable, he went to the garage and got a tow rope. He looped it over the rafters and stood on the hood of his car.

"I love you, Cora. We'll be together again soon." He kissed his fingers and pressed them to his heart. Then he jumped. The rope went taut and tightened around his throat. The fall wasn't hard enough to break his neck and for the next five minutes, he choked, struggling for breath until he passed out. Shortly after that, his heart stopped beating.

CHAPTER THIRTY

May 7th, 2018

Beatrice Caster put her hand on Jason's arm. "I recognized your eyes. It's a very well-known fact that Gregory Brook's son Scott married a woman who had lavender eyes. I met her a few times at the get togethers we had here when they would come with Gregory."

"But I'm not adopted," Jason insisted.

"Call your parents, honey." Beatrice patted him again. "Maybe they didn't want to tell you."

Jason stepped away and pulled out his phone. His expression was hard to read. "When the call was answered, he didn't tiptoe around the topic. "Mom, am I adopted?"

His serious expression dropped the longer the silence stretched on.

"Why didn't you tell me?"

Beatrice nodded to Kristina with a smile. "I knew it. That eye color is too distinctive to have popped up in another family. I knew Scott's wife died giving birth to a baby boy and he took his own life shortly after. The Ashers must have adopted him after that. So, Jason's a direct descendant from Gregory Brooks, the Hagenbeck-Wallace Circus's second in command."

"That's why he was able to see Baldy then when he came after me," Kristina whispered.

Jason stepped away from the group. From the bits of the one side conversation Kristina could hear, he begged his mother to tell him how he came to be in their family, but it didn't seem like she was ready to discuss it with him. His silhouette looked defeated as he stood under a large willow tree bordering the Showmen's League's property line. He braced himself against the trunk while the branches swayed around him with the slight breeze. She started to go to him but thought better of it when she saw his shoulders quake. A lifetime of lies laid bare all because of her.

"He'll be okay." Beatrice patted her arm in a motherly way and turned to rejoin her husband near Henry's graveside. The old man was in a crouch, tracing the raised letters with his fingertips. His knees jutted out like a frog and Kristina was worried he wouldn't be able to get back to his feet. The cane lay on the ground beside him.

"You come here every year for his birthday?"

Bea nodded her head. "Oh, yes. If we don't remember our dead, who will?" Her red lips turned up in a smile. "Besides, I think they like it. I would imagine it gets rather boring here with the same old spirits to talk to day after day."

Kristina pondered the statement, envisioning a bunch of ghosts sitting around a campfire exchanging tales. "You believe they're all still here? There isn't a circus performer heaven?"

Beatrice laughed, putting her dainty hand to the edge of her mouth. "I'm sure some of them have moved on, but most still linger. They died traumatically and didn't even have proper graves with their names on their stones. I can feel them walking beside us every now and again. Sometimes I can even see them."

Norman got to his feet with some effort and a grunt. "Looks like another storm's coming in." Holding a hand above his eyes, he surveyed the dark clouds overhead. "I hope it holds out so we can have our picnic."

The willow branches completely hid Jason from sight now. Kristina held back as Bea opened the basket and handed the large blanket to her husband to spread on the ground. A feeling of dread crept into her stomach as they walked, and it was reaching a point that couldn't be ignored. Bending at the waist, she searched the ropes of leaves, hoping to get a glimpse of Jason but there was nothing. She couldn't hear his voice anymore either and she was getting worried.

"Dear?" Bea questioned, settling herself on the ground.

"Did you see Jason wander off? He was just under the tree a moment ago." Taking a few steps forward, Kristina squinted, but it didn't help.

With a large sandwich in his hands, Norman waved to her to sit and eat. "I'm sure he'll be along any minute now. Seemed like a pretty heated conversation he was having. He probably just needs some space."

That didn't seem like Jason at all. Kristina wasn't sure he knew the definition of the word space.

"I'm just going to check on him. I'll be right back."

Beatrice swallowed her first bite and raised a hand up to stop her. "Don't wander too far, dear. There are a great many spirits in this place and one in particular who would love to get you alone."

Kristina's stomach soured.

Jason wasn't under the tree anymore. Pushing the whip like limbs away from her face, Kristina called out his name and received no answer. The further in she went, the darker it became. The leaves blended together, moving faster in the encroaching storm. The noise they made as they smacked into each other was almost deafening while inside the cocoon of branches.

"Jason? Where the hell are you?" Kristina screamed with her hands around her mouth like a megaphone. "This isn't funny."

A branch whipped across her face, slashing a cut under her eye. It stung and blood welled up instantly, dripping down her cheeks. Daylight disappeared, all there was to see was the great tree that hadn't seemed this big from outside.

"Jason, you need to answer me, now!" Tripping on a raised root, Kristina went down hard, hitting both knees on the knobbed wood of the roots.

"Jason, Jason, Jason!"

Freezing, Kristina felt her heart beating in her throat. That wasn't Jason's voice, nor was it the Caster's. The first thunderclap sounded like a bass drum being pelted in the heavens. The wind blew furiously, making the leaves blend together in a green cloud of flying razor blades. As Kristina watched, the color changed going from earthly to bright red until it was a single sheet and no longer many pieces flowing together. The canvas walls of the circus tent dropped down around her with no entry and no exit. Then the calliope began to play.

The tree disappeared entirely. Kristina placed her palms on the ground watching the transformation occurring around her. The tightrope rose into the air, obtaining a staggering height far above her head and trapeze swings lowered from the ceiling, seemingly out of nowhere. The stage lifted, three rings in all, and bleachers materialized behind her.

"Ladies and gentlemen, for our final act this evening—"

The voice bellowed, bouncing off the heavy canvas walls. A tiger roared from an elaborate cage in the first ring and twin elephants trumpeted on the far right. Baldy stood in the center, costume red and pristine barely covering his unnaturally round belly. His top hat was pulled down over one eye and he grinned with his face paint glowing under the spotlight.

Kristina struggled to get to her feet, looking for a way to escape. Clowns guarded the perimeter, arms crossed over their chests, each one staring at her, daring her to try to get past them. Upon closer inspection, each of them had the same face, Baldy's face. The bleachers that were empty moments before were now full of screaming spectators. Kristina screamed at them to help her, but they laughed and pointed like she was a part of the show. Each of them was dressed as if it were still 1918.

"What the hell's happening here?" Kristina panted, looking at each face in the tent. It was impossible to tell which person was the real Baldy and who was just a clone. Even the audience members now wore his face.

"Kristina!" Jason screamed from the other side of the tent. Kristina couldn't see him where she was, but she could hear the tremor in his voice. "Kristina, are you okay?"

The ringmaster clown sneered, raising one lip revealing his pointed teeth. "Don't you get involved, boy! The show must go on! The final act must take the center ring!"

"Go to hell!" Kristina screamed, feeling the burn in her throat from the exertion.

The clown's chuckle filled the room, assaulting her ears. "Only the wicked go to hell, I'm a savior! You and your kind go to hell, and I'll throw kerosene over your burning bodies."

"Jason! Where are you?" Lunging for the edge of the tent, the Baldy lookalikes groped for her, reaching their snake like fingers in her direction. Their eyes burned with the same silver fury of the original and their mouths dropped open with thick saliva hanging from razor sharp teeth. Kristina avoided each of them as she made her way around the tent.

"Yes! Run girl! Put on a show!" A second spotlight found her, following her progress with oohs and ahhs from the spectators. "Ladies and gentlemen, we have a real treat for you tonight! Tonight only, we have the elusive final soul! She's the last living relative of the four! The last piece of my collection! Tonight, you get to watch her die!"

The cheers and claps were overwhelming. Everyone wanted to see her die. Kristina fought to remember that the crowd wasn't real. They were all projections meant to terrify her. "Jason! Tell me where you are! I'm coming!"

"Here! I'm here!" His voice was closer than it had been.

"Hold on! I'm coming!" Kristina continued to run, scared to stop, not knowing what would be behind her if she did.

"It's your choice tonight, boys and girls! How should our main attraction die?" Baldy's voice came from every direction at once. "Should we burn her?"

"No!" The audience screamed in unison.

Baldy gasped. "No burning? How about we hang her?"

"No!" They yelled again.

Baldy twiddled his fingers from the main stage. "Well, my, my, my.

I can see you're looking for something truly spectacular, something amazing! How about we let the elephants tear her in half?"

The crowd got to their feet. "Yeah!"

There was a cage ahead of Kristina with a velvet cloth draped over the top. "Jason! Speak to me!"

The velvet cloth ruffled from hands on the inside. "Here! I'm in the cage! Get me out of here, Kris!" The elephants raised their trunks and trumpeted, the shrill noise sounded far louder than it should have. Kristina didn't look at them as she drew nearer the cage. She couldn't think about the clown's words.

"Get me out of here, Kristina!"

The velvet cloth was just out of reach now, if she stretched her fingertips, she could reach it. Just a little further and she'd have it. Another step and her palm hit the cage with a thud. She gripped the cloth in both hands and pulled. "I'm here, Jason!"

The cage door sprung open from the inside and strong phantom arms pulled her inside. Something heavy hit her on the side of the head and her vision went blurry. All she could hear was the chuckles. The eerie, evil laugh of the maniacal clown who'd captured her at last.

"Oh, sorry, girlie. Were you expecting someone else?" Baldy stood outside the cage, wrapping his gloved hands around the bars. His grin was wider than the space between the iron, looking like a crazed jack-o-lantern from where he stared at her.

Kristina got as close to him as she dared, forcing herself to be brave. "Where's my friend? What have you done with him?"

More chuckles. The air and Kristina's arms stood on end. "He's there." Baldy stepped out of Kristina's line of sight and pointed to the main support pole in the center ring. Jason was tied to it, a gag in his mouth. There was no way he'd been calling to her before, it was all an illusion. This could be fake too.

"How do I know he's real? Nothing else is real, how do I know you're not making me see something that's not there?"

"Oh, she wants proof!" Baldy slowly walked to the pole, the spotlight following his footsteps. Pulling a knife from his waist, Baldy twisted the tip into Jason's shoulder. The wound immediately began to bleed, and Jason screamed, his voice muffled from the gag, eyes wide and frantic.

"Stop!" Kristina pleaded. "I believe you!" Baldy pulled the blade free, throwing it to the ground dramatically.

"I'm tired of this game," he chuckled. "First, I'm going to kill him for getting in my way. Then I'm going to tear you limb from limb. I'm so close to the end of the show."

Ropes snaked through the cage bars and wrapped themselves around Kristina's wrists. The rough material burned, and she yelped in pain. Once secured, the door opened and two of the Baldy clones pulled her out. Each rope was attached to one of the elephant's halters and she was standing between the two massive beasts. The big male stomped his flat feet on the ground, grumbling.

"Please! Just let Jason go! Kill me or whatever but let him live!"

"Oh, doesn't that just warm my little black heart." Baldy grasped his chest and pretended to swoon." "She wants her lovers' life spared. You want to know a secret, girlie?" Baldy bent down close to Kristina's ear.

She pulled away, gagging at his rapid breath.

"My wife wasn't spared. Neither was my son. They died just like the rest. Just like me."

Baldy's mouth opened wide as he threw his head back and screamed. Jason was free and he was hanging onto the knife he buried deep into the clown's back. Baldy bucked and tried to throw him off, but he held on, refusing to let go.

The elephants began to walk in separate directions. The ropes attached to Kristina's wrists grew shorter and shorter as they pulled. When the rope was fully extended, she felt the pressure begin to build in her joints. The pain was slow at first but growing, the bones beginning to feel hot beneath her skin.

"Get out of here, Jason!" She screamed through gritted teeth. "Save yourself!"

"I'm not leaving you!"

There was a clicking noise coming from the bull elephant. Kristina struggled to see what was in front of the beast, stopping him from walking any further. The elephant bellowed, raising his trunk high.

The clicking came again and the animal stepped backward, easing the pressure on her bones.

"Tear her to pieces, you dumb animals!" Baldy yelled, still reaching for the blade. "Why did you stop?"

"The elephants respond to elephant trainers!" Norman Caster's voice raised above the clowns. He held his arms up high in front of the bull, directing him where to go. There was another man before the female, arm's raised, mimicking Norman's posture. The two men grinned at each other, pushing the animals back until Kristina fell to the ground, caressing her sore arms.

"You can't stop me! Not now! What can the two of you do?"

"Three!" Jason hissed, plunging the blade in a second time.

"Four!" A woman joined the fray. Dressed as an acrobat complete with feathers in her elaborately styled hair, the woman rushed to Kristina, untying the ropes binding her. She winked and Kristina recognized her eyes.

"Bea?"

"In the flesh, darling," the woman giggled. "Well, sort of."

"You're all too late!" Baldy screamed. "Everything's already in motion! It can't be stopped!"

People began to file into the tent through an opening that hadn't been there before. Before long, the center ring was surrounded by faces Kristina didn't recognize. Each person dirty and burned, until there wasn't a space between them.

Baldy finally shook Jason off his back. The man hit the floor hard, hitting his head against the mast and staying down. The clown lunged for Kristina, narrowly missing her foot.

"Daddy?" The little voice came from the crowd. Baldy stopped, not moving a muscle. His eyes moved to the side, slowly. "Daddy is that you?"

Getting to his feet, Baldy turned his back to Kristina. "Reggie?"

The boy was covered in soot, his face painted black from the ash. The woman holding his hand was equally dirty and staring at the clown with tears in her big, brown eyes. As he walked forward, the tent grew brighter.

A beautiful gray-haired woman held her hand out to Kristina. The warm feeling she'd felt in the cemetery enveloped her once again. Taking what was offered, she stared at the woman, curious why she looked so familiar to her.

Beatrice stepped aside and nodded to the woman. They both stepped in front of Kristina, shielding her.

"Baldy." The woman's voice was soft, but it carried. It held an air of authority that wouldn't be ignored. The entire troupe turned to her as she spoke. "This ends today. You will not hurt my granddaughter or anyone else. This has gone on long enough."

"No!" Baldy screamed, turning back towards Kristina. "She's the last one! We're so close!"

Adelaide stepped forward, one silver slipper extending beneath the blue hem of the wispy, ghostly gown she wore. "I revoke your permission for revenge!"

Baldy laughed. "One old ghost can't stop me!"

Beatrice Caster stepped forward beside Kristina's grandmother. "I revoke your permission for revenge."

Baldy's smile faltered.

Norman Caster followed suit. "I revoke your permission!"

The other man with the elephants raised his voice with the rest. "I, Henry Caster, revoke your permission."

It resounded around the ring, the unanimous decision to end the murders until there were only three voices left to be heard. Martha stepped forward and laid a gentle hand on her husband's face. She smiled at him and kissed his cheek. "I revoke your permission. I love you. Come back to us."

The boy, Baldy's son, joined his mother. "Daddy, I revoke your permission. I miss you."

Everyone turned to Jason's form still motionless on the ground.

Baldy chuckled. "You all lost. His spirit didn't stick around. Without his say, I'm free to kill her!"

First, there was a grunt, then Jason's fingers twitched. His eyebrows furrowed, and his muscles tensed. As Kristina watched, begging him to be alright, he pushed himself up on his elbows and knees. His head hung down, too weak to lift it above his shoulders. "I revoke your permission," he whispered.

A bright light shot out of Baldy from all angles.

"How dare you! All of you! Her kin caused your deaths! You're all traitors!" His skin cracked like porcelain. "She has to die!"

"We revoke your permission to kill!" All the voices rose at once.

Adelaide led Kristina to Baldy's side. She looked into her would be killer's silvery eyes, the last part of him unfractured. "It's over. Go home to your family. They need you."

With the noise of a shattering window, the cracks in the clown exploded, turning to dust. It coated Kristina's hair and face and she welcomed it. It was a baptism in ash, all her sins and the sins of those who came before her forgiven. A new life granted. The red nose lay at her feet, a grim reminder of what almost was.

The ghosts disappeared one by one until Adelaide was the only one remaining.

"My darling one, I'm so proud of you." She ran a finger down Kristina's cheek and slowly faded away with a smile. Kristina picked the clown nose off the ground and shoved it in her pocket.

Jason got to his feet. He was wobbly but alive. Kristina ran to him, launching herself into his arms and knocking them both to the ground. As they embraced, the circus tent dissolved, leaving the sweeping branches of the willow brushing against their skin.

"We're still alive," he mouthed against her lips.

Kristina grinned, kissing him again. "We are."

The storm had passed, and sunlight glittered through the branches like diamonds. "Help me up, will you? Let's not forget I've been stabbed."

"Oh, God! Do you need stitches?"

Jason looked at his shoulder and rotated it. "I'll live. Let's get the hell out of here. I don't ever want to see this place or a circus ever again."

Kristina laughed. "Me either."

Outside of the tree, they found the bodies of the Casters. After the paramedics were called, it was discovered that Norman suffered a massive heart attack. No one was sure what caused Beatrice's death, but Kristina believed the old woman couldn't let her darling husband go into the afterlife without her. After answering all the questions they could for the authorities, including how Jason managed to get stabbed which they explained away by saying he tripped on the willow roots while holding the blade, he and Kristina were cleared to go. Jason refused to go by ambulance, opting to drive Kristina home himself.

"Let's go home," he kissed her again as he fastened his seatbelt gingerly over his injury.

On the way out, Kristina looked in the side mirror, getting one last glimpse at the cemetery and silently saying goodbye to her grandmother. Beside the wrought iron gate, Baldy stood waving at them.

THE END